Sexy Street Tales Volume 1

Flexin & Sexin

Stories By:

ERICK S. GRAY

ANNA J.

K'WAN

BRITTANI WILLIAMS

JUICY WRIGHT

ARETHA TEMPLE

A Life Changing Book in conjunction with Power Play Media
Published by Life Changing Books
P.O. Box 423 Brandywine, MD 20613

This novel is a work of fiction. Any references to real people, events, establishments, or locales are intended only to give the fiction a sense of reality and authenticity. Other names, characters, and incidents occurring in the work are either the product of the author's imagination or are used fictitiously, as are those fictionalized events and incidents that involve real persons. Any character that happens to share the name of a person who is an acquaintance of the author, past or present, is purely coincidental and is in no way intended to be an actual account involving that person.

Library of Congress Cataloging-in-Publication Data;

www.lifechangingbooks.net

ISBN - (10) 1-934230-95-2 (13) 978-1-934230-95-4

Concept & Project Coordinator: Nakea S. Murray - Literary Consultant Group
Cover Design: Davida Baldwin

ACKNOWLEDGEMENTS

HIT EM' UP - Erick S. Gray

Be strong!

I like to thank God and those that supported me over the years through my trials and tribulation, even though I'm still going through tribulations…but to keep it short and express myself in a better way…here a little poem I wrote called, Be Strong.

Some days I try to be strong, need to be strong when I feel the world is against me, people dead set against me-trying to fade a legend I'm soon to be, trying to become that positive brotha from Jamaica Queens, determination I bleed, I'll breathe my last breath to continue on with my dreams, y'all can hate, but I'm moving on with better means, got success building in my blood stream, my anger and rage I now press down on a pen, spread my word like a trend, won't let a negative situation eat me from within. With God on my side, I can carry twice the weight, ignore the nay say, and guarantee my fate is for better days. Look into my eyes and you know I'm serious with this, and watch me touch you wit' the pen, have you hook on my book like a new drug, and daze you wit' a some urban love, keeping my head above the skies, as I hit you with my urban style-creativity burns through my skin, and to let you know, I'm sentenced to life wit' a gift.

FOR THE LOVE OF MONEY - Anna J.

I'd like to thank God for giving me the talent and the imagination to keep coming up with stories to entertain the readers. Thanks to my entire family for believing in me when I didn't believe in myself. To Nakea, K. Elliott, Mark Anthony and Azarel, thanks for giving me room to express myself and for constantly giving me outlets to keep my name out there. Last, but not least, thanks for any and everyone that has picked up a work of fiction by Anna J. Trust and believe, there's more where that came from.

LITTLE NIKKI GRIND - K'wan

As always, gotta thank God and my mother. Without them, I'd never had discovered my gift and probably still be running around crazy, begging for death or caged.

I'd also like to thank my wife, Charlotte, who encouraged me to stop being squeamish about writing love scenes, which in turn led me to explore the genre of erotica, and my sister in-law Tabitha Hamilton, who is always willing to keep her niece when I have deadlines to meet.

To my readers who hold me down in everything I do. You guys are like my extended family and I hope to never fall short of your expectations for me.

Special thanks to Ms. Nakea Murray for thinking of me when they were looking for writers on this project. Told you I can write anything, now the world knows it too.

RIGHT HAND BITCH - Brittani Williams

First and Foremost I want to thank God for the talent to write and the drive to keep going. I dedicate everything that I do to my son Kristion because it is all for him. I thank my mom & dad, Curt, all of my family and friends. Nakea Murray, for hooking me up and being a wonderful friend. Mark Anthony, Azarel, K. Elliot Thanks for letting me shine. Anna J, K'wan, and Erick S. Gray I'm glad to have worked with such great authors.

THE COOKOUT - Juicy Wright

This moment seems surreal… I finally did it, and on my own! Thanks to all who have encouraged me and believed in my writing (you know who you are). Look for your names in bold writing in my upcoming novel, *A Piece of Sunshine,* when I can give you the props you deserve. But, I must give a special thank you to Azarel for believing in my work. JUICY WRIGHT is now officially on the map!

HONEY DIP - Aretha Temple

First I will like to thank my father in heaven, if it wasn't for him none of this would happen for me.

I would like to thank all my on line friends who read and comment on my stories.

I would also like to thank Nakea Murray for giving me this opportunity to write for this anthology.

Thank you Noire for your friendship and you too Jme. Melissa I see you sissy poo.

Last but not least I'd like to thank my two little men who were patient with me while I'm on the computer. Mommy loves you.

HIT 'EM UP

ERICK S. GRAY

"How will you be paying?" the petite desk clerk of the Westin hotel asked us.

"Cash always luv..." Tommy said, pulling out a wad of hundred dollar bills from his jacket pocket.

The clerk looked at him for a moment, shocked he was carrying so much money. The cost for three nights at the Westin for both of us came to twelve hundred dollars. We wanted separate rooms, which was almost two hundred per night.

Tommy began counting out what we owed as I just stood there clutching my duffle bag staring at the clerk. She was a beautiful young thing, clad in a green blazer, with a gold name tag pinned above her right breast. It read Michelle. She sported a bob and waited patiently while Tommy removed twelve hundred from his wad.

The plush Atlanta hotel was almost booked, so we were lucky they still had rooms. Places like these mostly go on reservations and credit cards, but Tommy has the gift of gab. He knows how to talk to people and looks important. He sported a bald head, wore a grey Sean John track suit, and was blinged out in diamonds and jewelry. Tommy's about 6'2, with flawless black skin and has a way with the ladies. But he's hood, really hood. We come from Queens Bridge—born and raised—and have seen our share of the ghetto. I've known Tommy since the sixth grade.

Tommy passed her the cash, as she processed our room keys.

"You good Bay?" Tommy asked me.

"Yeah, I'm good," I replied.

We looked like we came to ATL for pleasure, but on the real we were in town for business—business that in my mind was totally immoral.

"Here you go gentlemen, your rooms are 6314 and 6315," she stated, passing Tommy the keys.

"Thanks beautiful. You looked out for us fo' real," Tommy said, staring into her eyes. His voice was deep and masculine. When he talked to you he always gave you direct eye contact. "What time do you get off?"

She smiled.

"We're new in town. We need to go out for a drink or sumthin'. You are the epitome of what a beautiful black woman should look and act like," he continued, throwing that New York swagger and accent her way. "How much they pay you here?"

I thought she was about to curse Tommy out for prying into her personal business. She showed a smile and replied, "I get paid enough."

"Nah, you need to be a manager or sumthin'…I know you have grace and smarts to run this place better than your boss. I bet you he some tight ass white boy and a jerk too," he said.

She chuckled.

"Call him down here and I'll talk to him for you. I'll get you a raise beautiful. I'm gonna look out for you while I'm here."

She continued to chuckle with a bright smile and said,

"You're too much."

"You got a man?"

"Tommy, man, c'mon, let's go already," I said, feeling he was taking his flirting too far.

"Aight, man," he said, then turned his attention back to the desk clerk. "Listen, my boy is an impatient dude…he's on medication or sumthin," I heard him say. "But we should link up sometime. Make an extra key to my room for yourself and come see me when you get off."

She continued to smile.

Tommy then pulled out his large wad of cash again, peeled off a hundred dollar bill and passed it to her. "In case your boss doesn't give you that raise, here's a lil' extra sumthin' from me."

"Sir, I can't. I'll get in trouble," she stated.

"Nah, just take it."

"We're not allowed to take tips from customers."

"So we can tip the bell-hops and waiters, but a beautiful woman like yourself who's been so much help to me, can't allow herself to take a lil' sumthin' extra for herself?"

"They have cameras watching us," she said.

"Oh, so I got you when you get off work beautiful," he said. He put the wad back in his pocket. "What time do you get off?"

She smiled. "Ten o'clock."

"Aight so at ten, I'll meet you at the bar down here," he said. "And don't worry, I ain't no serial killer…my mama ain't fuck my childhood up. I had girlfriends before," Tommy joked.

She laughed.

Finally, Tommy began walking away.

When we got near the elevators he said, "See that Bay, too fuckin' easy. She's cute too."

I nodded.

"Afrika knew what he was doin' when he recruited me for this business. He knows a playa wit' game when he sees one. I got these bitches eating out the palm of my hand, like I'm a fuckin' rap star," Tommy said.

"Tommy, you need to let shorty be. She ain't what we're lookin' for."

"Niggah, I'm just tryin' to fuck her…you know what I'm sayin'? That bitch probably had one or two boyfriends in her life. She needs some New York up in her, cuz I know she's tired of dealing with these country bumpkins down here. Look how I had that bitch open so easily on my accent alone," he said.

I just shook my head.

The elevator doors finally opened, and we were the only ones to get on. I pressed the sixty third floor and we quickly ascended.

The Westin was one of the most luxurious and opulent hotels in the heart of downtown Atlanta. We needed a place like this if we wanted to impress the ladies. It is seventy three floors and located on Peachtree Street. I was starting to feel like the fifteen hour drive from N.Y. in a sleek black Escalade sittin' on twenty inch chrome rims, was worth it.

We hit the sixty third floor shortly and began looking for our rooms.

"6315, here we are," I said.

Tommy was right next door in 6314.

"What are you about to do?" I asked Tommy.

"Yo, that drive was long as fuck. A niggah needs a nap right now," he said.

"Aight, so I'm gonna get settled and call your room when I make moves."

"Do that," he said, then disappeared into his room.

I walked into my room, dropped my duffle bag in the corner and looked around. "Nice," I muttered to myself.

The room was fit for a baller with floor to ceiling windows which gave a fantastic view of downtown Atlanta. My room came with a king sized heavenly bed and a mauve marble heaven bath with a curved shower rod to give more room inside and dual showerheads. Near the windows was a plush upholstered loveseat to relax and take in the view.

I walked to the windows and peered out at the city, admiring the view from sixty three floors up.

"ATL," I said to myself.

This city is supposed to be filled with bitches and ballers. I came on a mission and we had three days to accomplish it or Afrika would have our heads.

***

I took a five hour nap and woke up around ten that night. My room was so comfortable and that bed was softer than a woman's tits.

I got up and walked towards the window. I stared down at beautiful downtown Atlanta illuminated for miles. The view from my room was just so breathtaking, I never closed my blinds.

I was ready to go out and explore the night life that waited for us. I picked up my cell phone from off the desk and dialed Tommy's number.

"Niggah you up and ready?" I asked.

"Yeah niggah, I'm down at the bar already," he replied.

"And you couldn't come get a niggah?"

"Niggah, I dialed your phone. You were knocked the fuck out."

"Aight, I'll be down there soon."

I hung up and went into the bathroom. I took a quick shower and changed clothes. I wanted to get fresh and clean for the night. I had to come correct in ATL and was ready to show these bitches how ill N.Y. niggahs get down. I wanted so much attention that night.

I threw on a blue and white Sean John sweat suit over a crisp white-T with a diamond encrusted cross dangling from my neck. My kicks, straight up Vintage Air Force One Premium, white, light and dark blue—cost a mere $300.

I stared at myself in the bathroom mirror, combed out my small fro, and secured my fifty-five hundred dollar stainless steel watch with seven floating diamonds around my wrist.

"Bay, you are too much…you look good baby," I said to myself, staring at my brown skin, six one frame in the mirror.

I got the rest of the things needed for the night and walked out my hotel room with twenty-five hundred dollars in my pocket.

I met up with Tommy at the bar in the lobby and saw that he had company. It was Michelle, the desk clerk from earlier. She was lounging around still in her work attire.

"I see you finally got your tired ass up my niggah," Tommy said. He came up to me and gave me dap and a masculine embrace.

"You remember Michelle from earlier," he said.

"Of course," I replied.

"Hey," Michelle happily greeted me.

"Damn, niggah, you tryin' to go hard tonight. You wanna bag all the honeys huh? Niggah came out with the Vintage Air Force Ones and the bling," Tommy said. He looked me up and down from head to toe.

I smiled and asked, "What y'all drinking?"

"Nuthin' but some Hennessy now, but you know how I do later on," he said.

I ordered a Rum and Coke, and placed a twenty on the bar counter.

"So Michelle, we're tryin' to get into some things tonight," Tommy said. "I keep hearing about this Magic city. I heard it's supposed to be the spot out here…with the finest bitches and shit."

"Y'all fittin' to go there tonight?" Michelle asked, in her southern accent.

"Hell yeah! You can roll with us, beautiful, if you want," Tommy said.

"I would love to, but I gotta pick up my daughter soon," she said.

I took a sip of my Rum and Coke and admired Michelle's petite figure on the low. She had to be about 5'6, with a little butt and some hips.

"We need directions baby. You know this is our first time in ATL," Tommy stated.

"Well, from the hotel y'all can hit up south Peachtree till you see Forsyth St. and make a right. That'll take ya straight down to Magic City. It's right by the bus station. You can't miss it."

"Bay, you got that?" Tommy asked me.

"Niggah, I thought you were writing the directions down."

"Niggah, just write 'em down," he said.

"Niggah, you helpless," I countered. I grabbed a napkin from the bar and wrote down the directions Michelle gave.

"Damn, I wish we could chill tonight, you know what I'm sayin'. We could have so much fun," Tommy said to Michelle.

"I know, but I gotta get my youngin," she said.

I was ready to go. It was already close to eleven, and down here in the south, shit closes too early for me.

Tommy pulled out his huge bankroll, peeled off two hundred dollar bills and shoved it into Michelle's hand. "Take that beautiful. Buy that precious little girl of yours sumthin' nice on me."

Michelle took the cash easily this time and smiled. From my point of view, I was looking at a completely different woman. Behind her work desk, she was a professional and talked with elegance. But seeing her now with Tommy down at the bar and gettin' her drink on, I knew Tommy had that on smash. It was just a matter of when and where he was going to fuck her.

"Luv, we're 'bout to be out, but I got that number so you know I'm definitely gonna holla at you," Tommy said.

"Dats what's up! Do that Tommy," she said. She then walked up, placed her arms around him and began kissing the niggah like he was her man.

"Damn," I muttered.

I watched Tommy shove his tongue down her throat like they didn't just meet this afternoon. Michelle smiled as she pulled herself away and strutted toward the exit.

"That bitch got my dick hard right now, Bay," Tommy said. He grabbed his dick and looked at me.

"Niggah, don't look at me. I can't do shit for you. You better go up to your room and rub one off real quick," I told him.

"Niggah, shut da fuck up," he said lightly.

He went up to the bar, downed the rest of his drink and said, "Niggah, you ready to do this?"

I nodded.

"Let's be out then."

***

It was looking crazy outside Magic City—cars, trucks, bitches, and niggahs were everywhere. Tommy drove and I looked around in awe. Every bitch we drove by was a dime. We got there in fifteen minutes. Michelle's directions were on point. They weren't lying when they said it be some ballers in ATL. As Tommy and I pulled up, it was looking like a Funk Master Flex car show outside the place—pimped out rides and trucks riding on hydraulics with customized paint jobs and systems blaring. Some cars were so exotic they didn't need to be pimped out. Niggahs were pulling into the parking lot in Aston Martins and Bentleys. I even saw a yellow Lamborghini, and a bitch was pushin' it.

They tried to beat us in the head in the parking lot, charging us forty dollars to park. They saw out of state N.Y tags and tried to rape us. Tommy talked the dude down to thirty. We had it, but it was the principle. We were always trying to get over.

We stepped out the truck and made our way to the entrance. I was excited to get inside. I couldn't wait to see what all the talk was about.

At the door, they wanted a dub. We weren't getting in without us both paying the fee. The 6'5 grizzly looking bouncer was certain about that.

Anyway, once we were inside it was on. The place was packed with beautiful butt naked hoes, niggahs, and bitches who just came to chill and have a good time. It was a nightclub and strip club. Inside, the DJ spun some Lil' John, Twista, and Trick Daddy's 'Let's go.' Hearing that jam blare throughout the joint had me hyped.

But you know how we do, Tommy and I walked through with our New York swagger and all eyes were on us, especially from the bitches.

I saw four naked strippers in clear stilettos on stage doin' it up. All four were so gorgeous that I was ready to take 'em home and fuck 'em all. One bitch on stage had a knot of money in her garter-belt as big as the one I came in with. She saw me and gave me a wink. She danced in front of me, moving to Lil' John's raspy lyrics. Her bare hips swayed from side to side. I wanted to reach up and grab her fat ass and push my finger up her pussy.

The stage was covered with money and literally the floor was too. I was stepping on bills like it was nuthin. Nobody attempted to pick up any bills because bouncers were all over the place waiting for a niggah to do something stupid.

Shorty got down on her knees and moved closer to me. I smiled. I pulled out my wad of bills and passed her two fifties. Her pussy looked sweet, like fruit from a tree. She continued to dance in front of me for the next ten minutes, making me come out my pockets a little.

"Yo, Bay, what you drinking?" Tommy asked me. He threw his arm around me and eyed the stripper in front of me.

"Whateva, niggah!" I said with my attention still on the girl.

"I'm gettin' a bottle then."

He made his way to the bar as I stood by the stage tossing ten and twenty dollar bills at shorty.

Twenty minutes later, I made her two hundred dollars richer. She asked if I wanted a dance when she got off stage, I told her I had her on the rebound.

Tommy tapped me on my shoulder and said he'd gottten a table for us. He had a bottle of Moet in his hand. I followed him toward the back of the place, navigating my way through the dense crowd of naked women, horny men, and other patrons. "I Gotta Stay Fly" by Three Six Mafia blared throughout the club. The DJ was pumping music from the south heavily in the place.

We made it to our table. I plopped down on the funky red velvet couch and stared out at the sea of beautiful ladies in front of us. Tommy placed the bottle on the table and soon after a lady appeared and placed another bottle of Moet on the table with some champagne glasses. Tommy gave her a fifty dollar tip. She smiled and walked off.

"This is what I'm talkin' about," Tommy said.

I quickly poured a glass.

"Yo, remember niggah, don't get too caught up. We're here on business," Tommy reminded me. "We have three days to do what we came to do, and then it's back to New York. And you know we can't leave this bitch empty handed. Afrika, that's a niggah I don't fuck wit'."

I nodded. I then downed my glass and poured another drink. I looked around, eyeing one stripper after another.

It wasn't long before we were getting so much attention. Shit, the way we were spending money, it was inevitable that bitches would come to our table. We bought drinks and tipped big, as a few other ballers in the place did.

I even went up to the stage, pulled out a knot of one dollar bills totaling a hundred and began making it rain. I tossed every single bill in the air until it landed. I did this a few times, acting like money was nothing to me. I definitely had bitches attention.

As I was about to leave the stage area, she caught my attention. She was across the room, on the other side of the stage dancing naked in a pair of red stilettos for a crowd of men. She was Latina. I have a hunger for Latina women. It was something about them that started a fire in me that never stopped burning.

I couldn't stop staring at her. Her petite nude body was glistening in baby oil. She had beautiful long, black curly hair that bounced off her shoulders.

She turned and saw me staring. She gazed back at me with her saucy bedroom eyes and light red lipstick covering her sexy full lips. Her exotic look stunned me.

I wanted her, but she was busy entertaining the men on the other side of the stage. They were throwing money at her like crazy. For the next ten to fifteen minutes, I never took my eyes off her. I watched her every movement as she danced and moved her body to this southern music like a sista, never missing a beat.

Finally, after waiting patiently, she started my way. She had a smile on her face, as she sauntered across the stage in her stilettos. Her eyes were fixed on me. I had a wad of hundreds in my hand and was ready and willing to spend it all on her.

I stared up at her as she stood over me. "You like what you see? I see you keep staring," she said. Her accent was not from around here, but her voice was sexy and enticing.

I smiled. "You're too beautiful. What's your name?"

"Sweet," she said.

Of course I knew that was her stage name. I wanted to know her government. Up close, her body was even more immaculate—from her perky tits to the neatly trimmed pubic hairs above her pussy. She had my dick hard.

"That's your stage name. I wanna know the name your mama gave you," I said.

"Sorry honey, but I don't know you like that to be giving that out."

"So how much would it take to get to know you like that," I returned, flashing her a wad of bills.

"You think you can afford me?" she asked.

"I'll try."

She smiled and began dancing for me, moving her body in ways that caused me to wish we were under some bedroom sheets fucking. She was sprawled out on stage, her long refined legs stretching up to the ceiling. I dropped three hundred dollar bills on her breasts. Her hand brushed against the side of my face. Her touch along with her beauty was angelic.

For me, now it was game time. I wanted her to come back with me to my hotel room. I wanted to spend the night with her, even if I had to pay for it, but I wasn't going to look desperate. Being desperate turned the ladies off.

I dropped a few more tens and twenty dollar bills on her and whispered in her ear, "Let me buy you a drink."

She looked at me as she rested on her hands and knees. "All I drink is Alize, Moet, and Cristal."

"And? Come join us at our table in the back. We got bottles of that shit," I told her.

She looked to see where I pointed, and then said, "Because you're cute, I'll come."

I smiled.

Shortly after, she followed me to the back and joined us and four other ladies around our table. We had four bottles of Moet, two bottle of Cristal, and about five hundred dollars in tens, twenties, and fifties spread out on our table.

I poured Sweet a drink as she took a seat on my lap. I began massaging her thigh. Her skin was smooth like silk. My dick began to swell the more she moved her ass around on my lap.

The conversation all around was good and the ladies loved us. We came here for attention and that's exactly what we got.

"So what y'all do?" this thick well rounded stripper asked, sitting across from us, with her breasts free and throwing back Cristal and Moet like it was water.

"We're in the music business," Tommy answered.

"Oh word," she said excitedly.

"Yeah, you know, we direct, promote, and scout the ladies and all that good stuff," Tommy said. "We came down here because we're lookin' for a few girls to be in the next 50 Cent video."

"Oh word," one of the wide-eyed ladies said.

"Where y'all from?" another asked.

"N.Y., ladies," Tommy responded.

I let Tommy do his thang, while my focus was on Sweet. I wanted to know her real name and spend some private time with her. But the only way that was happening was if we stepped outside the club.

"You cool Sweet?" I asked her.

"I'm okay," she said. Her voice was soft and her accent was driving me crazy.

"So Sweet, what's it gonna take for me to really get to know you, starting wit' your name?" I asked.

"First, you tell me yours and I might tell you mine," she said.

I chuckled. "They call me Bay?"

"Bay?"

"Yeah, when I was younger I liked to fish. My uncle use to take me out to the bay all the time. The name kinda stuck with me."

She smiled.

"So where are you from, Sweet?"

"Venezuela."

"Never been there, maybe we need to take a trip out there someday. My treat of course," I stated.

She gave me a look as if I was lying to her. I just shrugged it off.

As the night went on, Tommy and I felt like celebrities with all the cash we were spending and the attention we got.

Around two a.m., the DJ announced the bar was closing soon. It was last call. We went through six bottles of champagne.

"Listen ladies, we got rooms back at the Westin, let's say we continue this party over there," Tommy proclaimed.

Some were down and some were reluctant. I only wanted Sweet to come. The rest I didn't give a fuck about. Tommy had them on lock down.

"So you down Sweet?" I asked nonchalantly.

At first she looked hesitant, so I said, "You still owe me your name; let me at least get to know a beautiful woman like yourself. I don't bite, unless you want me to."

"I'll think about it," she said.

I fought to convince her to come. I stuffed another hundred dollar bill down her panties. I wanted to let her know I was for real when it came to spending money. I was attracted to her.

At exactly three a.m., the lights came on in the club and the music stopped, indicating the party was over. People started heading to the exit, while some lingered behind in the club still socializing with the ladies. I was one of those who lingered behind.

I finally convinced Sweet to join us back at our hotel. I promised to take her out shopping in the morning. She was down.

She went to get dressed and I told her I would wait for her outside. Swarms of folks loitered outside like it was the club. Traffic was dense as cars were leaving the parking lot simultaneously, and niggahs stood around trying to salvage the rest of the night by gettin' at those sexy ass females who flooded the streets and parking lot.

Tommy walked back to the Escalade wit two ladies under his arms, both dark-skin, thick, and curvaceous. I stood around by the club exit waiting for Sweet.

Moments later she came strolling out. She was wearing a short denim skirt, open toe sandals, and a tight white T-shirt with spaghetti straps which accentuated her tits, and legs gleaming like the stars.

She had me in awe—I was like DAMN. And I wasn't the only niggah staring at her. By her style and strut, I knew she had, or was about money. Around her neck she sported a diamond and platinum necklace; a lady's style de Chaumet white gold watch, with diamonds on a satin strap, and pear shape diamond earrings. She was high class or high maintenance. By lookin' at her, I wasn't sure if she was a gold digger, but I knew she wasn't fuckin' wit' no broke niggah.

She walked up to me, and the first thing out my mouth was, "Damn, you are so fine."

She smiled.

We walked side by side to the truck. For me the night was still young. It was three-thirty in the morning and in New York I'd still be in the club drinking and dancing.

"I'm kind of hungry," Sweet said.

"Same here, what's to eat around here?" I asked.

"I know the perfect spot," she said.

I dropped Tommy and his two hoes off at the hotel and took the truck. We went to a 24/hour spot in Buckhead on Roswell Road called Landmark Diner. It was some swanky diner with a full bar.

The food was pricy, but I had it, so I spent it. I ordered chicken and rice and she ordered fried seafood.

The conversation was good. She finally told me her real name, which was Carmen. She had a daughter who was three, and the father moved back to Venezuela. Carmen was twenty two and lived in Atlanta for two years. Her daughter, Olivia, lived with her grandmother in Jacksonville, Florida. She came to Atlanta to make some money for her and her daughter. She wanted to go to school, but had no idea what she wanted to major in. She'd been around, dating mostly NFL football players, niggahs from the Falcons and point blank, getting money from them. But one of her relationships went sour, when one of the players started putting his hands on her. He became jealous and controlling. She ended up leaving him and his money and started dancing at Magic City sixteen months ago. The money was too good.

"So do you really work in the music industry? Or was that just game you and your homeboy play to get some pussy?" she asked.

"Do I look like I gotta lie about what I do? We do our thang in N.Y. I've done a couple of videos with 50 Cent, Busta, Fat Joe, and Jay Z," I lied.

"I'm so in love with Jay Z's sexy, big lip ass. I would move to New York just to meet him," she proclaimed.

I smiled.

"He don't know, I'll give that niggah some kids and suck the shit out of his dick. Beyonce ain't got shit on me," she said.

I laughed. "She damn sure don't."

"See, this gotta be fate for us to meet. It so happens that I know the niggah personally."

She gave me a disbelieving look.

"Nah, I'm for real," I replied. I pulled out my camera phone and showed her pictures I took with Jay Z a year ago at 'Summer Jam.' With the connections we had, we got back stage and met up with him, Nas, 50 Cent and etc. and took pictures with them on our phone.

She looked at the pictures of me with him and her eyes got big. "Oh shit, you really do know him."

I lied and told her it was taken at one of the video shoots I helped put together for him.

"See, I'm fo' real, boo," I added.

"I'm so hating right now," she said.

"You know what, I got you, beautiful. It so happens that next week, Tommy and I are doin' another shoot wit' him in Brooklyn. Why don't you come through, and I'll introduce you to him."

"You serious?"

"Like a heart attack."

"Oh my God, you can't be. How am I supposed to get to New York?"

"We'll pay for your ticket to the city. All you gotta do is bring yourself," I said.

"Oh my God, please don't play with me. I've always wanted to see New York and to come up there to meet Jay Z—this can't be happening."

"It's fo' real Carmen. You gotta chance right now wit' me to make your dreams come true. Now I know you ain't gonna pass it up."

She beamed with excitement. I had her—hook, line, and now I was reeling her in. I knew it would only be a matter of time before I was able to crack through her shell. She tried to put up this front, this shield around her and I was easily penetrating my way into her zone. As time passed, she started to feel more relaxed and comfortable around me. I could taste that pussy in my mouth already.

It was five in the morning when we left the diner. I drove back to the Westin. We both had a few drinks in her system and I was horny and antsy. Carmen made my dick hard just by sight alone.

I pulled up to valet parking down at the entrance. We both got out and I noticed the valet gawking at Carmen with a slight smile as she strutted over to me in her short denim mini skirt.

I gave him a head nod with a smile, and he gave me the same back, knowing what time it was. We moved up the escalator and strutted through the empty quiet lobby to the elevator. Carmen walked ahead of me a little, her shoes clicking and clacking against the hard marble floors, leaving an echo throughout the lobby. I stared at the back of her long beautiful developed legs and watched the back of her skirt rise with every step she took.

We got on the elevator and I pushed sixty three. When the elevator began to ascend, I pulled Carmen into my arms and was all over her. I pressed my lips against hers, shoved my tongue in her mouth, and moved my hands up her skirt, grabbing and squeezing her juicy apple bottom ass. She smelled so good—like a rose garden after rain. I then cupped one of her tits and squeezed it like it was a grapefruit. I pulled up her T-shirt, exposing her breasts and stiff nipples and started sucking on them like they were candy. I had her skirt pulled up to her hips, exposing her blue thong. I wanted to fuck her on the elevator.

We came to our floor, stepped off the elevator and went straight for my room. I wasted no time sliding the key card key in the lock and pushing Carmen into my hotel room. Once inside, I was all over her again. She unzipped her skirt as I pulled her T-shirt over her head.

I moved her towards the window, where the blinds were pulled back and the view of the illuminated city was in our sight. I positioned her doggy style on the floor as the glare from the city lights gleamed in the room. She placed her hand against the window, leaving fingerprints on the glass, and I quickly removed her thong. I then unzipped my jeans, came out of them and my boxers and had my hard black dick gripped in my hand.

Carmen's pussy was so thick, wet, and fat that it looked like 3-D in motion. She was waiting for me to fuck her. I moved my dick near her goodies as I gripped her hips. I was wild'n out and slowly began penetrating her insides without any protection. She let out a slight moan as I pushed more and more inches into her.

"Oh my God," I cried out. Her pussy felt so good that after a while I didn't care about not having on a condom.

"Aaaaaahhh, Aaaaaahhh… Aaaaaahhh," she panted. I thrust into her, feeling my shit swell up with the more dick I pushed into her.

Carmen's hands pressed flat against the window, her ass pushed against me and my nuts. My dick slid in and out of her rapidly. I gripped her hips and stared out the window at downtown Atlanta, not giving a fuck who saw us.

"Ay, papi…Ooooooooh. La Vida es muy corta—so fuck me," she cried out.

"Oooh, I like that Spanish shit," I said. I cupped her tits and continued fucking the shit outta her. "Say sumthin' in Spanish again."

"Cojer…cojer….Caray! Caray…tu maldita madre," she said.

I ain't no what the fuck she said, but it was turning me the fuck on. I continued to thrust in and out of her, having her sweet juices drench my dick. As I fucked her doggystyle, I reached my right hand around her, moved it in front of her near her pussy and began massaging her clit, with me still hitting it from the back. She went crazy and that Spanish began pouring out her mouth.

"Cojer…hijueputa …hijueputa…you concha tu madre…fuck me, you concha tu madres!" she exclaimed, as I was fucking her so hard from the back I made ripples in her ass.

Her pussy was so good I could've stayed in the doggy position all night. I pulled out, dick dripping and shit, and got completely naked. Carmen took off the remainder of her clothes and got comfortable on the bed. She was on her back, propped against the pillows with her legs spread, knees up, and pussy dripping like Niagara Falls.

"Umm, that's a beautiful sight," I stated. I walked up to her, climbed on the bed and positioned myself between her thighs. I thrust myself into her again this time in the missionary position, with her legs straddling me and began fuckin' the shit out of her.

We sweated, grinded, and fucked for the next hour—from position to position, it was on. The bitch was a freak. She sucked my dick, and the freak that I was, I let her stick two fingers in my ass. Now I'm not gay, but it was a trip to have her suck my dick and finger my asshole at the same time. I ain't never come so good before.

Afterwards we just passed out on the bed with her nestled against me.

The next morning I heard my phone ringing, but I didn't bother to answer it. It rang two more times, but a niggah was too tired to get up. Carmen was still snuggled next to me and it felt good having her in my arms. She was so soft it felt like I was holding a pillow in my arms.

Ten minutes later, someone was knocking on the door.

"Fuck," I mumbled. "Can a niggah get some sleep?"

I looked at the time. It was eleven in the morning. I didn't get much sleep the night before. The morning sun was glaring through the open blinds in my room intensely, causing me to squint when I got out of bed.

The knocking continued and I yelled, "I'm coming."

I put on some jeans and went to the door.

"Damn niggah, wake your ass up…pussy got you tired like that?"

"What do you want Tommy?"

"Niggah, I need the keys to the truck, we're 'bout to get some breakfast," he said. He was fully dressed and had both hoes he brought back to his room standing behind him.

I sighed and snatched the keys off the table and passed them to him.

"Yo, that bitch you had last night, she still in there?"

I nodded.

"Ladies, excuse us a second," Tommy said. Both girls walked down the hall toward the elevator while we stood in the hallway.

When they were out of earshot, Tommy continued with, "Yo, that's the type of bitch we need to bring up north wit' us. You know how much Afrika will give us for that. Where's she from?"

"Venezuela."

"Get on that Bay, that's payday right there," he said. "She still asleep?"

I nodded.

"Let me see that."

"Now?"

"Yeah, niggah."

I let him in the room and he walked up to the bed. Carmen was still asleep with the covers barely covering her body. She slept like an angel. I couldn't help but to admire her beauty.

"Don't lose this one Bay," Tommy said, once we were back in the hallway.

"I'm already on it. She's down to come to New York," I told him.

"That's my niggah." He gave me dap and said, "Yo, these two hoes I got with me, they're ready to ride back in the truck wit' us."

"Aight, that's what's up," I replied.

"But yo, I'm out. You continue workin' her and we'll link up in a few."

"Niggah, you takin' the truck, what am I supposed to do?"

"Niggah, take her to the mall or sumthin'. Spend money on her. Consider her an investment. You know what I'm sayin?"

"Yeah, I hear you."

Tommy walked off and I went back into the room. I went near the window and peered out at the city. The view was never tiring to me. The day was clear and sunny and the city came alive. I couldn't help but smile because from my window people below looked like ants scurrying around.

As I stared out the window I thought about the business I was in and the many women I came across and brought back to New York. I've made a lot of money in the past year. I'm involved in, how can I say, kidnapping and smuggling women forcing them into prostitution for a well known kingpin named Afrika.

Afrika scared me and I don't scare easily. He was Nigerian born and raised in Rwanda. He survived the Rwandan holocaust, but he was a Hutu extremist and had a lot of Tutsi blood on his hands. This man killed for sport. Murder was nothing to him because he'd been around murderers, rapists and extremists since he was six.

Afrika's image alone was enough to put fear into any man. He stood 6'1 and was black as tar, but his eyes were white like cotton. To see him in the dark, it looked like there were only eyes and teeth staring at you. He worked out, so his physique was sharp. He had chiseled features and smooth dark skin. His hair was short and kinky and he always sported red and black beads around his neck. He wasn't a flashy individual. The only thing close to bling he wore was a white gold yellow diamond pinky ring. He kept a low profile and surrounded himself with killers from his country.

He frequently traveled back and forth from New York to Africa and ran one of the largest prostitution rings in the world. I mean, this man was on Interpol's radar—fuck the FBI, if you were known by Interpol, you were into something big—so big they need an army to bring you down.

It's said that Afrika was responsible for sixty percent of the missing females in the country. If his crew couldn't get you by pure will, then they kidnapped your ass by brute force. I've seen them do it. If you were a woman and you caught his attention then there was no escaping him. He had brothels and clientele all over the world, even as far as Thailand and Japan. He preyed on American women, no matter what race, religion or ethnicity. In his eyes, they were money.

American women made him tons of money overseas because his list of clientele, mostly foreigners, craved for women from our country and they were willing to pay top dollar for them. Sometimes his clients would have specific requests for the type of woman they wanted brought to them—either it be a black curvy woman like Beyonce or a big breasted woman like Pamela Anderson. Once you were in Afrika's possession, there was a ninety nine percent chance you stayed. He owned you till the day you died, or until he decided to let you go—which was rare. He kept you until you were old and almost dead.

The majority of the women kidnapped in the U.S were smuggled out the country to some prince, millionaire, warlord, or drug cartel. Once they were out the country, they stayed out and became sex slaves for the men who paid for them. America was no longer home for them.

It's said that globally forced labor, which includes sexual exploitation, generates $35 billion, half in the industrialized world and a tenth of that in transition countries. Meaning, sex sales and it sells big.

Many of Afrika's colleagues, some in Bulgaria, Thailand, Japan, and in neighboring countries, run what they see as an export-import enterprise providing a sophisticated trafficking network for the sex industry.

And the sad thing is, I've seen girls as young as twelve and thirteen being forced into prostitution. Despite their age, they were all treated like women and expected to generate thousands and thousands of dollars for their owners. I've seen twelve year old girls in bed with men as old as fifty. And it always turned my stomach. Sometimes I wanted to knock these men out or put my gun to the back of their heads and squeeze, but I had to restrain myself and say its only business.

Tommy worked for Afrika first. He was doing a three year bid in Rikers Island for drug possession. Almost every week he had about two to three women visiting him on a regular. An associate of Afrika who was locked up with him noticed the countless women who came and liked his way with them. This friend of Afrika offered Tommy a very lucrative position in Afrika's productive organization. He jumped at the chance and got down without a second thought. Tommy was like that, when it came to making a dollar, he was always down no matter how great the risks.

Six months later, he brought me in. I'd just got out of Rikers after doing a two year bid for possession and assault. The drug game was changing and being on Rikers, I saw how many snitches there were in the game. I was disgusted and needed to change my career. I loved money just like Tommy, but I hated the risks.

I met with Tommy, Afrika, and a dozen of his killers in a Brooklyn loft a month after I came home. My first impression of Afrika was I knew he was serious and you didn't want to get on his bad side. He spoke with a thick African accent, and his eyes were cold like a winter chill. When he looked at you for too long, it made you very uncomfortable. But he liked and welcomed me into his organization with open arms.

"My friend, you make me lots of money, hey," he said. "Your friend Tommy, he tells me great things about you."

I was flattered he liked me.

"You work hard for me and I'll be good to you. I like honesty and one thing, mi don't like snitches. A snitch is no good, you hear my friend?" he continued.

I nodded.

"Come here," he said. He motioned me to follow him with his index and middle finger.

I walked with him to a back room in the loft. One of his workers pulled back a large black steel door opening to a dimly lit room. When the door opened, that's when the stench hit me hard.

"Damn, what da fuck is that smell," I said covering my face. I felt like gagging.

I walked into the room slowly, following Afrika and three of his men who were bulging with muscles and gripping micro Uzi sub machine guns. He turned on the lights and I was wide-eyed. I saw where the stench was coming from. I was surrounded by mutilated and bloodied corpses. On three shelves were the heads of women and men placed in liquid jars, their facial expressions lifeless, as they stared out from these jars with the last face they made before they were killed.

I saw dozens and dozens of fingers, ears, tongues, and hands in cups, ashtrays and bowls, with the owners of the limbs or parts nowhere around.

But what frightened me was a man hanging from a cross near the back. He was pinned up like Jesus on his day of execution. His arms were outstretched with a nail in both his wrists. His feet were crossed with two nails driven into them. They gutted him, cut him open like a pig. His intestines were sprawled out on a nearby table. His ribs cracked and his eyes cut out along with his tongue. They murdered and tortured this man like we were in medieval times.

"Look hard my friend....this man is mi brother," Afrika stated.

I was shocked.

"Wh-wh-what?" I stammered. I must have heard him wrong.

"Yes, my own flesh and blood. He betrayed me. He used to work for me, but thought trafficking humans was wrong. He said it was immoral, that women deserved their freedom. He wanted to snitch on me and seek God. So I helped him find God sooner than he wanted," he said, with a chilling tone.

I just stared at the poor sap hanging from the cross. I couldn't help but think, *a man can do this to his own brother?*

"I loved mi brother, so imagine what will happen to you if you ever betray me," he said, putting that frightful thought in my head.

I was speechless. I didn't have shit to say. I walked out the room and thought, *what the fuck did Tommy get me into?*

Despite the risks and our immoral actions, the money was really good. Afrika paid us ten grand for every girl we brought to him—which was pennies to him because the U.S and Europe alone generated up to fifteen billion dollars in profits from trafficked forced labor. He got a good percentage of that billion.
We mostly traveled throughout the south like South Carolina, Kentucky, Tennessee, Mississippi, Texas, and Georgia. Anything up north was too close to home. Besides the girls weren't as easy up north as they were in the south. We lied about everything, telling bitches we were music producers, looking for the next top model, shooting a movie in New York, or just promised to take care of them once they arrived in New York. The majority of the ladies fell for our bullshit. I mean we came correct in every town; spending money like it was water and getting these bitches atten-

tion who thought we were big time. Once we got that, it was on. We would produce pictures we took with certain actors, singers, and rappers, making our lies much more believable. We had false documentation and access to almost anything, thanks to Afrika and his financial backing.

Once the girls came to New York looking for their big break or making their dreams come true, they would never leave the city under their own free will again. We would meet them at the airport with one or two of Afrika's thugs on hand to make sure nothing went wrong. The ladies would get into the truck excited about being in New York and we would drive them to one of the safe houses in Queens or Brooklyn. Once the girls were inside, everything was out of our hands and Afrika's thugs took over. Sometimes they would beat on the women, but not too badly because they still had to look presentable for the clients.

Usually the ladies were hit with sticks across their backs or legs, or got smacked around a few times. In the beginning, there was always crying and panicking echoing throughout the stoned basement where they kept the women hidden and stored like luggage.

The ladies would be intimidated by the foreign thugs, mostly from Haiti or Africa gripping guns and shouting out orders. They would make the women strip down naked, and empty out all the contents of their purse or on them. They would take I.D and information from them, driver's licenses, passports, birth certificates, or any kind of papers valuable to them.

They were told if they didn't cooperate, their families would be butchered and killed. Once they were naked, with their information taken from them and their dignity stripped, Afrika would greet them. His presence made people fearful of him. His demeanor was straightforward and about business.

First he would just stand in the center of the room, quiet as a mouse with an ugly grimace on his face and stare down every woman in the room. They would be frightened, cold, and shivering but Afrika would just stare at them like they were his cattle.

He would then pull out a loaded .nine-millimeter handgun from his leather holster and order one woman to come to him. He would point her out and she better come when told so.

The unfortunate woman he pointed out would slowly walk up to him and he would just stare at her for a moment like he was studying her. He never looked excited about her nakedness—it was like Elton John standing in a room filled with naked women.

"Get down on your knees," he would command the girl.

She would get down on her knees, frightened as Afrika casually put the gun to her head, like he would to a wounded animal and pulled the trigger, blowing her brains out.

Seeing this, the girls would panic, cry and some would try to run—but they wouldn't take three steps before they were violently knocked down by thugs.

"That's what you bitches mean to me, nothing," Afrika said. "Your life now belongs to me. I own you. You escape or try to escape; we will hunt you and your family down and slaughter you like pigs. We have information on everyone. You listen and obey, you live."

His speeches were short, stern and simple. Out of every batch of new girls wh came to him on a monthly or sometimes weekly basis, he would execute one girl in front of the others to prove he was serious.

I was always disturbed by this action, but what could I do. I worked for him, and he was in control. He would shoot a girl in her head, cold blooded, and as she lay dead by his feet, blood oozing from her lifeless body leaving a crimson stain on the floor, he would talk over her like she wasn't even there.

***

I continued to stare out the window, deep in thought about the past year. I'd made over two hundred grand working for Afrika.

The money was good, but after a while seeing countless beautiful women being sold and forced into prostitution in this country or the next was getting to me. I had a mother and two sisters. Every girl I handed over to him, I thought about them. I would think what if my sisters were put into this predicament—what if I never saw them again. I thought about some man's nasty hands violating them in ways too unbearable to think about. No lie; I cried alone the first time I saw what went down in that basement and did so a few times afterwards. I would force myself out that weakened state and try to justify my actions by saying the bitches I brought to him were greedy gold-digging, druggy bitches who either had death or prison coming to them sooner or later.

Deep inside I didn't believe that because some of these girls despite their lifestyles had dreams and goals they wanted to accomplish. They had children, families, and boyfriends. They had rights and deserved their future.

I knew having a conscience in this game I was in was critical for me and my family. Afrika collected information on Tommy and me. He knew where my moms stayed at. He knew about my sisters, their jobs, their kids, and their husbands. I know if I fucked up their freedom or life would be in jeopardy along with mine.

I heard a slight moaning coming from behind me. I glanced at Carmen and she was starting to come out of her deep sleep.

I smiled as I watched her rise out of bed.

"Buenos dias," she said, which meant good morning in Spanish. I knew that at least.

"Buenos dias," I returned.

She moved slowly, while I tried to straighten up a few things in my room.

"Que' hora es?" she said. She was being cute, knowing I ain't understand one word she said.

She smiled and walked up to me in all her glory, wrapped her arms around me and gave me a kiss. "I said, what time is it?" she repeated in English.

"Almost noon," I said.

"A que' hora te despiertas?"

"Okay, you need to chill wit' that Spanish. We're in ATL, not Venezuela," I said jokingly, but the way her language flowed out her mouth turned me on.

"What time did you get up?" she repeated.

"About an hour ago," I replied.

"I need to teach you some words in my language so when you fuck me it can roll off your tongue too," she proclaimed.

"I'd like that."

We held each other near the opened window and stared into each other's eyes for a moment. Her eyes were different from last night. They told me something new about her. This wasn't the same woman I brought home and fucked the shit out of. In the physical it was—but there was something unusual about her. In the club she was Sweet, that get money bitch who could hustle a dollar and more out of a niggah. But in my room, I saw Carmen. She was more like wifey. The way she got out of bed and kissed me good morning, I never felt that before. The way we nestled together and held each other all night, I never did that with a woman I was trying to take back to Afrika.

"What are you thinking about?" she asked me.

"Nothing."

It felt good holding her in my arms, really good.

"You're thinking about something," she continued.

"Nah, I'm just admiring how truly beautiful you are," I said.

She smiled. "Well, let me give you something to really think about."

She pulled me onto the bed and pushed me down on my back. She mounted me slowly and started tugging at my pants. She slowly pulled them down around my ankles and had my Jones in her sight.

"I see he's up and ready to go too," she said with a seductive smile plastered across her face.

Her soft manicured hand gripped my hard on and stroked me gently until soft cries of bliss escaped my lips. She then moved her mouth near my goods and slowly wrapped her soft rounded lips around the tip of my dick having her tongue curled around my shaft.

She started off so damn gentle, with a little kiss here, a little lick there, and a little suck underneath my nuts. I just laid back on the pillow and relaxed with my eyes closed.

Her sucking increased—her licks became longer. She played with my balls with her fingers as her blowjob became rapid. She was sucking my dick from the tip to the base, half of my dick in her mouth as her tongue continued to twist around it. I was about to cum, so I tried to pull my shit from out her mouth. She wouldn't let me. She was in control and she knew it. I clutched the beds sheets, releasing out moans of pleasure. "Oh shit, Oh my God," I cried out.

When she put her mouth around my balls and started humming. I was about to lose it. I was on the edge. My eyes began to roll in the back of my head. I continued to clutch the sheets intensely. I felt my dick growing bigger and bigger inside her clenched jaws. I felt her tongue coiling around the tip of my dick, which was my spot.

"You gonna make me cum, Carmen," I cried out as I squirmed, trying to hold my explosion, but she was relentless. She attacked my dick with such skill and force that she had my toes spread out and me panting like I just ran a marathon. I felt her swallowing my dick bit by bit, so I stopped drawing back and let her go at it, which put me in heaven. This bitch definitely knew what she was doing because she sucked my dick until she felt it loading up to shoot. She backed off and put her mouth around my nuts again and started humming. I didn't know if I should scream or moan.

After that, she began stroking me again. I swear I didn't

know my own dick; it looked so much bigger and so much harder. I thought, what does she have planned next for me in her bag of tricks?

Carmen then covered my mouth with her hand, raised herself up and climbed on top of me. My dick still gripped in her fist as she floated her sweet pussy over the tip of my hard on and slowly brought her pussy down on me. I penetrated her slowly, feeling every bit of her juices and warmth engulf me. I moaned. Once she was on top, she was in control again. She started riding me, stretching my shit out with circular gyrations. When she rose, she pulled it with her and when she slammed down, she took it deep inside of her. She arched her back and curved it inside of her.

I cupped her titties. I grabbed her hips. I slapped her ass. I was just trying to keep my hands busy because the way she was riding me I needed to do something. No woman ever rode me like Carmen. She rocked back and forth on top of me, her hips continued to gyrate as she arched forward and dug her nails into my chest and grabbed my fro.

"Oh shit, I'm cumming!" I exclaimed, feeling my muscle below tightening and a rush I was far too familiar with.

She bounced on top of me, pulling my shit up and deep down in that pussy. She continued to straddle me with force as I felt her fluids pour all over me.

"I'm cumming!" I shouted again. I felt my body tighten. I grabbed her hips and felt my rush coming faster and faster.

"Fuck me Bay…Oooh fuck me," she said, with sweat dripping from her brow.

I felt her pussy muscle tighten around my dick and the more she fucked me, moving on top of me like NASCAR, the louder she became.

I couldn't hold it in any longer and that explosion that I'd been trying to control for the longest happened right inside of her. She felt it, as I turned and twisted under her, and she dug her nails so deep into my chest she drew a little blood.

She collapsed on top of me with her breasts pressed against my chest. We both were panting and sweaty. I was thirsty and hungry as fuck. I held her in my arms for a few moments, savoring what good fucking sex we just had. I glanced at the time and it was 1:15 in the afternoon.

I woke up two hours later. I propped myself against the pillows and noticed Carmen wasn't near me. I heard the shower running in the bathroom. A short moment later, she came out wrapped in a blue towel. She was drying her wet hair with another towel. She sat down on the end of the bed.

"You're up again," she said.

I stretched, staring out the window. I needed to start my day. I got out of bed and searched for my clothes.

"I need to go home for a change of clothes," she said. She dropped her towel and strutted around my room naked collecting her clothing from the floor.

"Give me a minute. I need a shower," I said. I grabbed some items from out my duffle bag and went into the bathroom.

In the bathroom, I peered at myself in the large mirror. I thought about her and knew she was definitely cash money back in New York. A woman like her, I could get at least fifteen thousand dollars for. I touched myself; my dick was still feeling the after effects of what she put on me.

I got in the shower and let the water cascade off me as I pondered so many things. I felt I was a rich man. I had over a hundred and fifty thousand stashed away back home, lived in a nice crib, and pushed a forty-five thousand dollar truck. So why did I suddenly feel so empty? It came to me that I was getting rich off other people's misery.

This game, like the drug game, was getting tiresome. Sometimes, I would have dreams, nah, nightmares about these missing women I was responsible for. I felt things were going to start spiraling out of control soon. I felt my past was going to catch up to me. I never told Tommy about the nightmares. I didn't trust him anymore. He loved what we did. I no longer desired the hunt. That's what he called it, "the hunt." We tracked and captured innocent women like lions with prey in the pasture.

One time I was in a supermarket in Greenville, South Carolina and noticed this missing poster of a young girl in her early twenties who's been missing for three months. Her name was Larkish Watkins and the information about her fit the same description of young girl we kidnapped four months before. She was a dancer in Charlotte who went by the name Creamy. She was a beautiful young woman who surrounded herself around the wrong company. I remembered her because of her blond hair and mole on the right side of her face.

Tommy slipped Rohypnol in her drink. It was known as the date rape drug. Later that night when she had no idea of her surroundings, we forced her into the back of a van as she left the club headed toward her car.

"Yo, I'm gonna rape this bitch real quick. We got an hour before Afrika's men come to scoop her up. Keep an eye out Bay," I remember him saying.

I was against it, but he didn't listen to me. Once pussy was on this niggah's mind, everything else was out the door. He climbed into the van where she was sprawled out unconscious, and he had his way with her for the next twenty minutes. I sighed as I kept an eye out with my gun on me.

He came out the van sweating and zipping up his pants with a devilish grin on his face.

"Yo Bay go get some pussy before these niggahs come and scoop this bitch," he said.

"Nah, I'm good," I replied. I was kind of disgusted by his actions.

"Yo, her pussy aight, son. She ain't a real blond though," he commented.

Man, I knew I was going straight to hell for what we did.

"You okay in there?" I heard Carmen shout as she knocked on the door interrupting my thoughts.

"Yeah, I'll be out soon," I replied.

I finished up in the bathroom and got dressed in twenty minutes flat.

We took a cab to her home not too far from the city. She had a place in Brookwood Forest condominiums on Alden Ave. She needed to change her attire. Afterwards we headed out to Lenox Square mall where I promised to take her shopping.

During the cab ride, she talked about her daughter. She even showed me pictures of her beautiful Olivia.

"I haven't seen my baby in six months," she said. "I miss her so much."

"She's beautiful," I commented.

"Yes she is, and she knows mommy loves her despite me living in Atlanta for so long while trying to make a better life for her. Every month I send my mother some money to help take care of her. My mother is becoming ill though, Bay. She has cancer and I know it's only a matter of time before she passes. I'm all my daughter has left. She has a birthday next month. My baby is going to be four years old."

Her face lit up with every mention of her daughter's approaching birthday.

"That's good," I said.

"I can't believe I'm telling you all this," she said staring at me. "I've never told any man about my daughter, not even the football players I dated. But you, there's something different about you. At first, I thought you were a cocky baller just flashing money around, but at the diner, you held my attention. I thought you were lying about being a music producer, but the pictures you have of Jay Z, I know you're for real and you'll keep your word about having me meet him soon?"

I nodded.

Then she chuckled and said, "God, I can't believe I fucked

you last night and this morning. I know you must hear this all the time, especially it being funny after what we just did, but I'm not a ho. At the diner, when we were talking, I looked in your eyes and I saw a kind soul. I saw a man conflicted with something in his heart, so he hides behind money and things. You're not a choir boy, but your soul needs help and improvement."

I returned with, "And you know all this about me so soon? You just met me. How do you truly know what I'm about? What do you know about my true intentions?"

"My grandmother, mother, and I, we have a sixth sense about people—I can decipher a good hearted man from a wicked one within minutes sometimes. You, I like, but your friend Tommy, he gives me the creeps. There's something about him that rubs me the wrong way."

I smiled. At first I thought this bitch was nuts, but when she continued talking, there was something unusual about her.

"Be honest with me Bay. Do you mean to bring harm?"

"Harm?" I repeated. I chuckled at the thought. "I like you Carmen. I've always been attracted to Latino women and you're my type."

"I'm your type, huh?" she said.

"I wouldn't lie to you."

The smile on her face was so generous and at the same time so seductive. "I like you too. If I didn't, then I wouldn't have gone back to your room with you and fucked you," she stated. Hearing this, the driver gave us a quick glance in his rearview mirror and continued to drive.

She nestled much closer to me in the back of the cab and started moving her hand up my thigh and placed it gently on my dick. She grabbed my bulge slightly and then whispered in my ear, "I want you to fuck me in the back of this cab right now. I don't have any panties on."

She took my hand and guided it between her legs letting it under her skirt. I massaged her pussy with the tip of my fingers as she moaned.

"You're a freak," I stated.

The cab made its way down Interstate 85, just as she began unfastening my belt.

"You buggin'," I spat.

"Am I?" she said, lifting her skirt with her pussy in full view for the driver to witness.

"Yo..." I uttered. I was in awe. I was thinking about the driver's reaction about me getting some ass in the backseat of his ride.

My actions were reluctant and Carmen noticed too. "You're worried about him," she said. "Driver, you don't mind if I fuck my man in your backseat." She went into my pants pockets, pulled out a twenty and added, "Here's an extra twenty for your trouble."

The driver took the money and glanced at us in his rearview mirror again. I guessed that meant yes.

Carmen straddled me, with my pants lying around my ankles. She slowly inserted my jones into her, and moaned as I thrusted upwards. Her cries of ecstasy, with her tight grip around me and her hips gyrating back and forth against my bare hips, had me 'bout to buss a nut.

The driver did 65 mph on 85, and she continued to ride me the same speed as the car. I couldn't help but notice him glancing back at us with a smile appearing on his grill.

"Oh God," I cried out. I clutched her hips and prepared myself for impact. "I'm cumming!"

"Oooh, papi....fuck...Cojer...Cojer...si....si...si...si, Oooh, si...yes, fuck me," she cried out. She slammed her pussy and body into me like a twister.

I clutched her butt cheeks with a tight grip as I continued to thrust upwards. I felt it coming. You could see the ivory in my eyes as that sudden rush in my dick was looming. The palms of my hands were indented into her ass cheeks, as I pushed her against me and came in her. It was crazy, fucking her in the back of that cab on the highway with cars zooming by us was an experience I would never forget. The driver didn't mind either. We gave him a good peep show.

We arrived at Lenox Square mall and stepped out the cab like nothing happened. I'd be lying if I didn't say she definitely had me open. I never met a woman like her before.

Inside, we hit up all the stores from sneakers, clothes and even lingerie. I spent two grand on her, but it was worth it. We strutted through the mall like a couple. I had one hand gripping her hand and tons of bags in the other. I noticed a couple of the fellows checking her out in her short jean skirt, sandals and halter top. She was a dime piece for sure.

We got something to eat at the food court. As I was about to sit down and enjoy a burger, my phone rang. I looked at the caller I.D. and it was Tommy.

"What's up?" I answered.

"You got that bitch in pocket yet?" he asked.

"Yeah…soon," I answered half-heartedly.

"Niggah, you ain't sounding too sure. We're gonna have to go brute on her ass, and just plain kidnap the bitch for Afrika."

"It ain't even like that," I said.

"His peoples called me earlier asking when they can expect delivery. I told them about your rice and beans eating mama-cita and they're willing to go up fifteen large for her alone," he informed.

"Fo' real," I said, staring at her as she stuffed a few fries in her mouth.

"Yeah, so you gonna be on it, or do you want me to get on that and make it a sure thing for the both of us?"

"I'm on it," I replied.

"Don't fuck this up for us Bay. We need this," he said, and hung up.

"Who was that, your friend?" Carmen asked.

"Yeah."

"What did he want?"

"Nonsense," I said flatly.

Tommy wasn't aware, but I was suddenly having a change of heart in this whole game. I looked around and saw men with their families and thought about a family of my own. I didn't have kids and I wanted a few. Seeing Carmen boast about how wonderful and beautiful her daughter was, I felt a small void in my heart.

"What do you have planned for us next babe?" she asked.

"It's up in the air, you tell me," I responded.

She smiled and said, "I know of a place."

"Really?"

"Yeah, it's quiet, hardly anyone's around, and you can meet my home girl too," she informed. "You down?"

"Yeah, but is your girl cute?" I asked.

"You can see for yourself," she responded.

The next hour we were back in the cab on our way to the outskirts of Atlanta. We ended up in a neighborhood called Little Five Points, about twenty miles from the city. The cab pulled up to this housing complex off Euclid Ave. Carmen got out first and I followed.

"Who you know up in here?" I asked.

"My home girl is cute too. She's cool peoples Bay," she said. She then took me by my hand and led the way.

I knew this bitch was a freak and I thought she was probably down for a threesome, which I had no problem with. I'd done threesomes before.

We walked up to a ground floor apartment and she knocked twice on the door.

"Who is it?" I heard a female voice shout from behind the door.

"It's me, Carmen."

The door opened. She stepped in first and I was right behind her. I noticed the apartment was dark, the blinds were closed, and there wasn't any furniture. I saw two shadowy figures in the corner. Carmen quickly walked ahead of me and then I felt a rush come at me and heard, "Niggah, don't you fuckin' move!"

I was forced to the floor violently. I looked up and saw a black glock aimed at my head. The owner of the gun, a large male wearing a black Nike skully cap and black army fatigues.

I knew they weren't cops by their demeanor. They were stick-up kids.

"Yo, what the fuck is goin' on?" I said. Soon after, I was pistol whipped with the butt of the glock.

"I said shut the fuck up!" he shouted, looking belligerent.

I was bleeding from the side of my head. I felt an open cut over my eye and my hand was covered with blood. I saw Carmen standing behind the men. She looked at me with no sort of compassion or sympathy in her eyes.

I looked up at my attacker, fearing I might not leave the room alive.

"Yo, check that niggah's pockets and see what he got on him," the gunman who had his weapon trained on me told the second man with a Desert Eagle gripped in his hand.

I felt my pockets being rummaged through. He pulled out my wad of cash, about twenty-five hundred. They took off my jewelry and even removed my sneakers.

I got careless. I should have seen this shit coming, but pussy clouded my mind and that one mistake fucked me. Carmen was good. Here I was debating if I should go through with bringing her to New York for Afrika and all this time the bitch was setting me up.

I looked up at Carmen and I had to ask, "Yo, everything you told me, was it real? Your daughter, your moms, and what you felt about me?"

"Niggah, hell no…that's a picture of my niece and she's in Philly with my sister. Niggah, this is business, nothing personal boo," she said.

I spit blood from my mouth and wished I could have gotten to her first. Now it would have been a pleasure to see Afrika get his fuckin' hands on her.

"Yo, bring that other bitch niggah out the bathroom," the man with the glock ordered.

I watched the second gunman walk to the back of the room. Carmen turned on a small lamp near the stairs, and came over to me. Her face illuminated from the small lamp next to her. She crouched down next to me and examined the damage her armed friend did to my face. She then smiled and had the nerve to ask, "How was I?"

"Fuck you!"

"Been there done that boo. Thanks for taking me shopping though. Just for that, I'll make sure it's quick and painless," she stated.

As I glared, I noticed them drag somebody from the bathroom. When I got a good look at who it was, I became wide-eyed. It was Tommy. He was butt-naked, beaten badly, with his hands bonded behind him.

"Fuck y'all niggahs…that's my word, y'all niggahs is fuckin' dead. You know who I fuckin' work for?! Get the fuck off me!" He screamed and squirmed in his captives' grip.

Tommy saw me and got quiet. I guess seeing me in the same predicament made him lose hope.

"Fuck," he muttered.

Carmen smiled at Tommy. "Remember me?" she asked.

"Fuck you, you cunt ass bitch. You're dead bitch…I'm gonna make sure Afrika fucks you up," he yelled.

"Yo, shut that niggah up!" the man with the glock said.

Tommy caught a quick blow to his head and fell to his knees. Next they wrapped duct-tape around his mouth. The room was tense. I knew I was going to die. I felt it was karma—what goes around comes around, I knew sooner or later it was going to catch up to us.

I heard a knock at the door. The gunman nodded towards Carmen. She carefully walked to the window and peered from behind the blinds.

"It's me," I heard a female voice shout out.

She opened the door and in stepped another girl. Her face was hidden in the darkness of the foyer, but when she continued into the room, I was in awe.

"Fuckin' bitch!" I muttered.

She smiled at me. It was Michelle, the hotel clerk who checked us in at the Westin.

"How are my two boys?" she asked with a smile. She looked at me and Tommy with a wicked grin.

I heard Tommy mumble something under the duct tape and went crazy seeing Michelle. I felt the same way.

"Ah, Tommy don't act that way, I thought we were friends. You wanted to fuck me, remember. You thought I was some naïve country girl who got wet off your money," she tormented. "Niggah please! Y'all murder this niggah first."

Tommy tried to fight and mumbled under the tape, knowing his fate was sealed. He sprang to his feet and tried to run, but fell to the floor once the gun shots rang out.

"Y'all got their room keys right?" Michelle asked the two gunmen.

"Room 6314 and 6315," he replied.

Michelle smiled, looked down at me and said, "Your turn cutie."

"Oh God," I cried out.

"It's gonna be quick baby and look at it this way, you got to fuck my girl Carmen here, right? I called her at work and told her all about you and Tommy. Tell me her pussy ain't worth dying for," Michelle said.

The man with the glock walked up to me and aimed at my head. I closed my eyes, preparing for death and…

TO BE CONTINUED...

Booty, booty, booty, booty rockin' everywhere!

Booty, booty, booty, booty rockin' everywhere! I found you, Miss New Booty. Get it together, and bring it back to me…

The music up in here is too damn loud and my head is pounding from all the bass in the speakers. That didn't keep me from shaking my ass and putting my pussy all in this nigga's face who was sitting in front of me giving me his hard earned money. As I went from one drunk ass dude to the next giving lap dances and letting them cop cheap feels, I briefly wondered if I was taking money from some hungry child or keeping someone's lights from staying on, but at the end of the day I didn't force their tongues on my nipples or their cash in my pockets, so I did what I had to do.

It was a typical Thursday night at *Club Splash!* and I was on my grind once again trying to get up money for rent, bills, and tuition for another semester. The club was run by Milton, this old ass grease ball, who looked like the character Fat Bastard from the Austin Power's movie. He just got a kick out of looking at naked ass women walk around his club and make money for him, and believe me when I tell you he had eyes all over the damn place.

If you thought you were going to make some extra cash and not break bread, think again. Milton was on your ass like flies on shit, and it was either give him his cut or give him head; and who wanted to suck a dick that smelled like old bologna? Furthermore, there really wasn't any need to try to rake money off the top because Milton took care of us, and from the stories I hear around the club from the other girls, this was the best spot to work in since *Club Oasis* burned down in a riot six years ago.

It was quickly approaching midnight, and that was around the time the infamous street boys showed up. Kardiq, the leader of the 21st Street crew came through like clockwork. He always had an entourage, and this week he was accompanied by Samire and Hasan, whom I personally named Mutt and Jeff. Not that they were bad looking, because these dudes were definitely on point, but neither of them had an original thought in their head. I think they would have forgotten to breathe if Kardiq wasn't in their ear to remind them.

Many of the women who worked here would flock over to them and they would get turned down time and time again. The most arrogant one was that damn Hasan. This nigga didn't think his shit stunk, and not even the prettiest performer, Like Butta, could get next to him. He just didn't look interested in the women here, and that was surprising since we were allowed to get completely naked and walk around. He always had some ignorant shit to say, though. To avoid confrontation, I totally ignored his ass since he wasn't the one peeling off them dollars anyway.

I didn't feel like their shit tonight because on the real, I had better shit to do like getting my biology paper done which was due the day after tomorrow, and I had yet to start it. At the same time I was stuck between a rock and a hard place, so it was either sit in the library and live in my car, or shake my ass up in this club and get this money. My parents died in a car accident when I was young and even though my aunt and I were cool, I just needed my own space. Two bitches in the kitchen never worked out.

As I approached Kardiq and his two flunkies I forced a smile on my face and hoped this would be quick. Normally Kardiq wanted a private session, but I just wanted to get this money and get gone. Yeah, I could easily come up on twelve hundred in an hour and call it a night, but once again, I was just ready to go home.

Milton had a second floor full of nothing but immaculate private rooms where we could take guys that were willing to pay the twelve hundred an hour; triple that if you wanted a threesome. The patrons weren't aware there were hidden cameras in every room so Milton could keep an eye on his money. It started getting interesting when politicians started showing up at the club and paying for services also. Let's just say it made it a lot easier to get licenses and anything else Milton needed for his establishment without ruffling any feathers. When you're a white man and your fetish for black pussy is threatened to be put on blast you become very compromising, if you get what I'm saying.

"What can I do for you fellas tonight?" I asked Kardiq in a husky voice, purposely not addressing the other two goons that were sitting with him. Samire looked like a kid on Christmas morning as one totally, or half naked woman after the other walked by. What amazed me was he had to have been here a million times and still had the same look on his face. Hasan, as always, didn't seem interested.

"You know what it's hittin' for Ma, what room is open?" Kardiq answered back in a deep voice. As fine as this dude was, it amazed me he actually paid for pussy. I'm almost certain he could have any woman he wanted at any time, yet he came into the club every Thursday and paid me. What was even more hysterical was if I'm not here on a Thursday, he won't even stay and let someone else hook him up; he'd rather leave and wait for the next week to see me. Of course that sparked all kinds of jealousy in the club because everyone wanted a piece of Kardiq. The things those lips could do was amazing and he saved it all for me. It didn't hurt that he had long money either.

I wanted to deny the visit, but at the same time he contributed to most of the money I made here at *Club Splash!,* making it possible for me to cover my monthly expenses and still floss a little.

"Okay, follow me."

I didn't even wait to see if he moved, I just made my way through the crowded club and up the stairs to see if his favorite room was open. Each room had a different theme and I knew he loved the "Bone Room." He said it reminded him of the movie School Days and the room they had in the frat house.

The one thing about Kardiq I didn't get was he never wanted me to freshen up before we got down to business. Never mind that I'd been rubbing on the laps of too many niggas in this club before he got here. Never mind all the finger tips that touched my coochie and the rest of me, and the dirty money that was stuffed down there combined with sweat. He liked it, like he was David Banner or somebody. *Bring it here sweaty, cause I like it when it's funky...*He would sing that line every time, and I would oblige, letting him eat my pussy until he had enough.

What was even crazier was we would never fuck. He would place me on the very edge of the bed after he paid me the room fee and then he would get down on his knees and do the damn thing to me. His only rule was I couldn't lie down. I had to sit up and watch, and that just made it better. Watching his tongue circle my clit and his lips sopping me up like a biscuit would drive me over the edge in no time. I would put the heels of my feet on his back between his shoulder blades and prop myself up with my arms behind me so I could lean back a little and watch all the action.

Riding his tongue was like going through wild water rapids. My pussy got so wet from my own juices and his tongue action, I would literally be dripping when I got up. He would sometimes push three of his thick fingers inside of me and Lord knows I was going wild up in there. That was the most draining sex I've ever had without actually getting the dick.

Kardiq would literally eat my pussy for all of forty five minutes, using the last fifteen to wash his face and brush his teeth with the complimentary disposable tooth brushes and wash towels provided by the mayor of New Jersey. Let's just say our friendly neighborhood Mr. Mayor was caught on tape with his face in one of our best girls, Amber's ass, and once he was done he couldn't leave to go home to his wife without cleaning up. Since that night we've had an unlimited supply of toiletries for the guest of *Club Splash!,* and Amber had a couple extra thousand dollars added to her tab to keep their secret safe.

After we finished, I walked Kardiq to the door where Samire and Hasan were waiting, then went to the back to change my clothes. Hasan seemed to have an attitude about something judging by the look he gave me, but ask me if I gave a fuck. There was never any love lost between Hasan and I, and I liked it that way. I decided to shower once I got home. Ever since that night I saw one of the other dancers at the club, Morning Dew, squat down in the shower and push out a tampon onto the floor without bothering to rinse the blood up, I stopped showering at work. That was just too much for a sistah to take in.

Taking my cash intake for the night over to Milton, I chilled in the lounge chair in his office while he counted my money out. It was a seventy/thirty split and I always counted out what I should get before I went in there just to make sure he gave me the correct amount. Sometimes he would slip me extra because he knew I was actually in school, and not faking the funk like most of these broads up in here. I always counted it out in front of him to let him know there was extra and he always told me to keep it.

Milton was cool in that kind of way. You look out for him, he looks out for you, but once a few of the other dancers found out we were cool, the rumors started. Of course it was the younger girls who worked here, because the veterans in the club were making their money regardless and it didn't seem to matter to them. The girls my age, though…those bitches were like crabs in a fucking barrel. As soon as you made it to the top, one of them was waiting to pull you back down.

When I got to work earlier this evening, I had to park about a block down because all the spots close to the door were on lock. I hated leaving this time of night because it was dark as hell up the block, and I could never find any of the wonderful bouncers Milton hired to walk us to our cars after hours. They were up on the stage throwing doe and fondling hoes with the rest of these nut ass men who came to the club, and tonight of all nights I left my damn mace in my glove compartment. I waited by the door for a while hoping one of their lazy asses would pop up, but after fifteen minutes, I decided to take my chances with the streets. I had a paper to start, and other research to do, and I wanted to get home as soon as possible.

Deciding to swallow my fears and get to my car as fast as I could, I held my key in my hand and walked swiftly up the dark street, regretting not getting a car that had keyless entry. All kinds of crack heads and losers were in the alleys around this way, and I couldn't wait to make it to my little Yeadon community and get in my apartment.

The further I got up the block the weirder I felt, like someone was watching me. At this point I was too far from the club to turn back, but not close enough to my car to feel somewhat safe. I didn't want to look like I was scared, but on the inside I was shaking like a damn leaf. The closer I got to my car the faster I began to walk, breaking into a smooth trot to make it up the street quicker. My heels click clacking on the sidewalk didn't help matters at all, and the sound seemed to be magnified by the quietness of the street. Once I got to the car, I was so scared I was fumbling with the lock and dropped the keys three times before I was able to figure out which key fit.

Just as I was about to put the key into the lock, a hard body pressed up against mine from behind and I dropped everything but my keys to the ground. I could smell the strong liquor coming from the stranger's breath and I had to remember to breathe before I passed out. That nigga must have been sipping on Henney his entire life because he smelled fresh out the damn tavern, and it was making me sick to my stomach.

"You always ignore me when I'm in the club, with your pretty ass self," the stranger said, in my ear. He used his right hand to squeeze my breast and his left to rub my ass and hips. For a split second I was hoping it was Kardiq, but all that went out the window when I heard the slur in the stranger's voice.

"Are you sure you got the right girl? You know we all look the same when in costume," I said with a nervous laugh hoping to God this drunk fool would just back up off me. My heart was beating fast as shit and I didn't know what the guy was going to do. I started sweating profusely in spite of the cool early spring weather and my body began to shake a little. I wasn't about to be giving out lap dances in a dark ass piss infested alley.

"Oh, I'm sure I got the right girl. No one else in there has nipples like yours," he said, afterwards circling my earlobe with his tongue before sucking it into his mouth and nibbling on it gently. My stomach was doing flips the entire time, and I swallowed hard to keep from vomiting on the side of my car.

"Damn, they look like they were dipped in chocolate syrup. And I would never forget a pussy like yours. I wanted to run my tongue up that pink slit and get some of that strawberry juice on my tongue," the stranger said.

By now, he's grinding his dick into my lower back and squeezing my breasts and hips even harder. I'm damn near about to piss on myself at this point, but I'm still trying to hold it down. I can not get raped out here, that was out of the question. Furthermore, I was wondering why no one had exited the club yet. That door normally swings open a million times a night, but on this fretful evening it appeared that everyone was staying inside.

"Well, if you'd like, I'll be performing tomorrow night and you know we have private rooms. You can fulfill all your fantasies and more."

"Yeah, that's true, but Milton done bumped his fat head if he thinks I'm paying twelve hundred for some pussy."

By this time, the stranger had undone the bottom three buttons on my shirt and loosened my belt buckle. His grip on me was getting tighter by the second. I couldn't even move an inch without him pressing back against me.

"I could work a deal with you for a shorter time. Milton is understanding," I said, still trying to get him to back up off me a little so that I could at least try to run. At this point I'm pressed up so close to my car, I can feel the coldness of the glass through my shirt on my bare nipples. His breathing was getting harder and so was his dick. I just wanted to go home, why was this happening to me?

"I don't need a deal, because I'm about to work it out with you right here."

It happened so fast I didn't have time to react. This faceless stranger had the strength of ten men because before I could elbow him and run he snatched my button down shirt from my body, and grabbed me by my hair throwing me onto the ground, my breasts exposed to the night air. I tried to roll over real quick, but he dove on top of me out of nowhere, and his weight pressed my bare back into the ground.

I was trying to push him off of me, but my punches didn't faze him in the least. He continued to try and pull my jeans down, and his mouth somehow found my right breast. He latched onto my nipple like a damn vice grip. I started kicking and screaming for help, but all I heard was the loud music blare from the club every time the door opened.

I couldn't believe it had all boiled down to this. I was just trying to get some quick money so I could get out of school. And now I'm out here in the fucking gutter fighting an obsessed man off me. I remember thinking back to my childhood, and wondering how the hell I ended up at this point in my life. Just as I was going to give up and just let him take the ass, the stranger was yanked off of me and thrown in the street. I breathed a brief sigh of relief as I peeled myself from the glass filled concrete and scooted up to the curb.

I sat up on the ground and covered my chest, my back on fire from being scraped by the broken glass and jagged concrete. I was too shaken to get up and thankful for the three men that were beating the hell out of him. I could hear bones cracking because they were stomping him so hard, and as bad as I wanted to join, in, I couldn't even get up because I was so sore.

When they were done, the three men began walking over to me and I became scared again. I couldn't even get one man off of me, so I knew I had no chance with three. I drew my knees up tight against my chest, mad as hell because I was laying in the damn gutter and my three hundred dollar *Seven* jeans were fucked up beyond repair. My legs burned from the combination of broken glass and rocks that penetrated my skin during the struggle. The sweat that was now beading my body made me feel extra cold from the night air beating on me.

I didn't look up until the men got closer and when I did Kardiq, Samire and Hasan were all looking down at me. Never have I been so grateful to see all three of their faces, and I just broke down in tears, thankful for someone saving me, even if it was them.

"Damn, Ma. I'm so sorry this happened to you. Come on, let me help you up."

Before I could move, Kardiq placed my ripped shirt over me to cover my chest, and he scooped me up off the sidewalk, and carried me to his car. Samire passed me my pocket book and Kardiq instructed him and Hasan to drive my car and follow behind him. I was still shaking when he put me in the passenger seat of his winter white Bentley. The seats felt like butter and I sank into them after I turned my shirt the right way and got as comfortable as possible. My hair was all over my head and my damn lip was busted. I was more pissed than anything, but it was finally over, and I was on my way home.

I gave him directions to my place, and he got us there in no time. Hasan gave me my cars keys after securing my vehicle in a spot close to my building and Kardiq gave them his whip, instructing them to look out for his call later on. He wanted to make sure I was cool before he left. I heard Hasan mutter something under his breath, but I couldn't quite catch what he was saying because Samire was telling him to shut up and just get in the damn car.

Once inside my apartment, Kardiq stripped me naked and put me in the tub, carefully washing my back before cleansing the rest of me with a tender touch. The water burned my open wounds like hell when I first got in causing a fresh stream of tears to flow for a few minutes. Kardiq rinsed off some of the blood before soaping the rag, and gently washing and inspecting my body. He even went as far as drying me off and moisturizing my skin before I stepped into my thong and he tucked me in for the night.

"Kardiq, I really appreciate this. I can't believe that happened like that. How can I repay you?" I asked while holding back my tears. I could have been dead or something if he and his friends didn't show up.

"Don't worry about that right now, just get some sleep. We'll talk later."

I didn't say another word; I just closed my eyes and was out like a light. I found myself tossing and turning a few times during the night I got up the next morning shook because I had a bad dream I was being chased down a dark alley with one of my costumes on. No matter how fast I ran, I couldn't make it to the door at the end. There were a bunch of men chasing after me and they all had the same face as the guy who tried to rape me last night. Once I reached the end of the alley, I tried to open the door but it was locked and just as the men surrounded me and began to rip my clothes off, I jumped up out of my sleep.

When I sat up in the bed, I didn't see Kardiq. I thought maybe he left, but once I walked into the living room I saw him sitting by the window looking outside. I was still in my thong, but I did put on a little baby doll shirt to cover my breasts.

"Good morning, Ma. How you feeling?" he asked with a look of concern on his face. I wasn't sure if it was genuine or not, but it didn't matter. If it wasn't for him, I would have been ass out last night.

"I'm feeling better. Thanks again for last night."

"Hey, think nothing of it. Let me talk to you about something, though."

All kinds of thoughts ran through my mind and I knew for sure it was payback time. I figured he might just want to eat my pussy again, being as though he never wanted to fuck. Of course, I wondered why, but I never asked. Taking a seat on the chair closest to him, I made myself comfortable and looked his way to see what was on his mind.

"So this is what I need you to do, Ma," Kardiq jumped right to the point. I didn't know what to expect and was shocked to say the least at what he was requesting.

So many men come through the club and Kardiq wanted me to push coke through the private rooms for him. He explained that a lot of men he dealt with wanted eight balls and those could easily be stuffed into a balloon and pushed into my vagina without anyone knowing. I was looking at him like he had lost his mind and he gave me the same look right back. I wasn't made for the jail life and shit like this could definitely land me there in no time.

"Kardiq, I'm thankful for everything you've done for me, but you can't expect me to put myself on the line like that, I have too much at stake to get caught up in some shit like that."

Man, I could see my ass in jail now hugged up with some butch named Red Bone because I needed protection from the rest of the chicks who were trying to get at me. I had too much going on and I wasn't about to throw away all that college education I paid for to pay back a damn debt. He must have bumped his head.

"Listen, it won't be hard. All you gotta do is this..." He explained to me he would let his clientele know where to meet me and it would only be on Thursday and Saturday nights. He would be in the club and whoever wanted the drugs would pay for a private room. He would slip the balloon in me during a lap dance, and I would then go up to the room to meet the client. He would then get the balloon out while he was eating my pussy, and Milton would never know what was going on. He also told me I could fit at least three balloons in me at one time, just in case the client wanted more than one.

"What if the balloon breaks? I might die from an overdose."

He looked at me like I was the dumbest person on the face of the earth and continued to tell me what needed to be done. He would be using those thick latex party balloons and informed me they wouldn't be in me long enough to burst. On top of all that, I would be getting licked down in the process, so all I had to do was sit back and enjoy it. He insured me no one had ever died from their pussy getting over dosed, so I had nothing to worry about. I was just trying to find any excuse not to go along with it, but he had it all planned out for me already.

The money did sound nice though. I was already counting in my head what kind of money I would be making per night if I did like five or six transactions. I would be able to trade my car in sooner than I thought. I was still a little concerned about getting caught and I was concerned about Milton. He was good to me and like I said, there wasn't too much that got pass him in his club, but Kardiq seemed to have it all figured out.

"How long do I have to do this for?" I asked. I just wanted to stack some doe and be done with it because I didn't plan on working at *Club Splash!* forever. This was my last year of college and once I graduated I was walking away from it all.

"Just for a little while. Why, how long do you plan on working at *Club Splash!*? I'm sure you should be almost done with school. What has it been, four years now?" he said, with a smirk on his face like he didn't really believe I was a college student.

"First of all, if you doubt I'm a student take a look in that heavy ass bag of books on my kitchen table. And for your information, I graduate in June and then I'm done!"

"Well, until June it is. Take the rest of the week off and I'll see you at the club next week. I'll explain to Milton what went down and you give him a call too. Until then, stay sweet."

I didn't say anything else, although I was grateful for the time off. He dropped a knot of money on my coffee table before he kissed my lips and exited my apartment. Soon after, his entourage pulled up with his car and I called Milton to bring him up to speed on what happened. He gave me his well wishes and I told him I would see him on Thursday of next week. That gave me time to catch up on my school work and get some much needed rest.

Thursday came around too quickly and before I knew it, I was back at the club. This time when I pulled up, Milton had a parking space open for me so I wouldn't have to walk down the block once I got off. He asked me a few questions to make sure I was cool and then it was back to work as usual.

Just like always, Kardiq, Hasan, and Samire showed up at the club around eleven. We had a brief conversation in the corner to go over what I was supposed to do and then it was on from there. Between him, Hasan and Samire they took turns pushing the product into me during lap dances, a couple of times with Samire rubbing my clit with his thumb a little too long for comfort. Hasan, on the other hand, was rough with the insertion several times pinching my clit hard and shoving his fingers in my ass hole. I tried to let it slide, but after getting in Kardiq's ear about it, he straightened it out.

I met up with seven guys that first night. Six of them only ate my pussy, and one of them wanted to fuck since he was dropping twelve hundred on the room. The room price was also my payment for moving the product since Kardiq received his money ahead of time.

One night while I was getting dressed to perform, one of the other performers walked up to me and was watching me put my make-up on through the mirror. I looked at her with a *"Can I help you?"* expression, especially since she wasn't amongst the few I actually got down with. These bitches are cut throat and I ain't got that kind of time.

"What's up Cinnamon? Was there something you wanted to ask me?" I asked her with slight agitation evident in my voice. She didn't look as if it fazed her in the least and continued to stare at me through the mirror.

"So, word is that you and Kardiq got a thing going," she said, watching my expression closely for any signs of a lie.

"Oh, that's the word, huh?" I said not taking the bait. She looked at me for a moment longer before she spoke and the expression on her face turned from that of a jealous hoe to a concerned mother.

"Girl, I'm only going to tell you this because I know you have a bright future ahead of you. Plus, you got a chance to get up out of here. Don't hook up with Kardiq's crazy ass. That man don't mean no good to anyone in here. Get out while you can because the rest of us are trapped in here. What kind of job you going to get when all you can put on your resume is a pole dancing job and no education?"

"How you figure he's trouble? He's up in here flossing doe and spending money like everyone else," I said, trying not to let on that our relationship was more than services being provided. I briefly wondered if she knew what I was doing for him. I quickly tossed that thought to the side. Kardiq wouldn't tell on me because he'd be telling on himself.

"All I'm saying is watch your back with him. Yeah, he's tossing money around like it's nothing, but his comes with a price."

I saw her in a whole new light after that and had to turn and look her in the eyes. There was a sadness there so deep it couldn't be removed. Maybe she saw herself in me and wanted better. I reached over and gave her a hug, a tear escaping from both our eyes.

"Thanks, Cinnamon. And my plan is to get out as soon as possible. The moment I graduate it's over."

"Okay, baby. Just be careful out there and remember what I said. Run while you can."

I felt bad for all the women who were sucked into this lifestyle. I made a promise right then to myself and my parents that once I'm done with Kardiq and Milton, I'll be leaving and won't look back.

This went on for a few months with the same guys coming back. Some guys just staying in my room long enough to get the product out and others to enjoy the ride. Around mid-March a new guy started coming through the club. I saw him and Kardiq talking one night as I walked by. I didn't say a word; I just kept working the men around the club and collecting my money until I got the signal from one of them for me to come over.

About a month later the same guy came back and this time

with friends. He spent some time at the stage watching me perform and later on that night I got the signal from Kardiq to come over and get the product from him.

"Listen, this guy is a new customer," he whispered in my ear as loud as he could over the loud music. "Make sure he's feeling good before he leaves. It'll be a tight fit, but I'm pushing four balloons inside of you. You know what to do. I'll reward you later."

I didn't say a word, I just clenched my pussy muscles as tight as I could and signaled for the guy to follow me up to the rooms. Once inside, I freshened up for him and made myself comfortable on the bed. The guy didn't say a word, he just went to work teasing my clit with his tongue and using his fingers to pull the balloons from out of my coochie. I thought he would stop once the balloons were out, but he pushed my legs back and kept going until I came in his mouth at least three times. When he was done he didn't even bother to wash his face, he just straightened his shirt and left me laying there.

Later on that night, Kardiq followed me home. Once inside my apartment we talked a little about what was going on with his drug business. I serviced at least five to seven men per Thursday and Saturday night over a three month period. Minus the other two nights I worked there, I was making a killing! Even Milton told me to keep up the good work, naïve as to what was going down, which was surprising taking into consideration all of the surveillance he had going on around here. That also made me wonder if Kardiq was breaking Milton off.

It was late, and being that it was already early Sunday morning I was trying to lay in the bed, wanting to use Sunday to get some homework done. Kardiq and I chatted for a while longer and before I knew it this dude was on his knees in front of me with my thong to the side and my clit in his mouth. Totally caught by surprise, I leaned further back on the couch forgetting his rule to watch, and I threw my legs up on his shoulders.

He rotated between licking up and down my pussy and putting his tongue in me to sucking on my clit, and finger fucking me. I couldn't control my hips from grinding into his face. As I got closer and closer to my orgasm, I called myself trying to make it last longer because I know he ain't fuckin', but the next thing I know I was depositing my sweet honey all over his lips and face. I'm grinding my wetness into his face until that last drop of cum released, and my body stopped shaking. He didn't protest at all and actually seemed to enjoy it.

Before I could stop shaking he stood up, and unzipped his pants. I was in shock because I couldn't believe I was really about to get it. The next thing I knew he was reaching for my arms and pulling me up from my position.

"Look at this," he said pointing to his dick. My mouth just about dragged on the floor from the size of it. Kardiq's dick made acquaintance with his knees without an effort. My mouth started to water from the anticipation of tasting it, but before I could grab it he pulled it back.

"What's the problem?" I asked him, getting a little impatient with this cat and mouse game. Why the fuck does he keep getting me all heated just to leave me high and damn dry? Fuck, my pussy felt as good as it tasted and I wanted to put it on him. This nigga must have gotten a kick out of being a tease.

"Once you finish getting this money for me and your debt is paid, it's all yours. Until then, keep this picture in your mind."

He didn't even wait for a response, he just put all that dick back in his pants and left me sitting there with a wet pussy and an open mouth. I had to finish the job in the shower, and I mentally tacked on another reason for June to hurry the hell up. If graduating wasn't good enough, riding Kardiq's dick would definitely put a smile on my face.

For a couple of weeks I didn't see Kardiq in the club, but I did see Samire and Hasan. They brought along two new guys who were working with them and I was pissed. How in hell this nigga just going to disappear out of nowhere and think it's cool to send some other niggas to put their hands in my pussy? I was pissed, but what could I do? I owed him a debt and I had no choice but to pay it.

The same guys I usually served came in for the hook up, and on a couple of occasions the new guy came in on days Kardiq and his crew weren't there. On those days he would still pay for the room, but we would just talk. He asked me a bunch of questions about why I was working in a strip club and about me going to school. He even went as far as giving me extra money for my classes and all that. I treated that shit as business, not thinking anything of it and kept doing what I was doing. I just automatically assumed he got his information on me from Kardiq and was using it to make small talk.

The end of April rolled around quickly. On my way out the club one Thursday night I saw Samire outside arguing with a bunch of dudes. I tried to dip back and listen to what was going on, but he already spotted me and I figured it would be best to mind my business. I said goodnight to him and the other guys on the walk by and drove on home, never giving the scene a second thought.

I wasn't in my apartment a good five minutes before someone was ringing my bell. I didn't know who it could be this time of night, but the way they were leaning on it made me think it was urgent. When I got back down to the door it was Samire.

"What are you doing here?" I asked him, as I leaned against the door jam indicating to him that whatever he had to say it could be said outside. You never know who's watching you, and I didn't need any haters going back to Kardiq with some shit that wasn't true.

"What did you hear?" he asked with a straight face like he would snap my neck if I said something he didn't want to hear.

"I didn't hear anything. I was going to ask you where Kardiq was hiding out, but you seemed to be in a heated debate so I let it go."

"Well, look Ma," he said a little softer this time. "I need to talk to you about something but I can't right now. Just give me a minute to get some things in order and I'll put you down on everything. Just make sure this conversation stays between me and you."

"Okay, no problem, but what about Kardiq. What happened to him?"

"He had to go out of town for a while, but he's back. You should see him at the club tomorrow. Just make sure you keep what you saw earlier, this conversation, and this visit between us. It'll be in your best interest, you dig?"

I made a motion across my mouth like I was closing a zipper and stepped back to close my door. The last thing I needed was beef from Samire or anyone else for that matter. I was just trying to get this job done as smoothly as possible without any interruptions. Some shit done went down, but I was lost as to what exactly. I wondered briefly if Kardiq was locked up all that time and no one wanted to say. Either way, it wasn't my problem, as long as the cops ain't come looking for my ass, I was cool.

As promised Kardiq was back in the club on Saturday night. I was feeling good because my classes were winding down and I only had a couple more weeks to go before my June 6th graduation date. That meant I was done working for Kardiq and Milton, and I could go on with my life. I got an interview for a nice six figure a year job as a fashion consultant for Iman, being that fashion and business were my majors in college. Pretty soon it would be over, and I'd be clicking my heels and haul assing out of here.

I walked up to Kardiq after my stage performance, and straddled his lap. I actually missed him and wanted to catch up briefly before I serviced the lust hungry men around the bar waiting eagerly for a quick dance. I must say, my performance to *Ring The Alarm*, Beyonce's new joint, was on point. I studied the video over and over again and had the moves down better than the singer herself.

"Where you been hiding? I missed you," I said into his ear while pressing my body against him, and grinding on his dick. Ever since he showed it to me, my mouth watered every time I thought about it. If it's the last thing I do, I will definitely make sure to give Kardiq some pussy. He wanted it, I'm sure, but you don't mix business with pleasure so I understood.

"I had to handle some shit, Ma, but I'm back. You been a good girl getting daddy's money?" he asked, while he ran his soft hands up and down the front of my body, stopping only to squeeze my nipples. Damn, I missed feeling his touch.

"I've been on my job."

"Good, I have a man that'll be here in an hour. Make your rounds, and get your juicy ass back over here. We got money to make."

I kissed him on the cheek before I got up, and when I turned around he smacked me on my ass, making my butt cheeks bounce. I smiled over my shoulder and went around the bar to please my fans. By the time I got back to him he was signaling me to go upstairs. Like normal, he pushed two balloons into me, and stroked my clit while promising me to wax my ass when this was all done. I was ready to cum, and could feel my walls getting slippery causing him to have to push the balloons back into me. I ran upstairs into the room before they slid out.

I didn't even bother to freshen up. I let this stranger, like so many others, eat my pussy until I came, he got the balloons out, and I went back downstairs to do my job. This went on for a few weeks and before I knew it, June was here. I was graduating on the same day as my retirement, so I was extra excited. I get my degree and walk into a hot job never missing a beat. The best thing is I'll finally get to feel all of Kardiq's dick up inside of me.

I spent the last week or so finalizing my plans and making

sure I got all the requirements done in order for me to start work on time. I didn't want to tell Iman I was working at a strip club for the past four years, so I got my aunt, who is a supervisor over at IBM in the HR department to vouch for me working there as a volunteer. This opportunity was too good to let slide and I didn't want anything to get in the way. Since I was a business major, she vouched for me doing billing and business for the past two summers on a temporary basis.

I also let Milton know I would be hanging up my g-string upon graduation and he was cool with it. We talked over a light lunch in his office and he congratulated me on making it out. He expressed his emotions sounding like a proud father. We talked before and he reminded me of what I told him the very first day I walked into his club.

"I don't plan on doing this forever," I told him with so much confidence an earthquake couldn't shake me.

I already had a four year plan figured out and I've stuck to it so far, never falling for the private parties and girl on girl action so many men wanted in this type of scenery. As tempting as that extra money was, I kept it moving. Aside from that, the lesbian thing just didn't appeal to me, so it was an easy decision to make.

"Prove me wrong baby girl because just about every woman you see wrapping their ass around that pole came in here with the same idea. Some of them have been working here for more than ten years and their goals are just as worn out as their pussies. So, like I said before, prove me wrong and do the right thing. You don't want this to be your life long career."

If felt good to be sitting here four years later and telling him I made it out. As hard as it was and as much money as I made here, it would be hard to walk away from, but I couldn't hide behind the pole forever. It was time to do my grown woman thing and I was ready.

On the day of my graduation, after I hung out with my family and classmates, I walked into *Club Splash!* feeling real good about my last night there. All I had to do was get through these last few hours and I was free. I was ready to bust up into Iman Fashions, Inc. and make it happen. Although I wouldn't be ripping the runway, I was responsible for the majority of new designs in clothing which was selected for the shows.

While I was getting dressed Milton walked into the room. We chatted a little bit more about me leaving and how proud he was, and before he left he gave me an envelope. I didn't open it until he left and to my surprise it was a check for fifty thousand dollars. The note attached to the check said the money in the envelope was part of what I made for him for the last year. He was putting money to the side for me to give to me if I graduated. It brought me to tears and I made a mental note to see Milton before I rolled out for good.

When I got upstairs I welcomed the loud music, and gave the men up in there the best show they would see in a long time. As usual, I made my rounds after my performance and when I saw Kardiq he gave me the signal to come over. Stuffing three balloons into my opening, he said we would finally hook up after the club closed, and thanked me for doing business with him.

When I got up to the room, the new guy I spoke to before was in there waiting for me. I didn't bother to freshen up, I just took my place on the bed, and let him work his magic. Just when I was about to cum for the second time I heard gun shots ring out in the club and the music stop abruptly. I heard a stampede in the hallway as the girls rushed to get out of harms way. The sound of police sirens in the distance let me know things were not good.

As I moved to get up, the guy I was in the room with looked at me like he was contemplating something. Before I could ask him what the problem was he pulled out a badge and a pair of handcuffs and told me I was under arrest. It was a struggle, but he finally got the handcuffs on after I begged him to at least let me put on some clothes and grab my pocket book.

On the way out I noticed the club was tore up, and I saw the

EMT putting a sheet over Kardiq's dead body. I don't know what happened down here, but I knew for sure I was in trouble. When we got down to the station I was asked a million questions about the drug activity going on in the club. After denying everything they showed me a tape of several men removing the drug filled balloons from my pussy.

They also had footage of me giving Kardiq and his boys lap dances, but at the angle the camera was facing you couldn't see who was putting the product into me. It just looked like they were fondling my pussy. There wasn't a lawyer in the world that could get me out of this one; Johnnie Cochran is resting in peace already.

I called my aunt and the police officers where nice enough to let her take my pocket book. I told her about the money and the check in my bag and she promised me she would use the money for a lawyer. That didn't work because I ended up getting ten years for conspiracy and drug trafficking and pretty soon my ass was shipped up state.

At the hearing everything was a blur. I remember being ushered into the court room, and my court appointed attorney giving a wack ass testimony on my behalf. I was deep in thought and just blocked out all the noise in the room. I was so racked with guilt from what my mom and dad would think of me if they were here that I missed the entire court proceeding. The next thing I knew, I was being ushered back into the holding cell.

The judge was nice enough to let me say goodbye to my aunt and give her a hug. Even a few of my friends from *Club Splash!* showed up to support me which made me cry even more. When I finally moved to leave, I saw Hasan sitting in the back of the court room, and he looked a little too happy at the outcome of this trial. I hated him at that moment, but it wasn't much I could do, I was on my way to jail.

I was so depressed I tried to kill myself on several occasions. They ended up putting me in the psych unit for close observation.

My hair started falling out in clumps from the stress. I cried so much at one point I had to be hospitalized for dehydration because I wouldn't eat or drink anything.

A few months had gone by and I refused all visits. By the fifth month I decided to finally read all the letters my aunt sent. I know my mom and dad are turning over in their graves right now. For the love of money my life is now a damn mess. The last letter my aunt wrote me informed me that Samire had been trying to come talk to me, and I needed to get with him soon, he had some valuable information that could help me get out.

Needless to say I contacted him immediately and within three weeks we were sitting in the visiting room. I couldn't believe the shit he was telling me. I was kicking myself more and more the longer we conversed.

"So, you're telling me Kardiq had that guy try to rape me so I could owe him a favor?" I asked, already in tears. It hurt me to even ask the question because I was certain Kardiq and I had a connection and I didn't want to believe he would set me up on some bullshit like that.

"Yeah, Ma. He asked a couple of the other strippers to do the same thing but none of them would bite. You were the most naïve and had the most to lose so he began setting that shit up months ago after the first time you let him do you in the private room," he said in a sad voice, afterwards apologizing for going along with it.

When the plan was first thought up, Samire said he tried to talk Kardiq out of the rape scenario, but Kardiq swore the person he got wouldn't actually rape me, he'd just rough me up a little. The night it all happened, the guy he hired got a little too drunk and was actually trying to take the pussy, forgetting the main plan they talked about. He said it wasn't even in their plan to come save me because the guy was supposed to have let me escape, but when they were walking up the hill to their cars they saw what was happening and jumped in to help, Samire being the first one to grab dude off me.

"Damn, you got to be kidding me," I said in shock not believing the shit I was hearing. A fucking set up. I fell for the game in a stupid way and all this time I thought I had shit under control. "Did he know that guy was a cop?" I asked, still in shock at how crazy it all went down. I still can't believe how all of that went on and I had no idea.

"No, not at first, but when he got locked up and disappeared for those couple of weeks he found out from someone in the clink with him."

"So, why didn't he say anything to me!!!" I asked, getting mad all over again. I swear if Kardiq wasn't already dead I would have murdered him myself. I couldn't believe how stupid I was.

"I don't know, Ma. And that promise of you getting the dick was bullshit because he and Hasan had been lovers for years. Him sitting up in a booty club was just a stunt."

The more we talked the more my heart dropped. Samire also informed me Hasan was the one who brought the cop in because he was jealous of me, and wanted me out of the picture.

The only reason he let me stay around as long as he did was because he wanted the money to finish getting that house built Kardiq was getting done for him. That and because he didn't have a pussy to transport the drugs in yet because the money Kardiq was making from me at the club was going to pay for Hasan to finally get his sex change.

"Kardiq loved pussy, but he loved men even more, so him going down on you was nothing. He had been sucking Hasan's dick for as long as I could remember."

I was ready to scream and ended up having to be taken back early because my hysterical crying was disturbing the other visitors in the room. Samire promised to get me out because there were loop holes in the case and he and his lawyer kept their word.

Before he left I asked him what went down in the club that night, but he said this wasn't really the place to talk about it and that once everything was settled he'd bring me up on how it all went down. He also said he had a surprise for me, too, but the only thing I wanted to be surprised about was my freedom.

I only ended up spending a year and a half in the clink. His lawyer found a discrepancy on the tape using the fact that even though they had me on film with countless guys pulling items from my pussy, it couldn't be determined that it was a drug transaction. He used that information by saying it was just a part of my act I did at the club and those items weren't drug related. The under cover cop they had covering the case mysteriously popped up missing so they didn't have any witnesses.

Samire also set me up with a sweet job with Iman, after explaining to his aunt who works with Iman the misunderstanding at the club. That was an experience I will never forget. Now, people are still admiring my body, but it's from the side lines at high fashion run-way shows. The look in my eyes now is from hurt, pain, and life lessons. As these cameras flick and pop all around me they take a piece of my soul with it.

I smile as I strut in *Designs by IMAN* down the glittering cat walk and at the end of the runway I blew a kiss to my aunt, a few of my cousins who came through to show some love, and Samire… my new man. He finally told me how he felt about me after the trial was over and it wasn't even a second thought for us to hook up since I had grown closer to him through this entire ordeal.

I worked the runway like I was born on it, giving everyone in the audience one stunning photo shot after the other. I may be just a beautiful face on the surface, but underneath there is a quiet storm brewing, just waiting…for revenge.

LITTLE NIKKI GRIND

K'WAN

Rome lounged on the leather sofa with his shoes off and his ankles crossed. Between his lips dangled an expertly rolled blunt that was packed to the brim with neon-green buds. The Cush went for six-hundred an ounce, but was well worth it. New York had one up on LA with most things, but when it came to grades of weed, Cali won the contest hands down.

Footsteps on the hardwood floor drew his attention to the hallway. The young lady who appeared at the mouth of the living room was a tender thing with butterscotch skin. Her dark hair cropped just above her ears. Her silk robe swung freely as she moved exposing the sheer watermelon colored Teddy beneath. It was a sexy number that barely covered her stripper sized ass. She flopped on the couch next to Rome. He could smell the sweet scent of vanilla over the Cush. His dick got hard but his face stayed neutral.

Her name was Helen if he remembered correctly. At five-six with a mean walk she was knocking a lot of chicks out the box. Rome had met her earlier that day working the cash register at Duane Reade on 94th and Columbus Avenue. Even beneath the red smock and loose fitting slacks he could tell that she had it and went in for the kill. Surprisingly enough, it didn't take much for her to give up the number, and with a bit of G, he found himself waiting outside her job to take her home that afternoon for God only knew what kind of fun.

"Damn, you rocking that shit Ma," he said, running a hand along her thigh.

"This is just a little something I picked up in the Bahamas," she said, as if it was no big deal. In all truthfulness a lot of thought was put into the outfit. She had planned to wear it for her man on their one year anniversary, but catching her best friend giving him head two days prior changed the plan.

"You know, when I saw you standing behind the register today I knew there was something special about you," he said in his Billy D voice.

"Nigga, knock it off. You saw me and thought I had a phat ass and that's why you pushed up," she said, letting him know that she was bullshit proof.

"Come on, Ma, it ain't always about a physical attraction. How do you know I didn't just dig you for your personality?"

Helen smiled then her face went very serious. She scooted closer to him and whispered in his ear. "Let's cut the bullshit, daddy. You saw me and wanted to fuck me. Ain't no shame in it cause I thought the same thing when I saw you. So lets not be coy about the whole shit."

Rome was surprised and turned on by Helen's directness. Usually he had to apply at least a little game, but in this instance it was Helen who took the initiative. Not one to be out gamed

Rome opened his mouth to make a snappy comeback, but she hushed him by placing her mouth over his. Helen's breath tasted like peppermint sticks as his tongue explored her mouth. Helen purred from somewhere low in her gut before biting his bottom lip playfully. Rome immediately jerked away.

"What's the matter, did I hurt you?" she teased.

"So, you like the rough shit, huh?" he said, touching his lip to make sure it wasn't bleeding.

"If it ain't rough it ain't right," she said flatly. That was all he needed to hear.

Rome grabbed Helen by both arms and lifted her. For all the ass that Helen had he was surprised by how light she was. Rome placed her on his lap and began to run his tongue up and down her neck. Helen hissed in approval and began grinding on his lap. Through his jeans he could feel the call of her warm pussy. Rome's hard dick pressed against her through his jeans only making her grind with more force.

Gracefully, Helen slid off his lap and knelt before Rome. She ran her hands up to his chest and back down, stopping at his crotch. She cupped his dick through his jeans and tested the size of his penis. Rome smiled because he knew that he had a big dick and now she did too. Slowly she unzipped his pants and removed his penis from his pants. Sure enough Rome was very well hung and hard as a rock. Helen stroked it for a while to get a feel for the large muscle before taking him in her mouth. She started at the head, running her tongue in circles around the rim of it. Rome grunted, but wouldn't allow himself to show her how good it was feeling.

Helen took her time playing around the head before taking him halfway into her mouth. Rome felt his dick hit the back of her throat at about the halfway point, and was pleasantly surprised when she opened up and took him in almost to the balls. With wet, slurping sounds, Helen ran her lips and tongue up and down Rome's shaft. Rome shivered when warm saliva dripped down the side of his dick, beneath his balls, and into the crease of his ass.

"You like that, don't you?" she looked up at him hungrily, while still stroking his dick.

"Yeah," he gasped.

"You don't sound convinced," she said, sliding his jeans and boxers down to his ankles. "Let me see what I can do to change that." Helen stroked Rome's throbbing dick and began to juggle his balls in her mouth. Every so often she would go up the shaft with her tongue, but she concentrated on his balls. Rome let his eyes roll back in his head and enjoyed the ride while she sucked him off. He was on cloud nine until something wet around his ass hole caused him to jump straight up, knocking Helen to the ground in the process.

"Fuck is you down there doing? Bitch, I ain't wit that anal penetration shit!" Rome barked, trying to keep the near panic out of his voice.

"Relax, baby," she said, easing him back down on the couch. "I wouldn't even play you like that. I got something special I want to try. Just relax and enjoy it."

Reluctantly Rome sat back on the couch and let Helen go back to what she had been doing. She licked beneath his balls, tickling that thin layer of skin that went from the nuts to the ass-hole. Once she had him fully relaxed again she moved her tongue further south. She could feel Rome tense up a bit when her tongue brushed over his asshole, but he didn't bolt up like before. As delicately as she could, Helen began flicking her tongue around the rim of his asshole.

Rome gritted his teeth and grabbed the back of her hair force-fully. At that moment he was having very mixed emotions about getting his salad tossed for the first time. One part of him wanted to slap her and yank her away from his ass, but the other part of him was turned on. Shorty was doing her thing and he was half enjoying it. He couldn't help but to wonder if that meant he had homosexual tendencies.

Helen attacked Rome's ass with tongue and lips, stroking his dick the whole time. He cursed her under his breath as she made him feel like a bitch. He could feel the cum building up in his dick and prayed that he didn't cum prematurely, but doubted that his prayers would be answered. Helen must have felt it too because she started stroking and licking faster. As the first squirts of semen began to shoot from the head of Rome's dick, Helen moved from his asshole back to his dick. She took the head in her mouth and caught the cum as it came shooting out. Rome roared like a jungle cat as Helen sucked the last few drops of cum from him and swallowed hard.

"Shit, that was some good head!" Rome gasped, slumping further into the couch.

"Oh, that was just he beginning," Helen said, wiping her mouth with a dish cloth. She stood up and slipped out of her robe so that he could appreciate her body fully. She placed her knees on both sides of Rome and ran her moist pussy against his half limp dick and smiled. "The best is yet to come."

As Helen straddled Rome and proceeded to give him the fucking of his life, he quietly hoped that he wouldn't be too wiped out afterwards to meet up with his crew later that evening.

2

"This spot better be the mutha fucking jump off for as long as it's taking to get there," Alonzo complained from the back seat. He had to lean forward for Rome to hear him over the deafening music.

"Calm your ass down, and wait like everybody else," Rome called over his shoulder. He turned his attention back to the road, but kept glancing back to the rearview mirror to check himself out. Rome was the pretty boy of the crew, and thought very highly of himself. He was a high-yellow dude with curly black hair that he kept freshly shaped up.

"I don't give a damn how far it is, as long as the bitches are proper," Po-Boy said, dumping the Dutch Master filling into his old Heineken bag. Po-Boy had gotten his name because back in the days he was one of the poorest kids in the neighborhood. His kicks were always out of style or tore up, if not both, and the only time you ever saw him wearing name brand clothes, they had come from someone else. Those days had long gone since Po-Boy had hooked up with Rome and the crew. Though Po-Boy was getting cake, he still didn't put much stock in high fashion clothes. Instead of spending in excess, Po-Boy horded his money away like the miser he was.

"True story, kid, a nigga trying to go up in there and taste something," Felon said, smoothly pulling on the blunt. In contrast to Rome's yellow skin, Felon's was coal black. He wasn't particularly ugly, but he wasn't the most handsome cat in the world. Both Felon's skin and soul bore scars, representing his rough upbringing. What he lacked in looks he made up for in heart. Felon was the type of cat that you could get fifty-cents from if he had a dollar. To spite the dirty line of business they were in, Felon always tried to be tactful about how he carried it. Tact was something that he always stressed to the young heads. But to spite his generous heart Felon had a vicious spirit. There was a side to him that no one wanted any parts of, the devil incarnate if you will. If you fucked with him he'd come at you with everything but the kitchen sink.

"Listen to you," Rome said, whipping the Escalade in and out of the traffic rolling across the Verrazano Bridge. "You got the mouth of a player, but the heart of a trick. You'll probably end up spending all your dough on the first bitch that shakes her stinking ass your way," Rome teased him. He was one of the few people who could joke with Felon like that and not get his shit rocked.

"Leave that man alone, Rome, I thought we was heading to celebrate our good fortune? We finally did it, kid!" Alonzo spoke up. Being the youngest of the group he sometimes made the mistake of speaking out of turn.

Rome turned a sharp glare at him through the rearview, but just as quickly composed himself. When he spoke his voice was easy, but the mocking undertone was apparent. "*We?* Zo, you got more jokes than a little bit. I don't recall you kicking out no bread for studio time when we were trying to cut this CD, now you screaming some *we* shit. When this nigga started taking this rap shit serious," he jerked his thumb at Felon who listened quietly, "I was the only one to support him. Everybody knew what he was doing and what he needed to prosper, but did anyone step to the plate?"

Silence.

"Exactly," Rome continued. "I was the one who kept it gangsta with him. Me and my dude saw what it had the potential to become. We took the bull by the horns. We held the block in twenty-four hour shifts to get that studio money up!"

Everybody knew the story of Rome and Felon's rise, but at times they didn't seem to respect it. They had all thought that Felon had become afflicted with the '*I wanna be a rapper*' bug, but as it turned out he was good. So good in fact that he had went on a ten win streak in underground battles until he was derailed by a sour audience, and a kid who later went on to sign with J-Records. Still, Felon was recognized as a truly gifted MC on the underground circuit. Some even called him a freak of nature, which played a big part in naming their company.

Back when it was all still fresh, Rome had been one of the few to take interest, and the only one to actually try and help his friend recognize his dream. Together they had created Freak Show, LLC. It was a company that offered management services as well as ghost writing. Felon was the only client, but the bravado was bigger than life. They would hustle all day and hit the clubs at night, buying bottles and talking shit. They eventually accomplished their goal as being one of the most recognized crews in Harlem. When they had the public's full attention they hit them with the music. It took over two years of promoting and hustling, but at long last they were able to see the mountain top. Freak Show had just signed a distribution agreement with Sony's Urban Music Division and the sky was the limit.

"Why don't the both of you niggaz relax?" Felon tried to defuse the situation. "Rome, Zo is family so he shines the same as we do. Zo," he turned to the youngster. "I know you're excited, but sometimes you say stupid shit. If you can't say something useful, then don't say anything," Felon continued.

"That'll keep that mutha fucka quiet all night!" Po-Boy declared, getting a laugh from Rome and a dirty look from Alonzo.

The rest of the ride was spent in silence. Finally, they arrived at their destination. It was a somewhat desolate spot near the southern most tip of the island. Rome grumbled something that went unheard by the others as they pulled up. The dusty gravel from the parking lot coated the running boards and doors of the Escalade. The debris threatened to ruin the wash and wax Rome had subjected the truck to earlier that day.

Dominating most of the abandoned plane was a two story house, The Cat House, as was advertised by the neon awning. It was just plain. Cars parked along the perimeter of the house but none came within more than a yard. On the porch there were two males trying to blend in. The first was older, possibly early to mid forties, with cinnamon skin that hung slightly off his bones. His far younger companion had a copper skin tone and seemed to be of Latin descent, if one had to guess.

The four men exited the car, downed their last shots of liquor and tossed the flaming blunt clips to the ground. They were all feeling nice, but none of them were too tipsy. They made it a habit to always maintain some level of sobriety before entering an area where they weren't assured absolute safety. Even in some of those spots they had to be on point.

Rome led the way up the rickety steps that welcomed visitors of the house, and conferred with one of the men watching the door. Seconds later, the rest of the crew was summoned to be searched before being allowed entrance to The Cat House. Once they passed the security checkpoint they found themselves wondering a narrow hallway. At the end of the hall was another door, this one was manned by a young looking dude wearing a white t-shirt and heavy blue denim shorts. Again Rome leaned in to whisper something in the man's ear and the crew was motioned to proceed. As they passed, they noticed that they were getting funny looks from some of the spectators. They weren't looks of envy, but of curiosity, wondering who the newcomers were.

"VIP treatment, that's what I'm talking about!" Po-Boy slapped Alonzo's palm as they passed through the foyer and into the *main hall.*

The Main Hall was little more than a living room and dining room that someone had gutted and slapped a bar/stage in the middle as a divider. The bar was shaped like a thick horseshoe wide enough for the girls to walk on. This sat under a slightly elevated stage that doubled the bar in width. The girls did their thing on the main stage, occasionally stepping down onto the bar to press for tips.

A tall white girl stood behind the bar taking drink orders. She was rail thin but had balloon-like breasts that had to cost her a pretty penny. She strutted in her four inch neon heels, swinging a long blonde ponytail, making sure there wasn't a dry cup on the bar.

The smell of sex was pungent in the dry air of the house. Strippers in all shapes and sizes strutted through the joint making sure there was an extra jiggle to their assess whenever they passed a dude that looked like he was holding. A girl wearing a blue crotch-less thong passed the quartet drawing all their stares.

"Yeah, yeah, see about me," Alonzo blew a kiss at the bartender, which got him a disgusted glare.

"Dawg, don't come in here acting like no fucking square," Rome warned him. "The last thing we need is to have our crew looking silly. With the official launch of Freak Show we became made men."

"That's the kind of shit I'm talking about," Po-Boy said, looking past the rude stripper and admiring the bartender.

Felon tapped Rome's arm, and motioned for him to follow, "Lets get a drink." Without looking back he headed to the bar. By the time his three friends had managed to pull themselves away from the show, two of the girls were performing over on one of the side stages and the big breasted bartender was sitting the drinks on the bar. Two were straight shots of Hennessey accompanied by two Heinekens and the others were Long Island Iced Teas.

"Sweets for the sweet," Felon teased, as he handed the Iced Teas to Alonzo and Po-Boy.

"Nigga, stop fronting. Just because y'all prefer that fire water to some smooth shit don't mean that we can't drink!" Po-Boy declared, downing half of his drink in one gulp.

"Drunk mutha fucka," Rome said, as he took his shot from the bar. "Say, I propose a toast." He raised his glass.

"What we toasting to?" Alonzo asked.

"Mo money, nigga, what else?" Rome asked, as if he should've already known.

3

The main part of the house had a nice sprinkling of chicks that night. Black, Spanish, Asian, White. There was a little of every thing. Girls sauntered across the room wearing next to nothing, offering their goods to any who had the finances to blow for it. A molasses flavored stallion whose upper lip sexily curved upward, appeared out of nowhere. She eyed the quartet like a hungry jackal, but let her sultry gaze linger on Po-Boy.

He played it real cool, but only a blind man couldn't see how sexy this girl was. Her face seemed to be sculpted from marble with its chiseled features and black-glass eyes. Po-Boy's eyes followed her hourglass shape from waist down to her large ass and healthy thighs. The girl turned around so that he could see her entire ass and started clapping it left and right. She backed it up against him and started clapping it on his dick. The girl had so much control over her ass that it almost felt like she was giving him a hand job.

"I'll be back," Po-Boy said, allowing the girl to lead him off to a darker section of the club.

"That nigga don't waste no time," Alonzo said, tossing a crumpled dollar at one of the girls on the bar.

"Yeah, we're gonna celebrate in true don fashion tonight," he declared, admiring a fine redbone that passed him with a wink. Felon smiled at the thought of how much more pussy would come his way once his album dropped. "Freak Show till the world blow!" he mumbled.

***

The big butt stripper pulled Po-Boy to the back of the club, where there was a short flight of stairs leading to the VIP area. A bald man with broad shoulders and an attitude problem notified Po-Boy that the VIP admission was an extra thirty dollars, but Po-Boy managed to Jew him down to twenty, being that it was early and the club wasn't packed yet.

Inside the closed off room were several couches and a bathroom sat, there was a guy hitting a girl with the short stroke from the back, but other than them the VIP was still relatively empty. The big butt stripper sat Po-Boy on one of the couches and began doing her thing. She started out slow grinding on his lap until she felt him stiffen. Not being one to waste too much time on one trick, she dropped down to her knees and started tugging at his belt. It took a minute, but she was finally able to pull his dick out of his pants.

"What's good daddy, I can give you a dance or we can get into some other shit," she said, stroking his short, but fat dick. "Fifty for some head and a hundred for a lay, what you wanna do?"

Po-Boy immediately regretted coming into the back with her. It was always fun to try and fuck the chicks in the strip club, but there was something about when they asked for paper that made him feel like he'd been had. Fuck it, he said to himself. He could tell by looking at her that she was a real freak joint and would earn every dollar he spent.

"Let me see what that head is like and we can see about some of that trim later," he said, counting off fifty singles.

The girl took the bills and stuffed them into the bag that she had slung over her shoulder, before pushing his legs further apart. She examined his dick carefully before letting her tongue taste the head of it and frowning. Po-Boy's dick tasted like dry Salami. She produced a condom from her bag and popped it into her mouth. Carefully inserting him into her mouth, she slipped the condom over his dick. Po-Boy let out a gasp as she began bobbing up and down on his dick. The stripper made slurping sounds as she blessed Po-Boy, making sure to hit him from balls to shaft. She used one hand to jerk his dick and the other to juggle his balls.

Po-Boy rolled his head back in ecstasy as the stripper gave him a blow job straight out of Booty Talk 48. He gripped a hand full of her hair and thrust himself into her mouth over and over. The stripper had excellent muscle control over her throat, but his quick and erratic movements made her gag a bit. When she looked up and saw the vein that had popped up on Po-Boy's forehead, she knew he was about to blow. Now, instead of sucking his dick in quick jerks she slowed it up, elongating her strokes. Po-Boy grunted something biblical and blew his load inside the condom.

***

Felon sat at the bar flanked by Rome and Alonzo. Alonzo busied himself trying to flirt with a thick Spanish chick who was wearing a transparent body suit, while Rome was hunched over whispering something to the bartender. She came back a few seconds later and placed two bottles of Crystal and three champagne flutes on the bar. Rome thanked her and told her to keep the change.

"That's that good shit there," Alonzo said, holding his flute out.

"Nothing but the best for my niggaz," Rome said, filling the flutes. "Drink up, my niggaz, cause after tonight we say goodbye to poverty and hello to the fast lane!" Rome said, hoisting his glass.

The DJ's voice came in over the loud speaker. "Big shot to Felon and my niggaz from Freak Show Entertainment. Congratulations on the deal!" Rome stood up, holding one of the bottles and took a bow, while Felon raised his glass coolly.

He was just as thrilled as his team was about the deal with Sony, but he didn't crave the limelight like they did. To Felon it was about more than the money, getting signed was his dream. Ever since he had seen Nas, who back then still went by Nasty Nas, do his thing at Esso's, a few years back, he knew that music was his calling. He spent long nights after that writing, and sharpening his skills, until he felt that he was ready to step out from within the shadows. Many years later, as they sat dipping high priced champagne, he realized that his dreams were finally coming true. He wanted to cry tears of joy, but didn't want anyone who might be watching to get the wrong idea, so he just chuckled softly.

"Yo, check these bitches out," Alonzo said, tapping Felon's arm and pointing to the stage. Felon's eyes wondered to the stage where two thick ass strippers had just stepped up to do their thing.

They were standing on a sheet of blue plastic shaking their asses to a techno type beat. The first girl was the color of sun dried leaves with a long black weave that tickled the almond colored nipples of her perky breasts. The second girl was dark chocolate sporting a short blonde afro. Her breasts were larger than those of the dark haired girl, but not quite as firm. The dark blonde dropped into a full split and bounced to the beat. The second girl raised her leg skyward in a vertical split and began popping her ass. Using her teeth, the blonde girl removed the dark haired girl's thong and slowly began lapping at her moist pussy, drawing a low moan from her.

The blonde girl yanked off her own thong and started jamming her finger in and out of her snatch making a squishing sound. She delivered a vicious slap to the dark haired girl's ass, sending a ripple up it. The dark haired girl played with her nipples enjoying the oral she was receiving. The onlookers cheered and began tossing dollars onto the stage.

The dark haired girl slid down on her ass, with one leg over the thigh of the blonde. They began moving in a rhythm, grinding their pussies together. After a few minutes of cat bumping the blonde girl flipped over on all fours and began popping her ass cheeks one at a time. She reached her hand back and began fingering herself while the crowd looked on.

At some point during the show the dark haired girl had produced a can of Red Bull which she tipped up over her mouth and began guzzling. The excess ran down her body and dripped onto the plastic. Still holding some of the liquid in her mouth she leaned forward and began spitting Red Bull into the crack of the blonde girl's ass. The energy drink dripped down the crack of her ass and the dark haired girl caught it in her mouth as it trickled from the blonde's pussy.

By this point the crowd was damn near in a frenzy, but they hadn't seen anything yet. Slowly the dark haired girl began rubbing the can on the blonde girl's pussy, while playing with her own clit. Giving the crowd a mischievous smile she began sliding the can into the blonde girl's pussy. The can disappeared to the halfway point before she pulled it out and repeated the process.

The blonde girl backed her ass up while the dark haired girl smacked it, continuing to slide the can in and out at different speeds. Guys were going wild, cheering and tossing money onto the stage. Even Rome who considered himself the too cool for words found his dick straining against his jeans. The roar of the horny men in the bar drowned out the moans escaping the blonde girl, but her face told the whole story. She bit her bottom lip and cursed as the dark haired girl fucked her with the can. Just when no one thought it could get any better the can of Red Bull disappeared completely into the girl's pussy. Still holding the can inside her the blonde girl began bouncing her ass roughly on thc stage as if she was trying to mix a martini in her twat. Raising her ass heavenward the blonde girl began slowly expelling the can. The dark haired girl pulled the can the rest of the way out of the blonde girl's pussy and downed the last of the Red Bull. Bills of every denomination rained down on the stage as the girls wrapped up their little freak show with a kiss.

"You like what you see," a feminine voice whispered into Felon's ear. He turned around and found himself looking at what could've only been described as a goddess. She had an angelic face, with cinnamon skin and eyes the color of caramel candy. Her body was covered by a silk robe, but Felon could tell that beneath it, she was built like a stallion.

"Maybe," he said, trying to maintain his cool.

"Well, if you think those bitches were something special wait until you see me do my thing," she winked and disappeared into the crowd.

"Damn, shorty was bad," Rome shouted to Felon over the loud music. "Who was she?"

"I don't know," Felon said, with a dazed look in his eyes.

4

The sounds of the DJ's voice over the loud speaker brought Felon out of his daze. "Okay, you hard luck ass niggaz. I want your cock in one hand and your wallet in the other. You mutha fuckas act like you know and show some love for the lovely Ms. Nikki Grind!"

The lights in the club flickered twice and died. Slowly they began to come back up, with a pale blue light highlighting the stage. The same girl who Felon had just been talking to came out, still dressed in the silk robe. Under the lights her face had somewhat of a child-like innocence, but Felon doubted if there was anything innocent about any of the women working in The Cat House.

The woman stepped out onto the stage as if she owned the joint and dropped the robe. This drew a gasp from everyone in the room, including Felon. Her body was like something out of King Magazine. Beneath the robe she wore black thigh high boots with clear stiletto heels and a leather corset, which had a fringed mini attached to it. Beneath the pleats of her skirt you could see the cheeks of her apple shaped ass. The boots hugged her thighs perfectly, with the lights playing tricks on the buckles that held them up. The leather corset hugged her small waist and cupped her breasts nicely.

Felon had been so preoccupied with watching the young stripper move that he hadn't noticed the music playing. At first he couldn't place the fierce guitar strings or the heavy bass, but the melodic voice of the singer made him realize just what it was he was listening to. It was Prince's *Nikki Grind.*

The blue tinted light danced off her skin making her appear to glow under it. Felon found himself unable to take his eyes off her as she did her thing for those assembled. The sinful goddess swayed in place for a moment before going into her routine. As Prince whined out the story of Nikki Grind, the stripper moved in time with the lyrics. Before she had even gotten into her groove money came flying onto the stage in heaps. She executed a cross-legged strut around the stage. Her hungry eyes touched everyone assembled around it, but lingered a little longer on Felon. Her movements were as graceful of those of a jungle cat as she dropped down on all fours and swung her mane of dark hair in time with the drum strikes.

A man sitting at the foot of the stage looked up at her with a hungry facial expression. Skillfully, she went into a baseball slide, with one leg elevated just above his shoulder, the edges of her pussy's lips ever so visible beneath the thong. When the man reached up and touched her calf he shivered. She let his hand come within inches of the exposed flesh of her thigh before snatching it back. He tried to climb on stage only to have one of the bouncers snatch him back roughly.

Flipping over on her hands and knees she cocked her ass up and gave the crowd a view of her goods. She wiggled her large ass, making it clap, but changed speed popping one cheek at a time. Without even realizing that he was doing so, Felon reached out for her. A wave of vertigo overcame Felon causing him to run his hands over his face to try and clear his head. Only when his hand brushed against the moisture of his lips did he realize that he had been drooling a bit. Felon was so caught up in the show that he didn't notice that someone was approaching him from the rear until the stranger was right on top of him.

Felon spun around on his barstool with his fists balled. The man took a step back and held his hands up in surrender. "My bad, I didn't mean to startle you."

"Fuck is you running up on niggaz like that for!" Felon barked. He wasn't sure if he was angrier at the fact that the man was able to creep up on him like that, or the fact that he had taken his attention away from the show.

"Easy, my dude," Rome placed a hand on Felon's shoulder. "This is Gino, he owns the place."

Gino was a thin Italian man, who wore too much gel in his hair and reeked of cheap cologne. He wore a bleached-white wife beater beneath his purple and black jogging suit. Whenever he moved the tiny gold chains around his neck clanked together, like tin cans. Gino was the poster boy for your stereotypical mobster.

"Rome, what's up with your partner?" Gino asked, trying to regain his cool.

"You gotta excuse Felon, Gino. When you've spent as much time in the battle field as he has you're bound to come away a little shell-shocked," Rome joked. "Things are jumping in here tonight."

"Did you expect anything less?" Gino smirked, exposing teeth that were badly stained from too much smoking and not enough dental visits. "I made sure to tell all my girls that we had some very important people coming through here tonight."

Rome slapped him a pound. "Flattery will get you everywhere, my dude."

"Say, what're you fellas doing sitting at the bar like a bunch of humps? I've made special accommodations for you guys tonight." Gino motioned for them to follow and headed back through the crowd. Rome and Alonzo followed, but Felon hesitated. He took a moment to glance back at the sexy stripper only to find that she was staring at him. As Prince wrapped up the song explaining that Nikki had told him to call her up whenever he wanted to grind, the stripper mimicked a phone with her thumb and pinky and winked at Felon.

***

Gino led them through the crowd of people occasionally nodding or stopping to greet one of the patrons. From the love that he got you could tell that he was an important man, no matter how silly his outward appearance might have been. Felon learned a long time ago, that it was never safe to judge a book by its cover.

Somewhere along their trek, Po-Boy had caught up with the group. From the shit eating grin he wore, he'd done something freaky with the stripper from earlier. Alonzo took a minute to explain their destination to him and Po-Boy fell in step with the rest of the group.

Gino had led them to the far side of the room, just off from the DJ booth. A huge man sporting a bald head and an eye patch leaned casually against a door marked *private*. He nodded at Gino and stepped to the side, holding the door open for the five of them to enter. Felon almost gagged on the cloud of weed smoke that slapped him in the face when they entered the dimly lit room. His lungs were no stranger to good weed but the amount of it congested within the room made it hard to breathe.

The VIP room was nicer than the rest of the club, yet had a wicked feel to it. There were a few people occupying the VIP room, but most of them were strippers who pranced around in bikinis or totally nude. They all seemed to notice Felon and his team when they walked in, but kept their distance for the time being. Of course they knew who the guys from Freak Show were, but Gino had given them specific instructions not to act too much like the vultures they were right off the back.

There were booths along the walls and a small bar in the center of the room. A small stage was positioned a few feet away from the bar, where a young woman was cocked over shaking her money maker for anyone interested. Lining the back wall were several stalls with what looked like Christmas lights hanging from the doors. Some of the lights were red, while others were green.

"Those are the boom-boom rooms," Gino said, noticing Felon curiously staring at the stalls. "Don't worry, you'll get to see what those are about before the night is over."

Gino had finally led them to their booth, which was the furthest from the door. It was circular with heavily padded seats just perfect for lounging or doing whatever else came to mind in the VIP. On the table were a magnum of Hennessey and several buckets holding bottles of Moet. Gino bowed and swept his hands at the seat, motioning for them to sit.

"This shit is pretty fly, Gino," Rome said, sliding into the booth.

"I told you that I would take care of you guys tonight."

"I'm trying to run up in one of these bitches," Alonzo said hungrily, eyeing a short brown skinned girl.

"Help yourself to whatever you want; all these bitches will fuck for a buck," Gino told him. "Now, I got some things to take care of out on the floor, but if you need me for anything just send one of the girls." Gino shook the hands of the men seated and went on about his business.

"Where do you know that little greasy mutha fucka from?" Felon asked, watching Gino slither away.

"You know I know a little bit of everybody. Gino is a cool ass nigga though, for a guinea," Rome said, lifting one of the bottles from the bucket. "I don't know about you niggaz, but I plan on getting thoroughly fucked up tonight and waking up with my dick in one of these bitch's mouths tomorrow."

"I'll drink to that," Po-Boy said, grabbing a bottle of Moet and taking it to the face.

"Your drunk ass will drink to anything!" Alonzo joked, grabbing a bottle and doing the same.

For the next hour or so the four men drank and got high as

kites. The strippers started coming out of the woodwork, smelling money in the air. One dude sat at two booths over from where Felon and company sat, wedged between two strippers. In each hand he held a fist full of hair as the strippers took turns sucking his dick. He noticed Po-Boy looking over at the show and gave him a drunken smile. Po-Boy raised his glass and saluted him back.

"That's right, my nigga, double your pleasure!" Po-Boy laughed.

"I think I might have to make this one of my regular spots," Rome said, cupping the breasts of a light skinned girl who had taken up a perch on his lap.

"You and me both," Alonzo said, tossing dollar bills at a thick Asian chick that was pussy popping on their table.

Felon had a chocolate delight on his lap, bumping and grinding her large ass on his crotch. He slapped her ass playfully while she grabbed her ankles and wiggled. He was trying to enjoy himself, but was distracted. Ever since he had seen the girl who had danced to Prince's song, he couldn't get his mind off her. It was as if she had worked some kind of spell on him through her dancing. He was about to get up and go look for her, but found that he didn't have to because she came sauntering into the VIP. She had shed the robe, but was still dressed in her leather corset and boots. Almost every dude in the room stopped what he was doing and watched her make her way to the bar.

"I'll be right back," Felon said, sliding from beneath the chocolate girl. She looked a little offended, but her face softened as Rome invited her to join her friend on his lap.

"Where're you going?" Rome called after his friend, now cupping the breasts of both women.

"Got something I need to look into," Felon called over his shoulder. Rome shouted something else, but he couldn't hear him over the sound of his own heart beating in his ears.

5

Her back was to him, so Felon couldn't see her face, but he didn't need to. It was etched in his brain like the first time he had ever seen a kilo. Some dude was occupying the stool beside her, teetering as if he'd had too much to drink, so Felon decided to hang back and watch for a minute. He wasn't sure what it was about the young tender, but he couldn't take his eyes off her.

The way she was positioned, curved her back into an arch, making Felon think about what hitting her doggy style would be like. There was a tattoo of a cross entangled in thorns with sprouting roses on her back. This made her even more appealing. When she turned the dim violet hue from the bar, it played tricks on her profile, making her features look almost perfect. With her delicate jaw line and button nose, she may as well have been flawlessly sculpted from marble. *God I wanna fuck her*, he thought.

Shorty must've been a mind reader because no sooner than the thought manifested itself, she turned in his direction. Her eyes had laziness to them; possibly from the drink she was sipping on, but there was no doubt that she was on point. She gave Felon a bored look and leaned in to whisper something into the drunk's ear. He made a funny face before taking his drink off the bar and moving to the next chick.

Felon moved towards the bar, watching shorty thc whole time. She had again turned her back on him, but he could see her watching him through one of the mirrors. Instead of taking the seat, the drunk had vacated Felon and took the stool two spots to the stripper's left. He placed his bottle on the bar and told the waitress to bring him a shot of poison and a champagne flute. Shorty was thrown off by his move, but countered by moving down and taking the stool next to his.

"I see you like the good shit," she said, eyeing the bottle of high-end champagne.

"Only on special occasions," he said, tossing a twenty on the bar for the waitress. Felon slid the flute down to the lady and filled her glass. The stripper nodded in appreciation. She took a baby sip from her glass and smiled.

"What's your name, Ma?" he asked, knowing that he had her once she took the glass.

"First name, Cash, last name, I need that," she said, seriously.

"Damn, that's some cold shit to say after partaking in my drink and all." His tone was serious, but portrayed none of the offense he felt.

The stripper frowned and slid the glass back to him. "Not for nothing, I don't go gaga over every nigga in here popping bottles. Nothing personal, sweetie, but a bitch is in here on a hustle. I ain't really got time for the courtship."

Felon was surprised by her quick wit, but hardly thrown off. "Baby, I'd hardly call this courting," he motioned towards the naked women in the Cat House and the thirty cat's chasing them. "I'd prefer a more intimate setting."

She couldn't help but to laugh. "I hear you talking, big time, but that doesn't change the fact that I gotta make a tip before its all said and done. How 'bout a dance?"

"I might consider it if I can get a name," he shot back.

"It's Nikki."

"Like the song," he said, referring to the theme she had just performed to.

"Exactly," she slid the glass back over. Another cat walked over and grabbed her arm, but she waved him off.

"I see you've got the same affect on everybody?" Felon sipped his drink.

"Alcohol and flesh makes everybody a little crazy, but a phat ass helps too," she slapped herself on the ass making it jiggle. Felon laughed, showing off his perfectly white teeth. "You've got a nice smile," she complimented.

"Thanks, when you're in the public eye a nice smile means a lot," Felon replied.

"Public eye?" she asked, taking a long swig of her champagne.

"Yeah, I just got my label off the ground so me and my crew are up in here celebrating," he said proudly.

"I should've known," she huffed.

"What's that supposed to mean?"

She finished the last of her champagne. "Don't take this the wrong way, boo, but the majority of the niggaz I meet in here claim to be some kind of rapper or CEO."

"Well, I ain't the majority of the niggaz you meet up in here," Felon shot back.

"And what makes you so different?"

"Passion," he said flatly. "See, most niggaz are motivated by the money and women that come with this game, but neither of those things move me. It's my passion for the craft that drives me to do what I do. Real talk, Ma."

"You kick a good game, daddy," she said, looking around.

Felon noticed that she did that every couple of minutes as if she was expecting someone to jump out of the shadows and grab her. In her line of work he couldn't blame her for being a little paranoid, so he let it go.

"I ain't never been one for games, Ma. Games are for kids and I'm a grown man," he told her.

Nikki laughed at how serious he was. Suddenly the hairs on her neck stood up and she looked over her shoulder. A man wearing a fitted White Sox hat and a three quarter leather jacket had just entered the VIP accompanied by a large black man with a sloped forehead. He scanned the darkened room as if he was looking for someone.

"Listen, baby boy, it's been real, but I gotta boogie," she said, getting up from the barstool.

"Hold on, Ma," Felon grabbed her arm, "I'm not trying to

boar you to death. I just want a little bit of your time."

Nikki searched Felon's eyes for signs of bullshit, but only saw sincerity. When she saw him near the main stage she thought he was cute, but no different than the rest of the niggaz who came to The Cat House to blow their money on ass and booze. Listening to him talk, she knew there was more to him though. She found herself wondering about the dark skinned man, but checked it. The number one rule of thumb was that you didn't get emotionally attached to the tricks.

"Well, my time is money," she said, casting a nervous glance over her shoulder. Felon followed her eyes and spotted the dude in the fitted hat. He wasn't sure who he was, but he seemed to have Nikki rattled.

"Baby girl, I ain't pressed for bread," he assured her.

"If that's the case, let's take this conversation to one of the boom-boom rooms." She grabbed him by the arm and began pulling him towards the stalls before he could protest. When they reached the stalls almost all of them were occupied. They finally found one at the end that was free and stepped inside. Nikki secured the latch on the door before releasing the breath she was holding.

"Who was that, an angry boyfriend?" Felon asked, sitting on the padded bench inside the boom-boom room.

"Something like that," she said, hanging her purse on one of the hooks attached to the mirrored wall. "So, what's the deal? You talking or are you spending?"

"Damn, you get right to it, huh?"

"I told you, boo, I'm in here on a come up." She sat on his lap facing him. Felon could smell sweat mixed with something far sweeter coming off Nikki's skin as she slowly grinded on his lap. "It's thirty cash for a dance."

"What if I want more than a dance?" he asked, taking in her scent.

"Then I suggest you get yourself another girl. All I do is

dance, love."

She started to get off his lap, but he pulled her back down.

"A'ight boo," he fished a knot of singles from his pants pocket and fanned them. This seemed to ease her mind a bit.

The boom-boom rooms were sound proofed, so no one could hear what was going on inside. This was the reason that Gino had all of the rooms fitted with small speakers that pumped music into the rooms. Swisha House's *Still Tipping* came through the speakers as she went into her routine.

She started out by grinding on Felon's lap, occasionally popping her pussy when the beat kicked. Felon looked into her eyes and found himself sinking into the softness of them. She draped her arms over his shoulders and locked one leg behind his, while propping the other on the bench next to him. As Felon's hands ran over her soft ass Nikki started grinding her pussy on his lap. In seconds, she could feel his dick trying to poke her through his jeans. Dipping her hands between her legs, she stroked Felon's dick through the jeans and was pleased at his size. She couldn't help but to imagine what his dick would feel like slamming into the walls of her pussy. He must've been thinking the same thing because his eyes held a look that said he wanted to eat her alive.

Nikki flipped over and touched the ground with her hands. She wiggled her ass in his face while he rained singles down on her. The songs had changed to Rick Ross' *Hustling* remix, then Jim Jones' *We Fly High*. Normally you got three songs per dance, but she didn't stop. As long as he was spending she was dancing. Felon delivered playful slaps to her ass as she bounced it on his lap in time with the music. She could feel his finger slip under her thong, but didn't move to stop him. Slowly, Felon began running his finger in and out of her pussy, making her moan. She hissed as he added another finger, then another. Spots flashed before Nikki's eyes as she came all over his hand.

She remounted his lap and started licking down the side of his neck. Now, it was Felon's turn to moan. Her tongue felt like a warm feather tracing along the side of his throat and playing over his collar bone. Nikki drew back and kissed Felon while continuing to grind on his lap. They were both moving to the beat as if they could fuck through their clothes. Reaching down, Nikki removed his dick from his pants and gave it a gentle stroke. She took the throbbing muscle and began rubbing it against her pussy through the thong.

"You feel this hot pussy, daddy?" she breathed into his ear.

"Yeah, baby I feel it," he said, trying to suck the air from her lungs. Felon knew that he was playing himself for kissing a stripper, but he couldn't help it. Ms. Nikki Grind was like a drug and he was a hopeless addict.

Nikki continued rubbing Felon against her pussy until her hand was soaked with juice. She squeezed his throbbing cock, enjoying the heat it radiated. The head of Felon's dick accidentally slipped into Nikki, drawing a gasp from both of them. Just the slight penetration was driving Nikki insane. Reaching up into her purse, she produced a condom and held it in front of Felon.

"I thought all you did was dance?" he asked, out of breath.

"Nigga, shut up and take this pussy." She kissed him.

Not removing her mouth from his, Nikki reached down and slid the condom onto Felon's dick. He was so large that it didn't even cover his entire shaft, which thrilled her. Some girls didn't like oversized dicks, but Nikki preferred them. Once the condom was on securely, Nikki began sliding Felon inside her. The head felt like someone was trying to shove their fist into her womb. Nikki made a face, but didn't stop sliding him inside. Once they had gotten pass the head it didn't hurt as much. She settled down as far as she could on his dick and began riding him.

Felon couldn't help the little gasp that had escaped him. Even through the condom Nikki's pussy was one of the warmest he had ever felt. She rocked slowly on his lap, taking a little more of him into her with each stroke. Expertly, she began flexing her pussy muscles on his dick causing him to grunt. Felon looked into her eyes and didn't see a whorish stripper, but an angle of mercy.

Nikki unexpectedly hopped off Felon's dick, leaving it bobbing like a jack in the box. He looked at her confused, but understood what she wanted when she placed her hands against the walls and spread her legs. Felon moved behind her and slipped back inside her warm pussy. Being that she was shorter than him, his dick bent a little when he pumped making it slightly uncomfortable. He was careful that he didn't slip out of her when he moved her over to the small bench. Placing her hands on the bench, she bent all the way over so Felon could really dig into her guts.

In this position Felon was able to get the full view of her ass. It was heart shaped and perfect just like the rest of her. She cocked her ass up as far as she could so he could go deeper, but he still couldn't fit the whole thing. He had gotten his dick about three quarters of the way in before hitting a wall. Nikki let out a low scream, but this didn't stop her from throwing it back. Felon pumped and grunted behind Nikki, completely lost in the warmth. He wouldn't even have noticed that he was digging his nails into her waist if she hadn't slapped his hands away. He could feel Nikki's juices running down the shaft of his dick, soaking not only his balls, but the jeans he wore too. This only turned him on more, causing him to pump faster. A secret compartment opened somewhere in her pussy allowing Felon to go even deeper. His balls slapped against her ass as she begged for him to fuck her harder. Felon could feel the familiar tingling that seemed to go from his hips to the shaft of his dick as the room began to spin. He braced one hand against the wall and the other on her back as he groaned once and exploded. The cum seemed to flow in rivers as it filled the condom and almost to mid shaft. Finally it stopped and Felon slumped over on Nikki's back.

6

"That was the best shot I ever had!" Felon declared, while wiping his dick clean with one of the baby wipes Nikki handed him.

"Shit, I thought that big ass dick of yours was gonna shoot clean out of my mouth," she said, dabbing her sore pussy with a baby wipe.

"How much do I owe you?" Felon asked, pulling out his bank roll.

Nikki gave him an offended look. "I told you, all I do is dance. I don't whore myself for Gino like the rest of these bitches."

Felon gave her a confused look like he missed something. Unless the last half hour had been a dream, he could've sworn they fucked. "But didn't we…"

"Look," she cut him off. "I know you probably don't believe me, but I don't sleep with the customers. There was just something about you that moved me and I couldn't help myself. Now, if you wanna buy me a drink, or tip me for dancing that's cool. But don't try to offer me no money for fucking you because my pussy is priceless." Nikki stormed out of the boom-boom room leaving Felon sitting there with a stupid look on his face.

***

It wasn't until Felon took a step out of the boom-boom room that he realized his legs were weak. So weak in fact, he had to brace himself against the wall before continuing. He scanned the now semi-crowded VIP for Nikki, but saw no sign of her.

"Everything okay?" Rome asked, startling him. He was visibly tipsy, balancing himself between the two strippers Felon had left him with. "You're looking around like that bitch made off with your wallet."

"Nah, I just need to holla at her for a second. Have you seen her?" Felon asked, still scanning the room.

"I think she went out to the main floor, but don't jet off just yet. We're about to get the real party popping." Rome jiggled the breast of the stripper on his right.

"In a minute, my dude," Felon called over his shoulder as he made hurried steps to the VIP exit. By now the main floor looked like something out of a porno flick. The main stage as well as the floor, clamored with scantily clad women bending and twisting for the thirsty men tossing dollars at them. It took a minute, but Felon eventually spotted Nikki sitting at the bar.

"Why'd you dip off like that?" he asked, taking the seat next to her.

She glanced at him with saddened eyes. "I don't know, maybe it's the fact that I fucked a guy I hardly know, but for some reason I'm feeling in a major way. Or it could be the fact that he thinks I'm a whore. Pick one."

Felon felt a little embarrassed. "Nah, I don't think you're a hoe. I just thought…never mind," he said, figuring anything that came out of his mouth would only make the situation worse. "Listen, baby, I was digging you before I even sampled that sweet fruit. I might have been out of bounds, but I didn't know how to come at you. Let's try this again. I'm Felon," he extended his hand.

She looked at it for a minute, but eventually smiled and shook it. "Nikki."

"Now, that we've got that out of the way what're you drinking?"

"Hennessey," she raised her glass. Felon told the bartender to bring him two Hennessey's and a Heineken. "Sorry I tweaked out on you in there," she said quietly.

"It's cool. I think it was an awkward situation for both of us," he said, paying the waitress with a hundred dollar bill and instructing her to give the change to Nikki. She looked like she was about to say something, but he waved her silent. "Don't take it like that. I'm just tipping you for the dance, okay?"

"Okay," she said, stuffing the money into her purse. "Can I ask you something?"

"Sure."

"You've already got the pussy, so why are you still sitting here trying to be nice to me?"

Felon laughed. "Shorty, I already told you that I'm just trying to occupy a little bit of your time. Now, let me ask you a question."

"Okay," she said, a little suspicious.

"If all you do is dance, what made you fuck me?"

She lowered her head trying to think of the right thing to say. "I don't know." She downed her shot and frowned as it ripped through her chest. "It's just that I meet so many guys that can't see past a pretty face and a phat ass that it was kind of nice for someone to come at me like a gentleman."

"I wouldn't call myself a gentleman, sweetie," he joked. This got her to laugh.

"You know what I mean. You didn't come at me on some, *shorty how much to fuck*, shit. That and the fact that I think you're sexy as hell."

"I've never been called sexy," he said turning his face away from her. Felon knew he wasn't the most handsome dude in the world, so he had somewhat of a complex about his looks.

"I find that hard to believe." She turned his face back towards her. For a minute they just sat there staring at each other, each feeling something, but neither really sure how to express it. Nikki's touch produced a small feeling of warmth in Felon's gut. The feeling eventually grew and spread throughout his body. He couldn't deny the fact that what he felt for Nikki went beyond lust. It was something alien to Felon, yet special. Could he be lame enough to be falling for a stripper?

Their tender moment was broken up by someone spinning

Nikki around on the barstool. Felon turned and saw that it was the kid who she had been ducking in the VIP. He looked at Felon as if they might know each other, but then produced an angry look directed at Nikki.

"Fuck is you doing?" he barked.

"Bone, I'm just sitting here drinking. Why are you tripping?" she asked, trying to hide the fear in her voice.

"Bitch, it looks like you're doing more than drinking." Bone glared angrily at Felon. "Who the fuck is this nigga?"

"The question shouldn't be who I am, but why you're grabbing on the lady like that?" Felon said, matching Bone's stare. No sooner than the words left his mouth he wished he could have taken them back. He knew better than to come between a girl he didn't know and her man, especially a stripper. It was too late to take them back now. All he could do is deal with whatever came of it.

"Fuck is you, Captain Save-a-Hoe?" the man with the sloped forehead asked, moving to the other side of Felon.

"Duke, is you fucking crazy?" Felon jumped up, pushing the man out of his space. If it was going down, he wanted to make sure he had enough room to swing. The man took a step forward, but the sound of a bottle being broken halted him.

"We got a problem here?" Po-Boy asked, holding a broken beer bottle in his hand. Alonzo was at his side clutching a razor he had snuck in with him.

"You niggaz better fall back and let me worry about my woman!" Bone said. His voice was harsh, but his eyes kept going from the beer bottle to the razor.

"Fam, we ain't got nothing to do with what goes on between you and yours, but seeing y'all trying to form on my brother makes me think we've got a problem," Po-Boy said in an icy tone. "Now, do we have a problem?"

The tension in the air was so thick that you could feel it pressing against your skin as the four men faced off. Felon looked like he was ready to pounce, but Po-Boy was giving him a look that said to stay cool. When it looked like it was about to get ugly Gino appeared.

"What's going on, fellas?" he asked, flanked by two very large bouncers with Rome bringing up the rear.

"You need to be more selective about who you let in your spot, Gino," Bone told him.

"Nigga, I ain't really feeling that slick shit you're kicking." Felon took a step forward, but Rome placed a hand on his chest.

"Hold ya head," Rome whispered into his friend's ear.

"Come on, guys, you know I don't go for the bullshit in my club. Why doesn't everybody relax? Tina!" he shouted to the bartender. "Bring these guys whatever they're drinking, and it's on the house."

"I don't need no damn drink. What I need is my woman, so we can get the fuck out of this dive," Bone said, indignantly.

"Well, if that's the case take your girl and go," Gino said, not feeling Bone's tone. "As a matter of fact, Nikki if you're going to bring trouble don't come back to my club."

Nikki nodded. "I'm sorry," she said to Felon, gently tugging on his jacket pocket beneath the bar.

"Bitch, you disrespect me and he's the one you're apologizing to?" Bone snarled, grabbing Nikki by the hair. Felon went to move on Bone, but Gino stepped in front of him.

"Bone, I told you about that shit the last time you came in here acting up. If you wanna kick her ass, do it outside. If you touch her in here it ain't gonna matter who you work for, understand?" he said seriously.

Bone glared at Gino, but didn't challenge him. He knew that he had connections, but Gino was connected. It would take some heavy favors to be called in to squash a beef between the two of them. "Let's go, bitch," he said shoving Nikki.

"I gotta get dressed and get my stuff," she pleaded.

"Fuck yo shit! Get your ass in the car dressed like that. You wanna be a hoe then look the part." Nikki whimpered something, but no one heard it over Bone's screaming.

"Sorry about that, Gino," Rome said.

"Don't worry about it. That piece of shit Bone is always coming in here trying to throw his weight around. The last time it happened, he cost me a few hundred dollars in damages. I told Nikki the next time she caused some shit, she was out on her ass. You boys go on back to the VIP and enjoy yourselves."

"Nah, I think we're gonna get out of here," Felon said.

"Come on, Felon, don't let that asshole ruin our relationship," Gino said.

"It ain't like that, Gino. You've got a nice spot here, and we'll definitely be coming back, but that shit blew my high. I'm going home." Felon headed towards the door with his crew on his heels.

"Yo Rome, you guys are still gonna do the album release party here, right?" Gino called after them, but got no response.

***

"Man, what was that shit about?" Rome asked once they were all back in the car.

"Punk ass nigga caught feelings because I was sitting there talking to shorty," Felon told him. "I should've popped his ass in the mouth."

"Yeah, and we'd all be in cuffs right now. You know better than to be scrapping over these hoes," Po-Boy said.

"Nigga, shut up!" Felon yelled over his shoulder.

"He's right. That bitch was hardly worth the trouble that would've come with her if we'd got down with them cats," Rome agreed.

"Whatever, man," Felon said, tucking his hands into his jacket pockets. Inside the right pocket he felt something that hadn't been there before. He pulled it out and saw that it was a black business card. Scribbled across the front in gold letters was Nikki's name and phone number.

7

The three days since they had left the club felt like an eternity to Felon. He had called Nikki bright and early the next morning only to get her voicemail. He tried her back, but got the same thing. Not sure what else to do, he left her a message. It wasn't until the next day that she called him back and explained that she hadn't picked up the first two times was because she was with Bone. Just the mention of his name made Felon want to wig out. She told him how much she missed him and they made plans to meet the next afternoon.

Nikki chose the Magic Johnson Theater in Harlem as the meeting spot. This would allow them the privacy to speak and a good alibi if she was spotted. Bone had eyes all over the city and she knew she had to move carefully. Felon had wanted to meet at a more intimate space, but Nikki wouldn't budge on it, so he agreed to the theater.

Felon kept his meeting a secret as his boys would surely clown him for it. To them a woman was no more than a piece of meat to be used or passed around as the situation called for, but a stripper fell even lower on the totem pole. He could hear Alonzo and Po-Boy making fun of him for falling for a stripper. It bothered him, but not enough to let Nikki go. She was a girl who was beautiful and intelligent, but wanted an ugly street nigga like him. Logically, it made no sense, but he figured that God might actually be doing him a solid on this one. Regardless of what she was doing before he came along, he was confident that things would change once they got together. It was a silly way of thinking, but he refused to believe that the attraction between he and

Nikki was anything but real.

As Felon stood in front of the theater waiting for Nikki he couldn't help but to wonder for the millionth time how he had gotten so lucky? Felon had fucked quite a few chicks in his days, but never considered himself a lady's man. He wasn't as handsome as Bone or cocky as Alonzo, so he had to rely on kindness or paper to get close to a woman. Though they provided temporary comfort he knew that he couldn't give them his heart. Nikki threatened to change that.

After about twenty minutes of waiting, a taxi pulled up and deposited Nikki on the curb. She looked different fully dressed, more regal. Nikki sported a gray skirt that flared at the knee but hugged her thighs over a pair of thick burgundy tights. Her hair hung loosely about her face, which was now free of makeup, making her look younger. Her short bubble coat was zipped to the neck in an attempt to keep out the December chill. Felon was so choked up that he couldn't barely speak. As she drew near, he finally found his voice.

"You look nice," he said, with a smile. To his surprise Nikki walked past him without as much as a second look. With a confused look on his face, he followed her inside the theater. By the time he caught up with her, she was at the counter purchasing tickets. When he went to speak again, she waved him silent and motioned for him to follow. It wasn't until they were standing inside the darkness of one of the movie rooms that she even acknowledged him.

"Sorry about that, but I didn't want to risk one of Bone's people spotting me with you," she said hugging him.

"You act like that nigga is the CIA or something." He returned the hug.

"Something like that," she half joked, leading him down the isle to an empty row of seats on the left. Once they were seated, she nestled herself against him.

"Damn, I missed you," he said, enjoying the fresh scent of

her hair.

"I missed you too." She kissed him softly on the lips. Felon's lips felt like sandpaper in contrast to hers which were rose petal soft.

"Baby I..."

She placed a finger against his lips for silence. "We've got plenty of time to talk, but for now I just want to feel you, daddy." She kissed his chin. Nikki slid her hand down his stomach, undid his belt and pulled his dick out. With tender lips she planted a kiss first on the head and then on the shaft. Even in the dimly lit theater, she could make out the goofy grin on Felon's face.

The theater was almost empty at that hour of the day, so they didn't have to worry about anyone seeing them. Even if they had been spotted, Nikki didn't care. She was a girl that had to have what she wanted when she wanted it. Gently, she stroked it until it was good and hard. She mounted Felon's lap, facing him and hiked up her skirt to reveal that the tights she wore were crotch-less. She'd conveniently forgotten her underwear. She slowly began rocking on his lap building up the moisture between her legs. Felon's body shook with anticipation for her forbidden fruit. Releasing a gasp, Nikki slipped Felon inside her.

Her pussy was even tighter than Felon remembered it to be. Nikki rode him slowly at first and gradually picked up speed. Her tight pussy felt like a hand-job as she bounced up and down on his dick. Riding him like a bronco, Nikki salivated and cursed as she came over his dick and down his balls. Felon tried to hold on for as long as he could, but it took under ten minutes for him to blow his wad. If Nikki was angry with him for cumming so quickly she didn't show it as she laid her head against his chest. For a long while they held each other in the silence of the darkened theater.

Breaking the silence, Felon finally spoke, "Yo, what's the deal with you and son? I don't mean no disrespect, but he acts like he's your pimp or something."

Nikki lowered her head. "It's a long story."

"We've got time."

Nikki composed herself, trying to think of a starting point. She went on to tell Felon the story of how she and Bone had gotten together. She had been in her second year at NYU, studying to become a journalist when she met Bone. In the beginning he was a perfect gentleman, but once she fell for him the other side surfaced. As it turned out, Bone was a part-time pimp, and full time cocaine dealer, who specialized in turning young girls out. It wasn't long before he had forced Nikki to start dancing at the club and kicking her ass whenever the mood struck him. The only family she had was a drug addict uncle who lived in South Carolina, so there was no one she could turn to. She had tried to run away from him on more than one occasion, but he always seemed to track her down. At several points in the story she had to stop to break down and cry over what her life had become. By the time she was done spinning her tale, Felon was damn near in tears himself.

"You probably think I'm less than shit now," she sobbed.

"Quit talking crazy," he wiped her cheek with the back of his hand. "It's not like you chose this life. He forced you into it."

"I know, but I feel like I haven't done enough to try and get out of the situation. I thought about going to the police, but the last girl that tried that was found dead in a dumpster. Felon, I'm terrified of him," she trembled.

"Baby, you ain't gotta be scared of that nigga. I'll take care of you," he assured her. "I just got a shit load of money from this deal we did with Sony so it'd be nothing for us to get up outta here. Come away with me, baby, and you ain't never gotta worry about that dude again."

Her lips began to form into a smile, but it quickly faded. "No, I couldn't get you involved in this. Bone is a psycho. If I tried to run away with you he'd kill us both."

"Baby, I ain't so hard to kill," Felon boasted. "I'm doing this rap shit now, but I still got soldiers on the street. Ask about me and you'll find that Felon ain't nothing to be fucked with."

"I don't doubt that, Felon, but it would only make the situation worse. No, the only way I'm ever gonna be free of Bone is when he's dead. I wish somebody would just kill his ass or kill me. Either way I'd be free of this shit."

Nikki went back to her sobbing. It was breaking Felon's heart to see such a tender creature trapped like that. The hate he had in his heart for Bone multiplied with every tear she shed.

"Don't talk like that," he said, comforting her. "Death is something you can't take back."

Nikki looked up at him with swollen red eyes. "I'm serious, Felon. You don't know how many times I wished I had the money to pay someone to off him, but Bone takes every dime I make at the club. All I want is my life back and I'm willing to do anything to get it. Even if it means whoring myself behind his back to get the money up to see him dead," she said, seriously.

"Now, you're talking crazy. Nikki." He placed his hand over hers. "You know how long I've prayed for God to send me someone like you? Someone who I connected with like no other?"

She shook her head wildly. "Don't toy with me, Felon. How could you feel that way about someone as filthy as I am? I'm nothing but a whore who's getting just what she deserves."

"Nikki, you listen to me and listen good," he said, seriously. "This shit I'm kicking to you probably sounds lame as hell, but make no mistake about how serious I am. I'm feeling you, Ma, and I want to discover every dimension of you. Now that I've found you, do you think I'd ever allow anyone to hurt you or take you away from me?"

"Felon, I'd love to believe what you're saying to me, but I just can't. I know Bone, you don't. I'm like a possession to him and he'd never rest until he got me back or killed me. I know you'd do all you could to protect me, but I can't see you get hurt over my bullshit." She looked at him with tear-rimmed eyes and smiled. Even with her face streaked and swollen as it was Nikki, was still beautiful to him. It was at that moment that Felon decided that he couldn't live without Nikki and was willing to do whatever it took to keep her with him, even if it meant spilling a little blood.

"You hush, Nikki. I think I know a way to solve your problem, but I'm gonna need your help to do it."

"Me? What could I do?" she asked, as if she didn't know where he was going with it.

Felon leaned over and whispered in her ear. "I need to know everything about Bone. Where he lays his head, who he does business with, the whole run down."

Nikki composed herself long enough to tell Felon everything she knew. On that cold December afternoon, the two lovers sat in the dark recesses of the Magic Johnson Theater and pieced together a plan to free Nikki from her keeper.

8

Bone stood in the middle of the darkened warehouse smoking a Newport nearly to the butt. Big Keith, as always, guarded his back, watching the three Dominicans closely. On the table between them were twenty neatly packaged kilos of cocaine, which Bone was supposed to distribute through his men on the streets…or so the story went.

"This shit better be official, Papi. I'd hate to have my customers thinking I pulled a fast one on them," Bone told him.

"Man, how long have we been doing business together? I should be offended that you even made the statement," Papi said, coolly.

"Nothing personal, but that's a lot of money sitting on the table." Bone nodded towards the coke.

"Yeah, this is the most you've ever brought from me at one time. Looks like you're moving up in the world." Papi smiled.

"Can't stay small-time forever, Keith," Bone called over his shoulder. "Give him the money." Big Keith handed Papi the duffle bag he had been holding onto for dear life.

After taking a quick glance inside the bag Papi nodded in approval. "Okay, Bone. See you on the next go around."

Big Keith turned around to say something to Bone when his head exploded. Bone never heard the shot, but he saw his partner go down in a heap. The three Dominicans tried to duck for cover, but they too were cut down by the silent assassin. Bone drew his weapon and backed against a stack of boxes. He looked around frantically, but couldn't see where the shots were coming from. Deciding that he'd make too easy of a target standing still, Bone made a mad dash for the door. He had made it within two feet of the exit when pain exploded in his leg. Bone dropped to the ground trying to cover the muscle and nerves that were exposed in his thigh.

"Look at you," a voice came from the darkness. "Big, bad ass pimp all curled up like a little bitch." Bone swung his gun from right to left, but couldn't see anyone. "You should've let her go," the voice said. The hand Bone had his gun in suddenly exploded. "Now, you're fucked!"

"Oh, God, help me," Bone pleaded, trying to drag himself to the door.

"God ain't got no love for niggaz like you," Felon said, stepping out of the darkness. He was holding an AR15 equip with a custom silencer. Just another souvenir he had held onto from his days of killing to protect his block. The gun had at least five bodies on it, not including the four men he had killed in the warehouse, but Felon had paid too much for it to toss it away.

Seeing Felon advancing on him, Bone's eyes got wide. "You?" he croaked.

"Yeah, me, baby boy. All she wanted to do was go back to

school, but you couldn't have that. Now you're about to die because of your selfishness."

"Hold on, man. That bitch has got you fucked up in the head. Don't do it!"

"I ain't the one that's fucked up in the head, son. How the hell could you keep her caged like that? Didn't you realize what you had?" Felon braced the gun against his shoulder and took aim.

"Don't do it, man, I'm a police officer!" Bone tried to tell him, but Felon was too far gone to listen.

"Them petty ass lies ain't gonna save your life. At least have the decency to die like a man." Bone yelled something, but never got it out because the AR's bullets tore through his body. When the smoke cleared he was nothing but a mess of flesh and blood dressed in expensive clothes.

Felon hadn't even gotten a chance to admire his handy work before he was blinded by lights. As if by magic, the room was suddenly filled with people, all waving guns at him. He couldn't see their faces, but he could make out three letters stamped on their clothing: DEA.

"Drop it mutha fucka!" one of the agents shouted. Felon was so shocked that all he could do was stare. "I said drop it!" the agent repeated. Still not getting a response, the officer shot Felon once in the stomach.

Pain exploded in Felon's gut as he doubled over. A mob of DEA agents, as well as a few uniformed cops pounced on him, raining kicks and punches. Enough order had been restored for two of the officers to squeeze in and handcuff Felon, but he still didn't totally understand what was going on. Through his haze of pain he could see one of the agents squatting over Bone's lifeless body, screaming officer down into his walkie-talkie. It was only then that the pieces began to fall into place.

SIX MONTHS LATER IN THE OBCC VISITING ROOM ON RIKER'S ISLAND:

Felon walked into the visiting room dressed in a prison issued jumpsuit and a pair of flip-flops. Sitting at a table in the corner were his lawyer and Rome. Both of the men wore grim faces, but Felon didn't need to see them to know that he was fucked. He leaned into hug Rome, but winced in pain. He had survived the gunshot wound, but it left him shitting in a bag and wearing a nasty scar.

"How you doing?" Rome asked.

"Considering my situation, I guess I'm good." Felon tried to make a joke, but he was the only one laughing.

"We're almost done with the album," Rome told him. "Because we couldn't get you into the studio, we had to improvise on a lot of shit, but I think it's good. I even got my man at Hot 97 to agree to play the single. They won't air it until like three in the morning but hey," Rome shrugged, "you've gotta start somewhere."

"How ya doing, kid?" the lawyer asked, speaking for the first time. Felon just shrugged. "I hate to put it like this, but you fucked yourself pretty good. They're charging you with the murders of the Dominicans as well as the two DEA agents. I'm trying to put together a plea agreement, but because two of the guys you killed were cops the DA is being a hard ass about it."

"So, what else is new?" Felon shrugged, as if he really didn't give a fuck. Rome mumbled something, but didn't press the issue. "Any word from Nikki yet?"

Rome looked at him as if he couldn't believe what he was hearing. "I don't fucking believe you. These people are screaming for the death penalty and you're asking about the bitch who put you here?!" Rome shouted.

"Rome, you don't know what time it is," Felon said.

"No, you don't know what time it is. The bitch set you up!"

Felon was still looking at Rome as if he didn't believe his childhood friend. "Tell him," Rome said to the lawyer.

Adjusting his glasses the lawyer pulled out a folder and a small white envelope. "Nikki's real name is Nicola Stevens, the legal wife of agent Richard 'Bone' Stevens. From what I've learned, they were married shortly after the untimely death of her last boyfriend. Richard had a life insurance policy for two hundred and fifty thousand dollars, with his wife as the beneficiary. There was also a clause in the contract that stated she would receive an additional fifty thousand from the Drug Enforcement Agency if he were killed in the line of duty."

"So, what's this got to do with anything?" Felon asked, as if he still wasn't grasping what he was being told.

"Nigga, you can't be that fucking dense!" Rome said, harshly. "Nikki used you to kill her husband so she could collect on the money. The bitch set you up, Felon."

"Nah, this can't be right," he said, rocking back and forth in his seat like a mad man. "Nikki wouldn't have done that to me, she couldn't have."

"Afraid she has," the lawyer said, sliding him the envelope. "If you're still having doubts about what we're telling you, this letter should solidify the claim."

Felon snatched the envelope from the lawyer and tore it open. Inside there was a neatly written letter:

Dear Felon,

By the time you get this letter you'll probably be tucked safely away in someone's jail, which I guess is lucky for me since you'd no doubt be after my head for what I've done. You were one of the sweetest men I've ever met which made it even harder for me to send you off on a fool's mission like that. I know it sounds cold, but I was desperate. I'm sorry that it had to be you, but I needed someone to free me of my controlling ass husband. It was a simple case of you being in the wrong place at the wrong time. I put five hundred dollars in your commissary. The way I hear it, that'll get you a long way in prison. Take care of yourself, and try not to think of me too much. I'm hardly worth it.

NIKKI GRIND

Felon read the letter three times, but still couldn't believe it. He had opened his heart to Nikki, only to have her plunge a knife into it. Tears ran freely down his face, but he didn't give a damn who saw it or what they thought. His heart was bleeding and even the other inmates laughing at him couldn't make him feel any worse.

"I'm sorry," the lawyer said, patting his hand.

Felon looked at the lawyer as if he was seeing him for the first time. The sorrow in his eyes was replaced by madness as he slammed his fist into the little man's face. Blood squirted all over his jumpsuit, but that didn't stop his attack. He slammed his fist into the lawyers face over and over until three guards were finally able to pull him free. Rome was so broken up by the display that he couldn't even watch as the CO's half beat and dragged Felon back through the iron doors. Even after he was long gone, Rome could still hear his friend screaming Prince's lyrics, "Come back, Nikki, come back!"

RIGHT HAND BITCH

BRITTANI WILLIAMS

As I sat there on the barstool looking across the room, I had a million thoughts running through my mind. I thought about all of the shit I had to do the following morning and also about fucking this fine ass nigga sitting at the booth towards the back of the restaurant. The mood in *Ms. Gina's Kitchen* was calm, but instead I was anxiously waiting for Omar to break away from his woman. I continued to stare until our eyes met. It was then that I gave him the signal to meet me in the back. This was our meeting place and it had been for the past three months. Omar was one of the top drug distributors in Philly. I met him a few years back when he was first getting his weight up. I never had any intention of being his girl or anyone elses for that matter. My intention was to get paid and things had been working out perfectly up to this point.

I slid off the stool and finished off my drink. I watched Omar head out of the restaurant. As I walked past the table where his girlfriend was sitting, we both looked at each other and smiled. If this bitch only knew I was about to walk out of here and fuck her man, she'd wipe that fake ass smile off of her face.

Once I reached the dark street in the back of the restaurant, Omar was sitting on the hood of his car waiting patiently for me.

Without speaking, I walked over to him and stood in between his legs. I stuck out my tongue so he could bring his lips closer to mine. He opened his mouth and took my tongue inside of it. His tongue was thick and warm causing me to get extremely moist down below. I could feel his hands caressing my ass as he raised my skirt. I could feel his dick rising through his jeans and I began to unzip his pants to release it. I rubbed the pre-cum off the head and as I backed away, I stuck my fingers in my mouth to suck his juices off of them. He smiled as he pulled the condom out of his pocket and put it on.

Cars were driving by the street at the end of dead end block, but once he bent me over the hood and stuck his dick inside of me, they were no longer a part of my world. I bit my lip as he moved in and out of me with force. I liked it rough and the intensity of possibly being caught made the shit feel even better. I continued bouncing my ass back against him as he firmly gripped his hands around my waist. I knew that I was nearing an orgasm and the pulsing of his stick let me know that he was too. He increased his speed and dug deeper inside before pausing to release all of his juices. Each time we met the sex was better, so I looked forward to my end of the week treat.

He slowly pulled his member from inside of me before speaking. "You are on birth control right?" he quizzed while removing the condom.

"Yeah, why?" I asked as I stood up to fix my clothing.

"Cause the condom broke and I didn't realize it," he responded while zipping his pants back up.

"Oh, yeah it's cool, we're safe." I smiled.

"Well come give me a kiss before I go back inside," he instructed.

I moved closer to him and met his lips for a kiss. I was excited when he slipped a wad of money into my purse before going back into the restaurant. I went back inside to use the restroom.

I wet a few paper towels to clean myself off and thought back to his comment about the condom breaking. It wasn't cool, shit! I hated when that shit happened. What good are the fucking condoms if they break more often than not!

I got myself together before leaving the bathroom. I walked back past Omar's table before leaving as if I didn't even know him. Shit, she could have him for the night; I got what I needed, dick and a stack of doe!

The following morning I woke up to the annoying sound of the alarm. I damn near knocked the clock on the floor trying to turn it off. I had a 9:00 appointment at the hair salon and I needed to be on time or else I'd be in there all damn day. Going to the hair dresser once a week was like a job. I didn't work a regular nine to five so my patience was short when it came to being in one place for too many hours. Mina was my stylist and since she was one of the hottest in the city, her book was always packed. I threw on a pair of jogging shorts and a little half shirt since it was going up to ninety degrees outside. I had to be fly in case I ran into a baller. I had one of the fattest asses you could imagine, so when I wore shorts and stilettos I had niggas under my spell, immediately.

I strutted into the salon in perfect time. The shampoo girl was waiting for me and after my hair was blow dried, I hopped into Mina's chair.

"How are things going?" Mina asked while brushing through my hair.

"Everything is great, I'm living it up as usual! You know how I get down," I replied with a giggle.

"Well I'm glad to see you doing better now after being in the hospital."

"Yeah I'm good, I'm glad to be out of there. That flu really kicked my ass! That two day stay was the hardest days of my life. But it's back to business now," I commented.

"Girl, you are the same Miani, always about them dollars!"

"That ain't never going to change shit. This is me and anyone that doesn't like it can kiss my ass!" I replied, as we both began laughing.

She began to style my hair as I sat there looking out of the window at this chocolate brotha making his way towards the shop. His jewels were shining and that shit was ringing like a cash register in my ear. I wished that I was up walking around so he could see my ass jiggle, but my hair was still only half way done.

He stopped at the receptionist desk and she pointed in my direction after he bent over to ask her a question. He walked over to me and I was speechless, wondering how he pin-pointed me. I mean I knew I was the shit, but there were about fifteen other chicks in the salon.

"Hey how are you doing, are you Miani?" he quizzed.

"Why? Who wants to know?" I said with attitude.

"He said you would be sassy," he spat.

"Excuse me?"

"Look, my boss Keni wants to meet with you and he asked me to stop by here and give you this," he said, passing me a small bag from Tiffany's. "The address and the meeting time are on the card." He walked away.

I sat there stunned. How the fuck did Keni know where I'd be and what the hell did he want to meet about? All eyes were on me in the shop with the anticipation of seeing what was in the bag. Mina's nosey ass even stopped curling my hair to join in.

I pulled the box from the bag which contained a charm bracelet and necklace set. Here this nigga doesn't even know me and is already spending that change, He's definitely my type of man!

I pulled out the card that read: Meet me at seven sharp, at the warehouse on Cambria. I wished that Mina would hurry up and finish my hair so I could go change, because I was definitely going to be there at seven, and I was damn sure going to be sharp!

Getting niggas to spoil me was something that I had become a professional at. I ran into a few road blocks along the way, but I always managed to find my way around them. Since I'd witnessed my mother being trashed by men growing up, I vowed to avoid following in her footsteps. Instead, I was going to flip the script and take these niggas for everything they had. As far as my taste in men, first came the money and then the looks. I needed a fine ass thug, but I needed them to be paid first! Without the doe, the looks weren't important. I made a name for myself by running scams on any baller that had a major cash flow. My mother never pushed me to do anything growing up, so when I dropped out of high school, at the age of 16, she didn't seem fazed by it one bit. I regretted it the older I got, but at twenty four I wasn't going back to school to get something that I believed I didn't need. Everything I wanted, I could get and it came to me easily. All I had to do was flex my ass in front of a nigga and he'd be crawling to get a piece. Once they were caught up, I would take the money and run. I went years before I fell in love, since love wasn't something I looked forward to.

After finishing my runs for the day I rushed home to change. I was out of the house in record time and not a hair was out of place. I drove down to the warehouse where his workers packaged and shipped his inventory of cocaine. I was nervous as I approached the guards that were standing post outside. I had on my freakum dress of course, since I wanted to leave a good impression. The guards searched me and opened the door to let me in. As I walked in I noticed Keni standing towards the back. I switched over to where he was with a strut that had everyone's attention. Niggas were practically drooling over the ass as I walked past. Keni turned to look me up and down a few times before speaking.

"Well, the infamous Miani. You look damn good! I can see why the niggas are losing their doe to you," he said smiling. I nodded returning the smile.

"I know you're wondering why I asked you to come here."

"Yeah I'm definitely wondering about that," I responded.

"Well first let me thank you for coming."

"You're welcome, but I'd rather skip the small talk and find out exactly what it is you want from me."

"I see that you are all about business and I like that. That shit is a turn on if you know what I mean!" he said, while laughing before noticing my evil stare. "I'm just fucking with you ma, lets go to my office so we can talk. You don't have to be all serious and shit all the time," he said beginning to walk into the direction of his office.

I wasn't always this serious, but I wanted him to believe that so he wouldn't think that I was a pushover and take advantage of me. We entered the plush office that looked like it in no way belonged in the back of a warehouse. The office had thick beige carpet and a cherry wood desk with a coffee colored leather chair. He had a huge gun cabinet with at least ten guns and a large plasma TV on the wall. The pictures of Scarface and the Godfather displayed his strength. Shit like that turned me on because I knew a nigga that worshiped them was bound to display some of their characteristics. I walked around the room for a few minutes before sitting down in the chair opposite the desk. We stared at each other for a few seconds before he spoke. "So, I've heard about the way you like taking niggas money! I think that shit is foul…"

I cut him off because starting off the conversation dogging me was definitely not going to keep my attention.

"Listen, if that's all you called me here for, I can turn around and walk out of here."

He straightened up in his chair. "Well what do you think I brought you here for?" he quizzed. I was irritated at that point and I damn sure wasn't in the mood to play the guessing game. I began to rise up out of the chair without saying a word.

"Where are you going?"

"Look, my time is very valuable. I could be out somewhere getting paid!" I spoke loudly. "I wish you would just cut the bull-shit and tell me why I'm really here!"

"Have a seat and I'll explain," he said, pointing in the direction of my chair. "I know your game and I need someone like you on my team. I'm trying to make this a win-win situation for us both."

"What could I possibly do to help you?"

"All I need you to do is be yourself. I'll designate the niggas and you just need to work your magic. It's pretty simple."

"I still don't understand how that will help you."

"I've been in this game for a long time and I'm pretty success-ful, but I have to eliminate my competition in order to move to the next level."

"Eliminate?"

"Yeah, I have to get rid of them permanently if you know what I mean."

"No, I don't know what you mean. Look, all I do is get with these niggas and make them spoil me, Simple as that. The shit you are talking about isn't something I want to get involved in. I'm not going to jail for murder!"

"You won't go to jail, I promise that."

"I can't, I'm sorry, I just can't be apart of this. I'm sure you'll find someone else willing to do it."

"I don't want anyone else to do it. You are the best one for the job."

"I'm sorry, I just can't," I said, before walking to the door.

I couldn't believe what he was asking me to do. I had plenty of other ways to get what I wanted and killing someone was too extreme. My mind raced as I got into my car. *What the fuck was I thinking going there in the first place?* I knew about Keni's boss status and I also knew how much he was feared. He was paid and that's what attracted me, but the devilish grin he displayed as he riddled off the names turned me off. One name in particular rang in my ear and I wasn't going for it.

Meeno was well known in the South Philly section of the city and everyone knew about him, and instantly showed fear with mention of his name.

I, on the other hand, wasn't afraid at all. I loved a challenge and getting him to sport me on his arm would have been a major accomplishment. I knew that it wouldn't be easy to get him since he'd dealt with his current girlfriend for the last few years. I needed more than a fuck, so first I had to get her out of the way. It was easier than I originally thought once I did my research. I found out that she'd been fucking around with this hustler from Camden, and once I bought it to Meeno's attention, he was wide open. I gave him the pussy shortly after that and it was a wrap!

A year into our relationship his ex popped back up on the scene and reversed the game on me. Once she told him about my past, he walked out on me thinking that it was my plan to take his money and leave. Though it was my plan at the start, it was out of the window when he stole my heart. I was genuinely in love, but I was devastated when he left. I knew then that I could never let my heart get in the way ever again. I got over the heartache pretty quickly since I had to get back on the grind and locate a new victim. Everything was going as planned until my game was blasted all over the city.

I'm glad I walked out of that office and left the conversation right where it was, in his twisted ass mind. Once I made it home I decided to call up one of my money trains to get a couple of dollars. I became a little bit annoyed when none of them answered. My day wasn't going the way I'd planned since I thought I'd be laying next to a warm body with a fat pocket by now. After an hour of trying, I gave up and took my ass to bed. There was always tomorrow.

The following day I woke up and checked my cell phone for missed calls. There was only one number on the list and I didn't recognize it. I dialed the number to find out who called. The phone rung a few times before a deep male voice boomed through the receiver. "Hello!"

"Hi, did someone call Miani from this number?" I quizzed, in a sexy tone hoping that this was my next money train.

"Yeah, it's Keni! Did you think about what I said?"

Instantly, my stomach began to turn. I was going to hang up, but something about his voice wouldn't allow me to. I sat in silence waiting for him to begin speaking.

"What's wrong, cat got your tongue?" he asked.

"No, I'm just wondering what the hell you're calling me for if I told you yesterday I didn't want anything to do with that shit."

"Well that was yesterday and shit changes. I just wanted to make sure that you were serious. I know you're running low on cash since most of the niggas you had won't return your calls."

"How the hell do you know that?"

"Because I know everything. Plus I made sure your regulars were aware of your past. Now you need me!"

"Fuck you Keni!" I yelled in anger.

"Ooh...I love it when women talk like that! If you think you don't need me and you believe you can make it by yourself, I wish you the best of luck. But when you realize what I'm saying ain't no bullshit, holla at me." Click…

TWO WEEKS LATER

"Thanks for bringing me here. This is a really nice restaurant." I said, as I sat down in the chair and slid up to the small table covered in white linens.

"No problem shorty. I don't mind spending my money on someone as fine as you," Joe said, as he smiled.

I stared at him from across the table and had to admit I was pretty turned on. Joe was one of the sexiest thugs I'd seen in a long time. His caramel colored skin was as smooth as a baby's ass. His hair was shaped up to perfection and his body was tight. I could tell that he worked out often by how ripped he was. I knew that this was only a job, but I also knew I had to at least screw him once before Keni's plan of elimination went into effect. I felt sorry for Joe the longer we sat and talked, because underneath all of the gangsta shit, he seemed like a good man. Joe was a major figure in West Philly. He pushed cocaine throughout the area gaining him a lot of respect and of course plenty of cash. He practically had the bottom sewed up. He was well known throughout the city, so I'd heard his name once or twice before, but I never had the opportunity of meeting him until now.

Dinner didn't last very long since we were both anxious to get to the hotel. I didn't really eat much since food hadn't been agreeing with my stomach lately. I was wearing a dress that hugged my size eight frame. I didn't know a man alive that could resist me. Joe was all over me as soon as we hit the Double Tree hotel. I could feel his hands all over my back as we stood at the counter waiting for the room key. I was growing more excited as we walked to the elevator.

Once inside he backed me against the wall and pushed his body up close to mine. I could feel his hard dick pressed up against me as he placed his lips onto mine, right before pushing his tongue through. The elevator opened and he quickly grabbed me by the hand to guide me to the room. My heart was beating faster and my panties were getting wetter by the second.

After entering the room, he walked me to the bed and bent me over immediately pulling my panties down. He dropped his pants and massaged his dick to keep it at attention until he was able to open the condom and put it on. I was patiently waiting with my ass still up in the air. He took his dick and slapped it across my ass a few times before shoving it inside of me. He filled my insides completely, and I moaned extremely loud while he continued to move in and out of my juicy tunnel.

"This pussy is so fucking good!" he whispered in excitement.

I contracted my walls to hug his dick while he hit my g-spot continuously. He slapped my ass over and over again while holding onto my waist like a handle bar with his other hand. He used his strength to go deeper and deeper as I begged for more. He wore me out, and appeared to be unfazed by the workout.

Once I reached my climax, I was about ready to stop since the constant pounding was going to have me walking funny for days. I tried to slow him down a bit by making slow circles, but that didn't work. *Damn, this nigga was fucking me like a race horse.* I mean, he pounded with such force and speed for over a half hour in the same position non-stop. I wondered if his ass drunk a red bull or something because he wasn't slowing down a bit, not even for a second to catch his breath.

He was still banging my back out when I heard a loud boom. Afraid, I ran to the nearest closet and tried to hide when three huge men in black ski masks kicked the door in with their guns drawn. Two of them grabbed Joe, while he was fumbling with his pants to retrieve his gun, and began kicking him. I sat in the corner crying hysterically when the third guy came over and picked me up off the floor.

"This is a fine bitch here. If he didn't already fuck her, I would have sampled this pussy!" he said, before he began laughing.

The other two joined in the laughter as he pushed me down on the bed and began tugging at my shirt to get a peek of my breast. I didn't know what to expect as I lay there trembling.

While Joe was being beaten, I eyed the door trying to figure out a way to jet. I prayed that I would make it out alive as I closed my eyes and quickly said a silent prayer.

"Shut the fuck up!" the tallest one yelled at Joe, as he continuously told them they could have whatever they wanted.

"You see your punk ass man over there? He can't even protect you!" he yelled, gripping the back of my hair and pointing in Joe's direction. "Answer me bitch!" he yelled.

I sat there silent still in shock, while he screamed obscenities. I was afraid to speak since I didn't want to piss them off.

"Get up muthafucker and face me like a man!" the shortest one yelled at Joe.

As Joe stood up and turned around to look at me, a few tears fell from my eyes. Blood ran down his face and his right eye was damn near swollen shut. I felt sorry for him as I continued to cry. I noticed a strange look on his face, and I couldn't tell what it meant. Either way I knew that it wasn't a look of submission, and I was afraid of what would happen next.

Joe balled up his fist and knocked the shorter one off his feet. As he tried to attack the one left standing, the taller one let go of me and quickly ran over to interrupt their tussle. He put the gun to the back of Joe's head and immediately fired. I screamed and as I jumped up off the bed to try and escape, I was quickly pulled back into the room.

"Where the fuck are you going?"

"Please let me go, I promise I won't say anything," I cried.

"Sit your ass down. Ain't nobody going to hurt you! Take this phone and wait for the call," he said passing me a pre-paid Trac phone. "If you call the cops before that call comes through, we'll catch your ass and kill you. Do I make myself clear!" he yelled startling me.

"Yes," I said, speaking for the first time since they'd entered the room. I just wanted this to be over and would say anything to get them to leave.

"Take care! And stop fucking with punk ass niggas like him!"

the shortest one said, before they turned and made their way to the door.

I watched them like a hawk without moving. I ran over to Joe as soon as the door closed to see if he was still breathing. I leaned over him and told him how sorry I was when I realized he was dead. I would have never wished this on my worst enemy. I was glad to still be alive, but I was traumatized. I contemplated calling the cops, but I knew that they meant business by what just happened, so I opted to wait for the phone call. I waited ten minutes and when the call came I didn't know what to expect.

"Hello," I said, nervously as my voice trembled.

"Good job baby!" Keni yelled through the phone.

"What Keni, you set this shit up?" I yelled in anger.

"You should have known that. I told you what the plan was, so I don't know where the confusion came in at!"

"You could have at least warned me!" I screamed into the receiver. "I thought that my life was over!"

"I'm sorry you were scared, but if I would have warned you, you would have probably fucked every thing up by acting suspicious. I'm proud of you."

"Fuck you Keni!" I screamed.

"Maybe later, but right now I need you to call the cops and tell them what happened. They'll come talk to you and you tell them what went down. Once you get home holla at me, and I'll let you know what's next."

"I'm not doing shit for you after this Keni, I mean it!"

"Look you're upset and that's cool. We had a deal and I know that money sounds good to you right about now since you're damn near broke! Just do what I said and everything will be cool!" *Click...*

"Keni! Keni!" I yelled into the phone before realizing that he hung up. I was furious that he'd risked my life the way that he had. He never told me that I would be caught in the crossfire. I never expected to witness a murder, nor did I expect to be degraded in the process. I called the cops as I was ordered. It was the hardest thing that I'd ever done. To sit and lie about a man's murder and possibly risk going to jail for my part in all of it, made me sick thinking about it. I couldn't even sleep that night, and I tossed and turned for the week that followed. It took a while for me to get back to Keni, but I had to do what I had to do and Keni made sure of that.

I had been feeling sick for days following the incident with Joe, and though I had been keeping up with my meds they weren't working very well. I was weak and nauseous and had a fever for a couple of days in a row. I continued to take Tylenol to bring my temperature down which only worked temporarily. I couldn't possibly work for Keni feeling as lousy as I did; so I went down to the clinic for a walk in visit to see if I could get a different prescription.

The clinic was packed as usual and I kept my shades on to avoid possibly being noticed by someone I knew. I signed my name on the board and sat down. I was getting annoyed the longer I sat. I looked up at the clock and before I put my head back down to glance at the magazine I'd been flipping through, I noticed a girl named Shena from around the way. I wondered what the hell she was doing here. I definitely didn't want her to see me, but I soon realized that it was too late.

"Miani, is that you?" she quizzed, before walking over to where I was sitting.

"Hey Shena, how are you?" I said, before removing my sunglasses.

"What are you doing here?" she asked, though she probably already speculated.

"Girl I had to come pick up something from the doc."

"Why are you on this side? You know what section this is don't you?"

"I know girl, It wasn't any seats on the on the other side." I lied.

"Well its some seats now, you don't want people to think you got something!" she said, pointing out a couple of seats on the opposite side of the waiting area.

"You go ahead girl, I'm cool right here."

"Alright, well I'll be seeing you around," she said before walking away.

Shena and I had never been friends in any way so for her to think we would get all buddy buddy so she could find out my business was out of the question. Her name was called shortly after that and I was glad since I didn't want her to see me be called back. I sat in the room for about ten minutes before the doctor came in.

"Hello Ms. Washington. What brings you in today?" he asked, before sitting down on the stool in front of me.

"The medicine that you gave me before I left the hospital isn't working. I'm still having the same symptoms. I haven't even been able to hold any food down."

"Well, I can up the dosage and maybe that will help but as you already know that your condition has advanced, and there isn't much that we can do at this stage. I can prescribe you some other things that may keep the nausea under control along with it. Are the fevers still coming as well?"

"Yes, I just take the Tylenol to bring them down."

"Has that been working?"

"Yes, temporarily. I'm just tired of being sick."

"Well as I've said, I'll up the dosage on the meds and hopefully that will keep you comfortable."

"Okay."

He wrote out my prescriptions and I went straight to the drug store to have them filled. I decided to rest for the remainder of the day to get myself together. I knew that I would probably feel much better the following day and able to get back on track.

Soon it was back to business and Keni had me setting up at least one nigga a week. Eventually, I became immune to the fear and when they would come kicking the door down, the feelings I displayed weren't much more than an act. Keni was paying me well for my time, but I was looking forward to the big payoff at the end, and the faster I got it, the better.

I was a month away from completing the last job and Timmy was next in line. Timmy wasn't the romantic ‘take you out to dinner and a movie’ type Timmy liked to be alone to just relax. He wanted to show me the place where he went to clear his mind, and since I knew it would be secluded, I was game.

"So why didn't you get at me a long time ago? I mean I'm a fly ass nigga and you chose all of those bammas before me," Timmy spoke, while glancing at my figure, showing through my tight fitting attire.

"I didn't really think you'd dig my style. I thought I might have been too flashy for you," I replied, before sitting down on the park bench beside him.

"Too flashy, never! Who could be flashier than me?" he said, laughing as he flipped his collar up on his shirt. I joined in the laughter as I knew that he was absolutely right.

He was a flashy nigga. He had diamonds, chains, watches, earrings and pinky rings everywhere. He wanted it known that he was paid. I'd never really paid Timmy any attention since I ran into him around the time I was with Meeno. Had I met him first, I would have definitely given him a sample of the kitty cat.

Timmy was from North Philly and had the area practically sewed up. Niggas all around knew about him, so before Keni, no one would even think about stepping into his territory. Timmy's weakness was for women. A nigga like Timmy would give up the doe without hesitation and that's what I needed in my life. He wouldn't be caught dead with a chick that wasn't as fly as he was.

"So what is it that you want from me?" he quizzed, with a smile on his face.

"I'm trying to be with you," I lied, trying to gas him up.

"With me? You mean like my girl or something?"

"Yeah, why is that a problem?"

"I mean we've been kicking it for a couple of weeks now and I dig you. I just don't know if I'm ready to be with you."

"Well, I'm definitely not one to beg, but I dig you too and that's why I hollered at you in the first place."

"Is that right?" he said, before placing his hand on my thigh. I knew where this was headed and I was all game for it.

"Baby lets head to the car, so I can show you something," I said in a low seductive tone.

Timmy jumped off the bench before I could even finish my sentence. We walked back to the car parked a few feet from the park bench. After we got in, I went to work immediately loosening his belt to get to his bulging manhood. Once I pulled it out, I was shocked and excited by the size.

I massaged its length, while he laid his chair back and put his hands behind his head. His dick was at attention waiting for me to kiss it. I licked the tip of it before wrapping my lips around the head sucking on it. He moaned a little as I took the pre-cum into my mouth. I was soon deep throating his stick while playing with his balls at the same time. My pussy was so wet, and I couldn't wait to feel him inside of me. I picked up the pace and he loved every second of it. I wanted him to fuck me as I pulled my panties to the side, I stuck two fingers into my juicy tunnel. I finger fucked myself waiting for the orgasm that was nearing. I continued to suck his dick while moving my fingers in and out of my pussy until I exploded. The juices began to pour out, and when I was finally able to open my eyes to speak...

Bang, Bang! The glass from the window shattered all over my head. Blood sprayed everywhere. I jumped up to move close to the passenger side when I was forcefully pulled through the window of the car. Blood was all over my face and hands as I stood up straight.

"Get the fuck in the car!" the familiar voice yelled at me. I didn't waste time getting up running over to the black Expedition parked on the side with the ignition still running. Though I expected them to come, I could never fully prepare myself to witness a murder.

The two men grabbed Timmy's lifeless body from the car while the third man opened up the trunk. The two men threw him into the trunk of his car and slammed the trunk shut. The last man pulled out a can of gasoline and poured it all over the car. Next they lit a couple of home made bombs, quickly throwing them inside of the car causing it to burst into flames. As the three of them jumped in, I sat quietly in the car. I didn't know where the hell they were taking me, which at that point I didn't care. I needed to be done with this shit and I was one more job away.

We pulled up to a huge home off City Line Avenue. I figured that it must've belonged to Keni since I noticed his Benz parked outside. They beeped the horn and instructed me to get out. I obeyed, but stood there still for a few seconds before Keni came to the door. "Come on in," he motioned, with his hands. I had my arms folded across my chest with sadness in my eyes. I didn't want to do this anymore, because mentally it was breaking me down. He tried to wrap his arm around my shoulder and I quickly pulled away.

"You don't look too good, baby, are you okay?" he asked.

"No I'm not okay, what kind of a fucking question is that? They just blew a man away while I had his dick in my mouth! Do you think I should be okay after some shit like that?" I yelled. "Where is the bathroom Keni? I need to clean myself up!" He stood there staring at me for a few seconds.

"You sure you don't want to talk?" he asked, trying to show his sensitive side.

"All I need is a shower, a towel and a washcloth!" I replied loudly.

"No problem. I'll show you to the bathroom," he said, as he began to make his way towards the stairs.

I was shaken, as thoughts of Timmy slumped over replayed

in my mind. Once we reached the bathroom, he reached into the linen closet to hand me a towel and washcloth. I waited for him to walk out so that I could close the door behind him. I sat down on the toilet seat to remove my shoes and clothing.

After turning on the shower, I waited a few seconds for it to reach the right temperature. As soon as the hot water hit my skin, I began to cry. I cried because I was sorry that I'd ever gotten involved with this. I'd witnessed too many murders. Though I was no longer afraid of the situations, inside it was breaking me down. I had to build up the skin to handle the situations and I had done pretty well with it. I was just growing annoyed with the fact that Keni had been stringing me on for the past few months, telling me it's just one more job. Each time he would tell me the same thing.

I began to care about Keni and it was hard for me to walk away. The more time we spent together the more I needed to be around him. He never acted as if he cared about me, but I knew better than that. It was all a cover up. Instead of pushing him away, I fell back hoping that when this shit was all over, something good would come out of it. Keni had a way of reeling me back in even when I was furious with him. At one point in time, it was me putting people under a spell, now I was stuck in that position. I was going to get my game back one way or another. Keni wouldn't be able to stop me.

I heard a knock on the door and I noticed Keni's naked body through the glass door of the shower. It was just like Keni to try to fuck after a situation like that. I didn't say a word as he stepped into the shower behind me. I knew that I could use some dick, so I wasn't going to turn him away no matter how angry I was.

He rubbed his hands across my back, and I began to shiver imagining the scene that was about to play out. His hands felt good and the feelings that I tried to avoid were bursting through. I could feel his lips on my back as I pushed my face completely under the shower. He wrapped his hands around my waist and pressed his hardness against my ass as he held me tight.

"Do you want me to fuck you?" Keni whispered into my ear.

I could barely speak, but was able to moan, "Yes," as his fingers traveled down to my clit. As much as I hated him for getting me involved in this life, I embraced his strength.

Keni always took control, so it was that persona that won me over in the first place. He wrapped his hands around my neck not tight enough to hurt me, but just enough to get my adrenaline rushing. He sucked on the side of my neck before questioning me once more.

"You really want me to fuck you?"

"Yes," I said, as I reached around behind me to grab hold of his dick. I stroked the length of it as he continued to play with my clit. I put one leg up on the side of the tub to give him full access. He took advantage of it by sliding his finger inside of my wetness. I sighed a little as the warmness of his fingers sent chills through my body. He continued kissing the back of my neck, as I grinded my hips to get his fingers deeper inside of me.

"I need you inside of me now," I moaned.

He turned me around and looked me eye to eye. We didn't speak, but as our lips met, we both knew what the other thought.

The water was beating on my back as he continued to push his tongue into my mouth. At that point, I didn't care about the anger that I'd felt earlier. All I cared about was feeling his dick inside of me. Without hesitation, he turned me back around, bent me over and shoved his stick inside of me. The feeling was intense and he picked up speed once he realized how much I was enjoying it.

"You like this dick?" he panted, as he placed his hand on my back digging deeper inside of me. I couldn't speak as I was nearing an orgasm.

"I said do you like this dick?" he repeated, obviously annoyed by my silence.

"Yes, dammit! Just don't stop!" I responded loudly.

He was hitting all of the right places. I could admit that he was damn good. I knew that it wouldn't be long before he came since I was throwing my ass back at him, contracting my walls at the same time. I had learned a long time ago that there weren't too many men that could take what I called a recipe to put a nigga to sleep.

He removed his length from inside of me then expelled on my ass. I was satisfied, but I didn't know where it would lead. I knew that Keni wasn't one for serious relationships, neither was I at this point. I just hoped that maybe what happened would somehow steer him away from having me being an accessory to any more murders.

Keni quickly washed himself off, and without saying a word he stepped out of the shower. I followed his lead, then met him in his living room.

"So, does this mean that I won't have to do any more jobs for you?" I asked, nervously.

"What gave you that idea?" he said, before taking a puff of his cigarette.

"I thought that you saw what this was doing to me. I thought that you hopping in that shower with me was showing me that you cared."

"Look, I wanted to tap that ass from the first day I saw you and since opportunity presented itself, I took advantage. It didn't have shit to do with caring," he coldly responded.

"What?"

"Look, I have a business to run. You are definitely an integral part of that. I don't mix feelings with business. That's why I'm still standing, and that's also why these niggas I'm setting up are going down. I love pussy don't get me wrong, just not enough to let it interfere with my plan."

"So what if I said I was done?"

"That's not an option. Your only option is to do what you are supposed to do."

"Keni, I can't do this anymore," I yelled.

"Look, I know that you are upset right now, but if you want that 20G's you'd better get yourself together."

"It's not about the money anymore Keni. This shit is fucking with me mentally."

"I'll give you a week to get yourself together, that's the best I can do. After that, it's back to business."

I couldn't even respond. All of my anger was coming back because I could see how cold he really was. I had to figure out a way to be done with this shit. I knew that ignoring him would only piss him off. I didn't even know who his next target was but I knew that I didn't want to be involved. I left his house and made my way home with all sorts of different emotions going through me. All I could do was wait around for his call. It was exactly a week later when he got with me.

After I made it to the meeting, I walked in without saying much. I gave him the look of death as I sat across from him in his living room. I knew that Keni would try to pull a fast one on me, so I was ready for whatever he threw at me. With both of us having the same personality traits, we were destined to bump heads on this situation.

When he walked in the room, I had my game face on, and so did he. I was determined not to give in, but at the same time what choice did I have? I was ready to say damn the contract, but was my life really worth it? I was ready to say fuck it all.

"So, are you ready for the next job?" he asked, with a stern look on his face.

"No I'm not ready but I just want to get this shit over with," I replied.

"Well your next target is the nigga Menno from South Philly…."

"No Keni, you know how I feel about him. I thought we agreed that he was off limits."

"I never agreed to shit, I saved him for last! That nigga has to go and there ain't no ifs, ands, or buts about it!"

"We did agree to that, or I would have never went through with this shit! I told you how I feel about him!"

"Look, I know what I agreed to and you need to get on the ball so you can figure out how to get back in good with his ass! I want this job done, and I want it done right. I've tried to be cool but Mr. Nice Guy is gone, and if you don't do what you agreed to do, it's curtains!" he yelled.

"I'm through with this shit Keni! I told you from the beginning he was off limits," I yelled in frustration.

"What the fuck do you mean you're through? This shit ain't over until you do what you agreed to do!" he responded.

"I never agreed to hurt him. I care about him Keni," I explained, as I moved closer still trying to convince him to end this charade.

"Well let me give you a newsflash. He doesn't give a fuck about you. He dumped your ass before and he'll do it again," he yelled, while pointing his finger into my face.

"Keni please, let me go. I've done enough already," I begged, as tears fell from my eyes.

"Don't start that shit Miani. We had an arrangement, that's the bottom line. You need to go home, get yourself together and holla at me later. I'm not changing my mind so you can cut the tears short!" he demanded, before heading towards the door to let me out.

"Keni!" I yelled as he opened the door. "Please don't make me do this," I said, grabbing him by the hand.

"I said all I have to say," he said, snatching his hand away, pushing me closer toward the door.

I continued to beg before walking out. I thought that I could weigh him down and eventually get him to change his mind. As he pushed me out of the door he shut it behind me, I knew that I was fighting a war that I would never win. I walked to my car crying hysterically, because of the fact that I had no choice other than to finish what I started.

I pulled my cell phone out of my bag and stared at it contemplating calling Meeno and tipping him off. I scrolled through the phone book and pressed call. The phone rung a few times before he answered. When I heard his voice, I instantly froze. So, instead of speaking, I ended the call. "What the fuck are you doing?" I asked myself aloud, before turning off the phone completely. I knew Meeno would try to reach me and see why I had called.

After I made it home, I flopped down on the couch quickly closing me eyes. Tears were still falling as I thought about the conversation I just had with Keni. Though Meeno left me high and dry, I still loved him. I turned on the television before falling to sleep. It wasn't long before I was awakened by a knock at the door. Once I opened it, I was surprised to see Meeno standing before me looking sexier than I'd ever seen him.

"Hey Meeno, what brings you here?" I asked, while leaning against the door.

"You called my phone and when I tried to call you back, I couldn't get through."

"So, you came all the way over here because I didn't answer the phone?"

"No, because niggas in the street are talking and I was worried."

"What do you mean niggas are talking?"

"Look, let me come in so we can sit and talk," he insisted.

"Sure, come on in," I said, as he began to make his way into my apartment. "So who's talking? And about what?"

"About you being involved with these hustlers that are somehow popping up dead. Niggas think you have something to do with it."

"What?" I asked surprised.

"That's the word on the street. I was just worried since I hadn't seen you in a while. It was kind of weird that you called me."

"Well I apologize if I worried you."

"So what did you need when you called?"

"I wanted to ask you a question."

"About what?"

"About your feelings for me, I wanted to know if you ever really loved me."

"I have a lot of love for you."

"But I mean, did you really love me?"

"I still do," he responded, before turning his head to avoid staring me in the eye. I knew that I had touched a soft spot. It was that answer that made it harder for me to do what Keni needed me to do. Had he told me he never really loved me, I would have called Keni and told him to count me in. I wanted to tell him what Keni was planning to do but I knew that he would be furious at me. I needed to feel his touch one last time before he walked out of my life for good. I moved closer to him, looked into his eyes before I began to kiss him. I could feel him trying to pull away, but I wasn't going to allow it.

I slowly unzipped his pants sticking my hand inside to caress his dick. It was then that I realized how much I missed him. He began to get into it as he rubbed his hands across my breast. I wanted to taste him, so I got down on my knees and put all of him into my mouth.

Giving head was something that I enjoyed to the fullest since I had mastered my technique while dealing with him. You could hear the sound of me sucking his stick as the apartment was quiet as a mouse. I moved up and down as I showed his balls some attention with my free hand. As he became more excited he lifted me up and turned me around so that my ass was in his face. He pulled down my shorts before lying back on the sofa, instructing me to sit on his face. I obliged as he stuck out his tongue. I placed my clit on top of it and moved in circles. I quickly climaxed releasing all over his tongue.

He continued to suck my clit as I rode his face like a horse in a race. I leaned back so that I could stroke his dick while he took in my juices. I couldn't wait any longer, so I moved down to sit on his dick. I moaned as his thickness went inside of me. I grinded into him while placing my hands on his chest. He stared at me while taking handfuls of my breast. I breathed heavily as I picked up more speed. He then held on to me tightly and exploded. I laid there on his chest thinking about the future. I needed to tell him what I'd been doing, and I needed to tell him Keni's plans so that he could protect himself.

After he went into the bathroom and cleaned himself up, Meeno sat back on the sofa next to me. He looked at me and I could tell that he had something on his mind. "So why did you really call me?" he asked. "Because I know that it wasn't what you said earlier."

"I called you because I…" I froze up. Once he noticed the fear in my eyes he moved closer to me on the sofa. "I was helping Keni and that's something I'll regret for the rest of my life."

"What? You were helping Keni?"

"Yes, Keni came to me and offered me a chunk of money to help him eliminate his competition."

"So what the fuck does that mean? You killed people?"

"No, I distracted them and got them alone. His goons killed them," I said, as I began to cry. "I called because you were next on his list, and I told him I couldn't do it. I told him how I felt about you and he didn't care. I wanted to let you know how much I care about you, and to watch your back."

"So you were going to help that muthafucker kill me?" he yelled, before standing up from the chair.

"No Meeno, I wasn't and I'm scared as hell since he threatened to kill me if I didn't."

"I don't believe this shit Miani. What the fuck were you thinking about, getting involved with some shit like that?"

"I was broke. I had no other choice."

"You could have got a job or something, that's a bullshit excuse! You think you're built for this game and you're not. This shit is serious!" His cell phone rang and he paused to answer it. I sat there quietly as he talked on the phone.

He hung up and immediately began yelling,"You set me up, you fucking bitch!" he screamed.

"What are you talking about?" I responded. "I told him I wasn't going to go through with it."

"That muthafucker has three niggas on their way up here now! I have to get out of here," he said trying to get to the door.

"I didn't set you up, Meeno. I didn't even know you were coming here. Who told you that? Who was that on the phone?" He didn't speak another word before removing his gun from the small of his back.

I was nervous as I backed into the kitchen. Meeno opened the door to peek out and was immediately knocked down. His gun flew out of his hand. As he crawled to get it, one of the three men grabbed him and the other two began beating him. I cried and begged for them to stop. They continued to beat him. As I begged for them to stop, they ignored me.

A few minutes later, Keni walked through the door with a smile on his face. I was furious as he sat down on my sofa instructing his goons to keep beating. I was helpless. I realized there wasn't anything I could do to save him. Soon Meeno was unresponsive, I tried to get closer to him, but each time I was pulled away. To finish him off, Keni put four shots in his back. The blood immediately began to spill out onto the carpet.

"I told you that you were going to finish what you started!" he said, as he laughed. "Here's your cash!" He tossed a bag full of cash towards me.

"Fuck your money Keni! And fuck you too!" I replied.

"Fuck me? Bitch I just gave you enough money so you won't have to beg for that shit anymore. You should be thanking me!" he yelled.

"You just killed the one man I cared about, and I should thank you? You can take your money Keni because I don't want it!" I yelled, before throwing the bag across the room. "You are the one that's going to go down for this! I hope you know that!"

"I'm not going down for a damn thing. I'll kill you first!"

"Go ahead, but you're going to die anyway!"

"What?"

"You want to kill me? Go ahead but remember this, you fucked me raw in the shower that day. You should have known better!"

"So are you trying to say you gave me something?" he yelled, before walking closer to me. His eyes were opened wide and I tried to back away. "Yeah, that's exactly what I'm saying. I have HIV muthafucker and when your ass is dying you'll think of me!"

"What?"

"You heard me! You'll die thinking of me!"

I was nervous about what he would do next. I wanted this to be over and if dying was the only way, I was ready to go. I had done a lot of things in my life and it was too late to turn back now. I stood up off the floor with a million thoughts running through my head. I found out that I was HIV positive just months before I broke up with Meeno. I never pushed to get back with him for fear that he would find out. I was still addicted to sex and I made sure that I didn't purposely infect anyone, but condoms did occasionally break and once they did I stepped off.

As for Keni, I didn't care whether he had it or not. Over the six month period I worked for him, I had a lot of different feelings for him be it lust, hate or disgust. He ruined my life and after that there wouldn't be anything left to live for.

While we stood there staring each other down, I thought about the good times I had with Meeno. If only I could turn back time and never dialed his number, he would still be alive. My heart was broken as I glanced at Meeno's body. I wanted to hug him once more before it was all over.

I moved slowly over to his body as Keni continued to stare. I got on my knees and kneeled down next to him as tears began to pour out. I put my lips close to his skin and kept them there for a few seconds. The blood on the floor began to soak into my pants. Keni became annoyed.

"Get the fuck up off the floor!" he yelled. I kissed Meeno's cheek one more time before rising from the ground. I was no longer afraid of what would happen. I knew that I needed to be with Meeno to tell him how sorry I was. If death was my only option, then I was willing to take it. I could tell that Keni was nervous as he began to pace the floor. I knew that the words I spoke to him a few minutes ago were running through his head. HIV was definitely nothing to play with, so I knew that he would go crazy thinking about it long after I was gone.

"You might as well kill me!" I begged him to get it over with. As he raised his gun and pointed it in my direction, I closed my eyes.

"You did this shit the coward way. You got me to do your dirty work. If you were such a fucking tough guy you would have done the shit by yourself. For that shit you deserve to die and I hope you die slow!"

Soon I felt the bullet pierce my chest and the warmness of the blood ran down my shirt. I stumbled a little before falling to the floor. He took one more shot at me. The things that I should have valued I didn't, and even if Keni hadn't come into my life, HIV would have gotten me. I was fast to give up the ass for cash and look where it landed me. I had a new outlook on life once I woke up in the hospital and realized that God had given me another chance. The attitude I had toward my illness prior to being shot was definitely different now. I cared about my life and was going to make the best of whatever time I had left. We should never be so stuck on money that we step out of character to make someone else rich. Money, cars and clothes have value, but life is priceless. It was over, and it was the price I had to pay for being the right hand bitch to a conniving man who would have never been there for me. It's too bad I didn't realize it all before it was too late.

THE COOKOUT

JUICY WRIGHT

Sunny's back was flat against the wall of the shower as she cringed from side to side. The tile felt cold to her skin at first. The hot water was beating against her breast and hardened nipples. With both legs slightly bent and separated, Sunny clutched tightly her silver waterproof bullet in one hand, while using the other hand to separate her lips. Her clit was sitting pretty in pink as she teased it with the egg shaped vibe. Her moans were echoing through the bathroom as she fantasized that a complete stranger was in the shower with her, with his head buried between her legs. Her fantasy man was straight sexy as hell, resembling Morris Chesnut. His chocolate body was perched between her thighs as his tongue played hide and seek with her clit. Her moans became louder and drowned out the sound of the phone ringing in the background. The caller was persistent, calling repeatedly.

"Damn, who the fuck is it. Shit that phone is fucking up my cum." Sunny was becoming irritated because the ringing of the phone was seriously putting a damper on her excitement, and the man she had envisioned in the shower with her.

The phone stopped, and she got back on track. She continued to work the vibe on her clit, increasing its intensity, moving it back and forth. As Sunny felt tingles from within, she inserted the egg shaped vibe inside her pussy. She could feel her juices running down on her hand, mixing in with the stream of water and running down her leg. Massaging both of her 36 D breast, made her pussy pulsate, but she squeezed her pelvic muscle to hold back on cumming; she just wasn't ready just yet. She took her time and rolled her nipples between her fingers and then lifted her left breast so that she could lick around the areola and nipple. Her nipple stood erect, welcoming her tongue as she teased it.

She began to grind down on her bullet that was now engulfed inside her wetness, and her rhythm quickened. Sunny was imagining that the gentleman in the shower was groping her ass, and pushing her pussy into his face as his tongue was slipping in and out of her, while he sucked her juices from within. As she began to pant and make high pitch noises, she grabbed the sliding glass door handle with one hand while the other continued to dive deeply within herself.

Sunny began to tremble, "Oh, oh shit. Damn I'm cumming, hell yeah."

She looked down with a smile as if the stranger was really in the shower with her and she was showing her gratitude. Sunny was patting the air near her groin as if the stranger's head really existed.

As her juices continued to run down her legs into the drain below her, Sunny stood still as the water beat upon her and she basked in fulfillment.

Just as she was stepping out the shower after washing the

remnants of the explosion she had seconds ago, the phone began to ring again. She hurried to wrap a towel around her body and briskly walked to answer the phone that was in her room on the bed. The cool air gave her a chill as it hit her still damp shoulders.

Looking down at the caller id she saw that it was her friend Jazz. She knew she was calling to see if she was ready yet. She damn near fucked up her cum, ringing the phone off the damn hook.

Sunny answered, "Bitch, I just got out the shower. I will be ready in like 20 minutes, damn. Ringin my phone off the damn hook."

"Shut the hell up Sunny, I ain't got all got damn day to be waiting in front your house waiting on your half and half ass. I'm tryin to meet me some new dick tonight and I want first pickins," Jazz shouted back into the phone.

"I wuv you too, bitch. See ya when you get here." Sunny hung up not giving Jazz time to reply.

Sunny ran back into her closet to pick out something cute and sexy. Shit, she was hoping to get her some new dick, dicks, or pussy tonight too. Fuck, she was down when it came to sex, and variety only made it better. Although she loved her some dick, a lil pussy here and there ain't never hurt either. Shit, as a matter of fact Sunny loved to eat pussy. She could recall a few occasions in her past that another bitch called out her name as her tongue pleased them and their juices spilled all over her face. Just the thought made Sunny smile and made the space between her thighs become moist.

Whispering to herself, "Let me get my mind right before I have to get myself off again."

Sunny returned to the mirror after getting dressed, admiring herself and how damn good she looked from head to toe. She had her long dark wavy hair pulled up in a high ponytail, in preparation for the heat. She only needed very minimal makeup since her skin was flawless. Her golden skin tone was evenly spread over her entire body, like she had a tan all year round. She was always questioned about her nationality, but she would just simply respond that she was "black" in lieu of explaining her Latino genetics, since she knew nothing about that part of her life.

Just as Sunny was making it down the stairs she heard the horn to Jazz's car out front of her house. She opened the door quickly, and stuck her hand out to door to let her know she saw her and was on her way in a few minutes. She grabbed her shades and keys, slid on her new pink Chanel four inch heels and matching backpack. She gave one more look at her self on the way out the door and locked it behind her.

She quickly got into Jazz's brother's Range Rover. The truck was hot as shit. Peanut butter and jelly is what they usually referred to it as. The truck's exterior was a high gloss burgundy and the inside was tan leather. The chromed out wheels made the truck stand out from any other like it. Jazz asked her brother to borrow the truck cause she wanted her and Sunny to make a grand entrance at today's event.

"What up ho? Glad Terrance let you hold the keys to his ride, cause this shit is hot," Sunny said with all smiles. "I wish I had a whip of my own to push like this, but in due fuckin time, in due time."

Jazz looked at Sunny with a raised eyebrow and said, "Well I promised Terrance you would definitely give him some pussy one day soon if he let us use the truck." Jazz began to giggle. "I don't know why you won't give my brotha none, he been trying to get at your ass for years. Shit, he fine as all get out and paid out the ass. Shit I would fuck em' if he wasn't my damn blood."

"Jazz, I'm gonna beat your ass. How you gonna just offer up my pussy? But T is one gorgeous motha-fucka and I told you how I feel about him. He's somebody I would rather have a serious relationship with than just some quick dick. Plus he wit that new bitch Shanita anyway. Can't wait to see what this one looks like."

"Ah, fuck that bitch, I don't like her anyway. But I give it to her, she is sexy as hell. All you got to do is give me the word and me and you is good as sister in laws. That bitch aint got nothin on you."

Sunny looked at Jazz seductively, "Then will I still be able to lick my sister in law's pussy when I want, or would that be considered incest?"

Sunny and Jazz had been licking each other since they were fifteen years old. They started experimenting out of curiosity. Neither lady considered themselves to be lesbian or bi-sexual, instead they both liked variety and excitement to their sex life, and both figured who better to share it with than someone you can trust and are down with. It was their little secret, although they had participated in a threesome here and there with guys they had met.

Jazz rubbed the tips of her fingers across her braless breast that were sitting up nice and perky in a low cut halter top and replied back to Sunny, " Well if incest feels that damn good, then by all means sister…welcome to the motha-fuckin family."

Both girls laughed, but Jazz who was looking damn good in the driver's seat was turning Sunny the fuck on. Jazz wore a jean mini that accented her coco brown thick thighs and a blue, white and gold v-neck halter that she made out of a Gilbert Arenas jersey. The jersey was fitted and it hugged her waist tightly showing her navel ring. Jazz's stomach was toned and her waist was clinched. The plunge in the "V" neck was so deep if the top moved an inch in either direction a nipple would pop out. Jazz was absolutely gorgeous. Her hair hung to her chin and she had each side pinned back with a clip. She had gorgeous eyes that were dreamy and a slight cleft in her chin. Most guys couldn't resist her. Standing only 5 foot 2 inches, Jazz's legs were long and lean. Running track for years had definitely paid off.

"Why you lookin at me like that, mommi?" Jazz asked Sunny, calling her by her pet name.

"Cause your ass lookin good over there and I think I might want a taste," Sunny said bluntly, just as she did, Sunny placed her left hand in between Jazz's thighs.

Immediately Jazz spread her legs apart slightly and a sly grin spread over her face. Beyonce and Jay Z's, De'ja'vu was pumping and Sunny's hand began to creep slowly up Jazz's inner thigh, and her clit was tingling from excitement. Jazz relaxed her foot slightly on the accelerator so that she could coast at a safe speed.

Sunny leaned over and licked Jazz lightly on the ear, which sent a quick shiver up her spine and juices flowing in the seat beneath her. It was too much for her thong to hold. That was her spot and Sunny knew it. As Sunny continued to feast on her ear, with her right hand she began to gently massage Jazz's breast.

Jazz began to moan, "Girl u wanna pull over. You gonna make me wreck this truck and then you gonna have to fuck my brotha for the rest of your life to make up for it."

"That's a risk I will have to take, keep driving bitch. I don't want us to be too late."

Jazz did just as she was told as she felt Sunny's thumb began to massage her clit. Her legs opened wider and welcomed Sunny's performance. Sunny herself was moaning as she was giving her best friend pleasure and began to grind in her own seat. Jazz rotated her pelvis against Sunny's thumb and was hoping that it would slip inside her. Jazz was having a hard time concentrating on the road as she was getting a rhythm against the hand between her legs. While concentrating on the pleasures she was receiving, Jazz closed her eyes and laid her head back on the headrest. She was dazed and didn't realize she was rolling right through a four way stop sign, until a horn and loud screech made her snap back into reality. Jazz had to swerve onto the wrong lane to miss a head on collision.

"Damn bitch, you see what you almost made me do. My brother would kill me if I crashed this truck," Jazz said still confused.

Both girls were getting lost in their pleasures. Jazz now had her free leg propped up higher against the door so that she could be penetrated. Sunny loved teasing Jazz and she knew that Jazz wanted her fingers deep inside. Sunny moved Jazz's thong to the side as she teased the opening to Jazz's hole. Jazz began to thrust her pelvis forward in hopes that Sunny would stop teasing her, and start finger fucking her like she wanted. Instead, Sunny continued to massage and stimulate Jazz's clit. Jazz was gripping the hell out of the steering wheel, and could feel her explosion approaching. By now the truck was crawling at about 15 mph and the car behind her was blowing. Sunny was about to cum herself, just from bringing her friend pleasure. Thank God for red lights, cause just as Jazz stopped the truck, she squealed and juices ran out on Sunny's hand and onto the leather seats. Sunny then squirted her own juices and drenched her thong.

"Damn Sunny, now I feel like I need a shower and a nap." Jazz rolled her eyes.

Sunny leaned over and tongued Jazz just before the light turned green. Looking to the right, two teenage boys in a Jeep Cherokee were enjoying the festivities beside them.

Just then, the Range Rover reached its destination at the 'Biker Boyz' annual cookout. Jazz's brother Terrance was a member and invited both his sister and Sunny. This was the hottest event of the summer and only those who were top flight were invited. The 'Biker Boyz' was DC's finest and hottest hustlers around. The group consisted of about 75 dudes from Maryland, DC and Virginia, who all were down for doing their thang and being paid out the ass. They got much respect and would tolerate bullshit from no one.

"Damn, look at all these niggas that are up in here. The joint only started like an hour ago and it looks like over 300 people up at this spot." Sunny had to shout over all the loud noises and music.

Jazz nodded, "All these fine ass niggas in one place, to many to choose from. How the hell am I suppose to pick just one? I feel like I'm in a dick shop with so many flavors, colors and shit."

Bikes were lined up everywhere, along with cars sitting on chromed out rims letting you know that money was all up in the place. That put a smile on both girls' faces. As they walked by the many cars, the ladies looked at their reflections in the windows of the parked cars. Sunny knew she looked cute. Although her outfit was simple, she was looking hot in it. She wore a short Dolce and Gabanna jean skirt, a white wife beater that was tight to death and fitting her like a glove. Underneath the T, she wore a pink sequined bikini top that could barely hold her 36 D's. She put her pink cap on her head, and pulled her ponytail through the hole in the back. The platinum hoops with diamonds that hung from her ear gave just the right amount of bling and the matching bangles that hung on her wrist. She threw her backpack on her back and she put on her million-dollar walk with those thick beautiful shapely legs of hers, and the phat ass to go along with it.

Just as they were approaching the yard the ladies heard someone call their names and they turned in unison.

A light skin cutie that was standing with a group of guys yelled out, "Damn shorties, y'all lookin' hot as hell. Damn mommi, you working that wife beater. Damn!"

Sunny responded by giving the cutie a wink and blowing a kiss at the same time. Sunny and Jazz looked at each other and giggled. Feeling like movie stars they were recognized by others who turned to see who they were as well. It was Jazz's brother.

"Hey Jazz. What's up Sunny? Took y'all asses long enough to get here. Jazz you left the house almost two hours before I did and we only live like five minutes from Sunny," Terrance commented. “I hope you took special care of my baby while you were driving her.” Although he was referring to his truck, Jazz’s brother coyly looked over at Sunny and reached out and ran his index finger down her glossy lips.

Terrance, or “T” as he was simply named by his boys, was Jazz’s older brother. Sunny thought he was looking mighty fine as usual, and she all of a sudden got a visual of him in between her legs bangin her pussy and she immediately got wet. The expression on her face must have gotten his attention.

“Sunny, what up wit you, ma?” he said while looking her up and down and licking his lips while he did so.

She returned the same look; only she used her hazel green eyes seductively to flirt back at him, “Maybe you, one day soon.” She smiled, rolled her eyes, and the girls walked off to get in the mix of things.

The cookout was off the hook. One of the fellow ‘Biker Boyz’, Jump Man offered to have the cookout at his crib, since he had the space for it. He had just bought his new house in Accokeek Maryland; he had 6 acres and an 8,000 square foot home. The food was the shit. It was catered by one of the hottest soul food restaurants in the metropolitan area, Henry’s Soul Café. The grills were blazing and the air was filled with the aroma of bar-b-que ribs and chicken. Each way you turned you could see guests licking their lips and sucking their fingers clean of the thick sauces. And the DJ, Mr. B was off the chain, rocking the joint. He played hit after hit, and of course a party would not be a party in D.C. without legendary Go-Go. So, Chuck, RE and Junk Yard got their time on the turntable.

The night air was starting to settle in, and the long day was showing its affects on everyone. There wasn’t a sober soul up in the spot. Everyone was feeling lovely and by now, majority of the people knew whom they were trying to hook up with and was horny as hell.

Sunny had lost track of where Jazz went. All she could

remember was that she went after some light skinned tall dude, that was cute, but not Sunny's speed… she liked them dark. But for the last hour or so, some cute ass Spanish girl had been giving her the eye, and that shit was turning her the hell on. Sunny had her eyes on a couple of honies and a few had approached her, but she was really feeling Terrance tonight and was having thoughts about hooking up with him, especially since it seemed like he had elected to leave his girl at home.

The three glasses of Hypnotiq and one glass of Long Island Ice Tea Sunny had drunk, was helping her relax even more. It was causing her body heat to rise. As R. Kelly's, 'My Body's Calling' was playing in the background, Sunny began to gyrate to the music. Sunny danced all alone, but she didn't care. She closed her eyes and could feel the bass of the music deep down within her soul. She felt intoxicated. She removed her wife beater showing off her rock hard abs and toned back. The pink sequin reflected beautifully against her bronze skin and the dimples towards the small of her back could be seen as her low-rise skirt hugged her hips nicely. All eyes were on her. Terrance watched her from afar as did many of the guys there. In the corner near the bar, two guys were giving each other dap as they both wanted to fuck her.

Some guy sitting on the deck called out, "Work that body Sunshine," referring to the name she had tattooed on her lower back with a sun rising up above the word.

Sunny didn't even respond to him and didn't realize that Terrance was also watching her from a distance. He was craving to be with her. He wanted to be so close that he could smell her skin as if it were his own.

The Spanish girl also had her eye on Sunny and she wanted to lick and suck her too. She could tell that Sunny was down and into shit like that. When one enjoys that type of lifestyle, it is noticeable. The Spanish girl whispered to some of the guys nearby, but not once took her eyes off of Sunny's every move.

One guy wearing a 'Biker Boyz' jacket yelled from his table to the Spanish girl, "Is everything straight, you got my twenty right?"

The Spanish girl winked back and said, "Its all good. I got this and your twenty."

Many of the 'Biker Boyz' and some other guests gave each other high fives and the ones that had beers clanked them together in a toast.

The many drinks had finally caught up with Sunny and she had an extreme urge to pee. She tried to dance it off, but that didn't work. If she didn't hurry, she would be the fuckin joke at this cook out. The half breed bitch that pissed all over Jump Man's deck is what everybody would remember her as.

Sunny headed through the sliding glass doors to the bathroom on the main floor, but of course it was occupied. Squeezing her thighs together tightly and looking from side to side for a means of escape, Redds, one of the 'Biker Boyz' who was black as hell, and no one ever understood how he got his name, pointed up the steps.

"Damn Sunny, don't piss on Jump Man's carpet. Take your ass to the upstairs bathroom."

"Fuck you Redds. Thanks," Sunny said, looking over her shoulder and almost running at the same time.

Redds shot back quickly and followed Sunny to the steps, "When baby, when? I want a piece of that ass." He could see the lower half of her phat ass under her mini jiggling as she went up the steps. His dick stood front and center.

Terrance caught a glimpse of Redds eyeballing Sunny and he didn't like it. None of his boys knew how bad he had it for Sunny. He was known as a player, and he didn't want to jeopardize his status by letting anyone in on his real feelings. But honestly, it ate him up to see other niggas feanin' over her.

As the Spanish girl saw Sunny head up the steps, she made her way behind her. And as she did, the many guys she passed slipped her a twenty-dollar bill each. Some giving her dap on her way, while others saying not a word, but giving a nod of approval.

Sunny dried her hands, freshened her Mac Lip Glass, and was headed back down stairs. When she opened the door, the Spanish chick that was watching her on the deck was standing right there in the doorway. Sunny jumped back slightly because she startled her.

"Wha…" before Sunny could get it out, the Spanish chick reached for Sunny's hand and guided her to the bedroom next door without saying a word. Sunny didn't object.

The women stood face to face, with their breathing getting heavier from excitement and intoxication. Sunny reached over and touched the Latina's lips with the tips of her fingers and then slowly inserted her pointer finger into her mouth. The chick grabbed her hand and sucked her finger eagerly. The Spanish chick quickly removed her own top and then proceeded to help Sunny untie her bikini top. Instantly, it fell to the floor. The chick stepped back to admire Sunny's curvaceous figure. Sunny continued to undress. She unsnapped her jean mini and slid it down her full toned legs, then onto the floor. Unbelievably, Sunny became shy and looked away. The Spanish girl took the lead and took off her jeans as well. And from the mirror directly behind her, Sunny was able see the shapely ass she had glimpsed at several times that night.

The chick's light golden skin looked edible in the pastel purple thongs she was wearing and Sunny couldn't wait to grab it. As they both took time to admire each other's body, Sunny stepped behind the chick so that she could feel her plump rear press against her front. While behind the mamacita, she unhooked her bra and let it fall to the floor. Sunny wrapped her arms around the chick and cupped her breast as she began to kiss her neck. Just then the bedroom door swung open and startled both ladies. It was Fat Joe, Redd's brother. His eyes almost popped out his head when he saw the two beautiful ladies skin to skin.

"Oh damn. Sorry. Damn," Fat Boy apologized. He backed his way out the room, never letting his eyes off the scene before him. He gave the ladies a wink, but only the Spanish girl winked back.

Sunny was a little hesitant about continuing. But her hormones were raging and the alcohol was edging her to keep going. The little bit of soberness that she had left was telling her to get dressed, but her hormones won. The interruption was now just a thought and the ladies continued on.

Sunny rubbed each of her nipples and gave them both just the right amount of pressure. While holding and massaging the left breast with her left hand, Sunny took her right hand and slowly slid it down the front of the Spanish chick's body until she was able to reach the inside of her thong. With her middle finger, Sunny maneuvered in between the chick's lips and found that she was wet. This excited Sunny and she too became moist over the Spanish mama's excitement. Sunny continued to fondle the chick's clit until she grabbed a hold of her hand and pulled it from her panties. The chick quickly turned so that she could face her. She noticed Sunny's full size breast erect, and the chick could not help but to want to feast on the pink colored nipples. The chick leaned down so that she could nestle between the breasts and then began to lick each, as if they were a lollipop with the flavor of the month. Sunny's pussy became even wetter. The Spanish chick released the lip hold she had on Sunny's breast and escorted her to the beautifully made bed. There was a full-length mirror behind the bed. It captured the beauty of both ladies. They both seemed to admire themselves when they caught the glimpse of their mirror images. The Latina gave a wink to the mirror and Sunny smiled back. She helped Sunny out her panties before she sat down and laid back.

The Spanish chick stood above her and admired her clean-shaven pussy and licked her lips in approval. The girl then removed her thong and tossed it to lie on top of Sunny's clothes. What they did to each other was incredible. The women were touching and feeling, licking and kissing. They caressed each other as they discovered the others body. As Sunny positioned herself on her back, she scooted back some so that her entire body could lie upon the bed. Silence in the room was thick. You could almost hear the beating of their hearts. From time to time you could hear noise from the room next door. Almost as if a group of guys were together watching a football game. But just as quick as the noise would begin it would cease.

"Damn you're beautiful, mommi," the Spanish chick whispered loudly to Sunny.

Sunny just smiled. This was the first time she had heard the Latina speak since they came into the room. She also thought how this was the name Jazz used when flirting with her. "You're pretty damn sexy yourself, m-m-ii-sss," Sunny raised her voice as if asking a question.

"Oh, Miss Sunny, I'm Nita and I was trying to make it a pleasure to meet you all night. When I first saw you earlier I wanted to taste you."

From outside the door a voice shouted, "Hey Nita, count me, Big B, Donte, Crazy J, and Alonzo in. Its all there, plus a tip."

Nita looked at Sunny with raised eyebrows as if not knowing what that was all about. The room became quiet again as each lady locked lustful eyes on each other. The only noise was coming from down stairs and it seemed so distant. You could faintly hear the guys below fussing and cursing while they were playing pool. Nita stood and watched Sunny as she began to massage her own breast. Shockingly, she lifted her head and brought her own nipple upward, licking them, and they responded by hardening to the touch. With her free hand she parted her lips between her thighs with her fingers. With her other hand she released her breast and put two fingers in her mouth; that hand also found its way to her vagina. Then with moistened fingers she inserted them deep into herself. She moaned in the delight that she was causing herself.

The actions taking place before Nita's eyes were turning her the fuck on and she had to join in. She was turned on by the pinkness of Sunny's lips and the clit that was now swollen with pleasure. Her mouth began to pucker, as she wanted a taste of the sweet juices. Nita then climbed on top the bed. Looking into the mirror she licked her lips and blew a kiss. She went head first to drench her tongue in Sunny's garden. Sunny welcomed her by spreading her legs further apart and allowing her to lick and suck her thickness.

On the other side of the wall, loud banging and cheering could be heard. Sunny could have sworn she heard someone say, "Get that Nita." But then again she figured the guys were watching a game or something, and instead were hollering, "Get that nigga."

Sunny's juices were flowing and her breathing was uncontrollable. Nita was pleasing her body right. As Nita flicked her tongue back and forth on Sunny's clit, Sunny could feel the passion growing within. The throb in her pussy was beating harder and harder as she started to grind her pussy into Nita's face, wanting her tongue to reach deeper and deeper into her.

In the midst of it all, neither woman had realized that the door to the bedroom had been eased open and that Terrance was standing there, admiring it all. He stood there silently. He was amazed at how these two beautiful women entangled themselves around each other. The two shades of golden skin tones blended perfectly together. He didn't make a sound, but enjoyed the view as his excitement caused an immediate erection in his jean shorts. He was glad that his wrong turn to the bathroom landed him in heaven. He closed the door carefully behind him. Looking down at his feet, he realized he was standing on at least $300 or more. Almost all twenty-dollar bills. He thought how strange that was, but immediately his attention was back on the action before him.

He longed to join the women, but didn't want to disturb their moment. So, he patiently watched, waited and hoped.

He thought about how bad he had wanted Sunny for years and to see her like this increased his desires for her. He let his shorts and boxers drop easily to the floor in one movement, hoping that his slightest move would not cause a distraction. The girls didn't notice him. They didn't see him rubbing his hardness as he was watching them and wishing they would include him. He felt like a kid in a toy store, being told, "look but don't touch."

As Sunny reached her climax, her joy juices ran onto Nita's tongue and Nita licked it from her lips in delight.

"Damn Sunny, you taste good mommi."

When Sunny finally caught her breath, Nita lifted her head and they looked at each other. From the corner of Sunny's eye she spotted Terrance in the doorway but didn't say a word to him or Nita, instead she gave him a teasing grin as she slid off the bed.

With Sunny's ass sitting high in the air from the position she was in, Terrance was gaining the urge to push his dick into her pussy from behind. The excitement of feeling the wetness of Sunny's pussy on his dick made his knees weak. He could see the wetness of her pussy glistening from where he stood and wanted so bad to be drenched in it.

"Mmmm, ahhh," Sunny said seductively looking at Terrance.

Just then, as Terrance looked down he saw a few twenties being pushed underneath the door. Curiosity got the best of him this time and he opened the door. Standing before him was one of his biker buddies, Tank.

"What you doing nigga?" Terrance questioned him.

"Ahhhhh, damn dog. You's da man, no shit. I owe this to Nita," Tank said, handing him the twenty and giving him dap at the same time. He peeked in a little and grinned slyly. "You da mothafuckin' man fo sho."

Terrance took the money and tossed it on the night stand. His mind was so preoccupied about how he was going to get in on the pussy, he didn't even think twice about Tank giving him the money; besides, the girls didn't even let that scene at the door distract them.

***

Behind the full-length mirror, on the other side of the wall, there was a secret room. A theater room. Jump Man had the room specially designed to view the festivities of the guest bedroom. The same room that Sunny, Nita and now Terrance were in. The theater room was packed. Every 'Biker Boyz' VIP guest in the room was glued to the one-way mirror. Each guy had paid Nita $20 to entice Sunny to the room and seduce her. And they paid an additional $20 to Jump Man to view the girl on girl sex scene. Terrance coming into the scene was a bonus. He knew nothing about the plot that had been boiling all evening around this event. All the guys knew how he felt about Sunny and knew he would never be down for it. But he walked in on this one and now all the guys behind the glass wished they were in his shoes.

"Man, I cant believe this nigga up in my crib getting ready to have the time of his life. This shit suppose to be happenin' to me. I should charge y'all nigga's another dub," Jump Man said out loud to all the dudes up in the room.

Tank yelled back, "Shi-it, nigga, I ain't payin' nothin' else unless I'm gettin' some of that pussy too. But this room cool as shit. Only a pervert ass nigga like you would think to do some crazy shit like this. Not to mention the room is sound proof."

Big Donte sat on the front row with his mouth wide open and his hands in his pants. "Damn that Sunny is hot as hell. Man look at dem titties. And her ass is phat as hell. That is one bad ass bitch. I see why Terrance hot after her ass," he said to no one in particular, but they all agreed.

"Yeah and Nita is bad as a motha too. But the bitch is a freak. I don't know why T been takin' up time with that ho. I told him she wasn't shit, but his ass won't listen. But he'll see after tonight," Redds said out to everyone in the room.

"Yeah, but that fool gonna be hot wit all our asses when he finds out we been watching and paid to watch this shit. The way that dude feel about Sunny, mannnnn. He gonna flip," Tank shouted out.

Up until now Crazy J had been quiet, "Man fuck T. This some hot shit. And I wish all y'all bitches be quiet so a nigga can get into this shit."

They all laughed and agreed.

***

Sunny smacked her own ass, and looked over her shoulder, Her eyes begged Terrance to enter heaven. As he walked over she softly tapped Nita on the behind to get her attention, and pointed directly at the handsome man before them. Nita gave a nod of approval as she turned on her back. Sunny smiled a 'thank you', and backed towards him slightly, just enough that her ass grazed his manhood. Sunny motioned Nita to slide down some so that she could continue to indulge her on.

As Terrance slowly entered Sunny, he was greeted by an over flow of juices that had formed inside her vagina. They welcomed his presence. He moaned as he entered Sunny, and she paused in her breathing.

Loud cheers and chants could be heard through the walls, "That's my nigga! Hit that shit!"

"Damn girl, you feel better than I ever imagined," Terrance panted with shut eyes.

Nita grabbed Sunny's head and pushed it downward between her legs. She was turned on from seeing Terrance enjoying the pussy he was so deeply in. His face showed her that he was enjoying each stroke that he offered. He got a glimpse of his own face in the mirror before him. And thought to himself how lucky he was to be in this position right now. Sunny moaned in between the licks that she was giving Nita's pussy. Nita held on tight to Sunny's long hair that was no longer in the ponytail she came with, and with force held her into position. She grinded her pelvis on Sunny's face causing her juices to overflow onto her chin and nose. Her pace became faster and faster as Sunny's tongue dove in deeper and deeper.

With her thumb, Sunny began to massage Nita's clit. Nita arched her back, no longer able to control herself. She began to shiver as she came, and a flood poured onto the blanket beneath her.

Now with two free hands, Sunny reached between her parted legs and started to massage Terrance's balls as he continued to plunge deep inside her. He was now grabbing hold of both her ass cheeks, separating them slightly as he watched his dick slide in and out of her deepness. He could feel her inside muscle as she made her walls constrict around his meat, holding him tightly. He reached out and grabbed her hair, twisting it into his hand, causing her head to rise up and lcan back. As he pounded her, her breast shook from the body-to-body contact.

Nita rose to her knees on the bed and began to kiss Terrance's chest and slowly found his thick lips. As he tongued her back, he could taste the sweet juices that Sunny had left behind from her climax. The taste was sweet. Sunny moaned loudly and he could feel her explosion within all over him.

Nita, acting as if she knew Terrance oh so well, wanting to feed his appetite for more sex, laid flat on the bed opening her legs wide to invite him inside. As he kneeled upon the bed he entered her. She rose up her pelvis and began to take all of him in. He grabbed her at the waist to assist in his thrusting. Her moans grew louder as she could feel him fill her up. Their bodies moved in unison as if they were one.

Nita moaned, "Damn baby, fuck me. Yeah I like it like that."

After regaining composure, Sunny returned to kneel on the bed as she bent down to delight herself on Nita's perky breast. Nita's nipples stood erect, awaiting Sunny to taste and lick them. With very soft lips, Sunny nibbled each breast, giving each a slight squeeze. As Nita's back began to arch, Terrance knew she was about to cum, he could feel the liquids inside her becoming warmer and warmer.

Sunny continued to kiss on Nita's body, down to her navel…licking and sucking. Nita grabbed the covers into her hand and bit down on her bottom lip as her insides felt as if they were caving in and exploding at the same time. Her wetness increased and soaked Terrance's shaft. Her knees trembled and shook the bed. She lay lifeless from exhaustion.

"Damn, damn," was all Nita could manage to whimper from her lips while her eyes were closed.

As Nita regained her composure, Sunny on her knees bent towards Terrance, her head at his waist level. She looked up at him with her hazel green eyes and she took his rock hard dick into her hands. The boy was definitely blessed with at least nine inches. She guided his penis into her mouth and began to work her magic. He moaned in ecstasy as he felt his manhood touch the back of Sunny's throat.

"Fuck girl, damn. Shit, you gonna make a nigga cum," Terrance said to Sunny as they looked eye to eye.

As Terrance looked up and into the mirror, he could have sworn he'd seen someone on the other side. Seemed as if he saw something that resembled a face and a baseball cap. He shook his head slightly and closed his eyes, thinking his excitement was causing him to hallucinate. Once he opened his eyes the reflection was gone.

Sunny was taking in all of him and her tongue was dancing around the head. As Sunny was stroking his dick with her mouth, her hand was massaging his balls. Sunny was the best at givinig head. There weren't many bitches who could compete with her in the head game. Terrance grabbed her by the head with both hands to force her to take all of him, and to his surprise she didn't gag like most females that had sucked him off in the past.

"Take that shit, all that shit." Those were the words heard coming from the opposite side of the wall.

Sunny looked up at Terrance with questionable eyes, but he didn't respond.

As Sunny continued to give Terrance joy with her mouth, Nita came to join in on the action. She knelt beside Sunny, both women on all fours turned to each other to kiss passionately. As they kissed deeply, Terrance enjoyed the sight of seeing these two beautiful women together with their tongues intertwined and began to stroke himself. As their lips parted, Nita took in Terrance's stiffness. Her lips glided up and down his erectness as saliva drenched him. He moaned out loudly and she began to quicken her pace. The slurping sounds filled the room and the smell of sex surrounded them. He began to pound towards her, as he was near reaching an ultimate high. Sunny watched as his dick disappeared inside of Nita's mouth and her cheeks pulled him in.

Terrance's eyes were closed for a brief second as he was losing his self in his pleasures. He began to quiver as Nita was rhythmatically jerking him, and positioned his dick right above Sunny's perfect breast and pink nipples. Within seconds, his hot cream was pouring onto Sunny's breast and nipples, and Nita welcomed its presence with her tongue by licking her tits clean from Terrance's cum. He let out a loud sigh of gratification and collapsed on the bed between the two women.

"Whhhheeeewww, damn," that was all Terrance could managed to say for now.

Seconds passed without one word from anyone. But there were loud roars, cheers, and banging on the wall from the other side. Terrance and Sunny looked at each other confused and then they both looked at Nita, who was smiling.

Terrance began to speak in a groggy voice, "Well I guess you two have met, right?"

"Think it's a lil late for formal introductions, don't you?" Nita said with raised eyebrows to Sunny. Then gave a slight giggle like there was more to her statement then she let on.

Sunny responded with a questionable look on her face, "I think we passed formal introductions the minute you put your tongue on my clit. But it seems like I'm missing something here." Sunny looked at both Nita and Terrance.

"Wait, wait, wait, hold the fuck up. Nita, you didn't tell her who you were before you stepped to her? I know you ain't go foul on her like that?" Terrance said, with his voice raised slightly as if he were agitated.

Nita just laughed as she continued to encircle Terrance's nipple with her pointer finger. Each lady was on one side of Terrance with their heads lying on his shoulder.

Sunny sat up quickly and put some attitude in her neck, rolling her eyes, looking back and forth between the two before speaking. "Someone want to fill me in on what the fuck I'm missing here?"

Terrance looked at Nita who didn't say a word, but grinned then kissed his nipple.

Terrance began to speak, "Look Sunny, I had no idea you didn't know who she was. Nita has been watching you all night. She stepped to me asking who you were when she saw you with my sister. I gave her a lil info on you and told her that I thought you were hot. She asked me if she could get you to agree to a lil fun with both of us, would I be down. I told her hell yeah. But I had no idea she was referring to tonight. Shit, why wouldn't I want to get down with my girl and the girl I have been attracted to for years?"

Sunny sat up and interrupted, "What the fuck you just say? Your girl? What the fuck do that mean?"

Nita also sat up, "Ooops, I failed to tell you that I am Terrance's girlfriend, Shanita. Thought you might turn me down if I told you that, and I always get what I want. Am I right? If I had told you, would you still be here?"

"Not sure if I would have been here or not. I was attracted to you as well and had some thoughts going on in my head. But, you should have given me the chance to make that decision on my own, but what's done is done now. And shit, I enjoyed myself," Sunny said unfazed.

With shock all over her face, Nita didn't say a word for a minute. Thinking she would have ruined any possibilities that Terrance would have had of hooking up with Sunny alone were now crushed. Nita had overheard him earlier that night telling one of his fellow 'Biker Boyz', that he would drop her in a hot minute if he ever got the opportunity to be with Sunny. He said that she was a true woman and they deserved each other. Nita knew that Sunny went both ways because she overheard Sunny and Jazz talking while waiting in the line for the bathroom about their sex-capade in the car before getting there. Plus she had taken notice to the way Sunny had been checking her out all night. So, Nita with her bright idea thought if she could prove how low down Sunny was, and that she fiddled on both sides of the fence, Terrence would have second thoughts and see Sunny for the freaky bi-sexual bitch she really was. And then when she told Jump Man about what she overheard between Sunny and Jazz, he propositioned her to make it happen.

Sunny got up off the bed after realizing the stunt Nita tried to pull. She slipped back into her thong and jean skirt, tied her bikini top around her neck and back. Nita stared at her with a dropped jaw.

"Sunny, if it means anything to you, I didn't have anything to do with this bullshit Nita just pulled. That ain't my style. I ain't gotta trick no woman into givin me no pussy," Terrance said, to Sunny, but looking straight at Nita.

"No need to explain sexy, I've known you long enough to know that you don't get down like that. Fuck, to be honest, I had a really good time and that is exactly what I came here to do. So no harm done." Sunny smiled and primped her lips looking at Nita out the side of her eye who was now pouting at her failed plan.

Sunny bent down to Terrance so that they were eye to eye and could feel each other's breath. While holding his face with both hands, Sunny said to him in a low seductive voice, but loud enough for Nita to hear, "I've been wanting you for a long ass time, and your shit is good. Lets meet again on different terms, just you and me. This was only half as good as it can get."

Sunny let her lips find his and he didn't turn away. Their lips parted and Sunny was the first to let her tongue enter into his world. His mouth was warm and his lips were soft and gentle. Sunny reached down without breaking contact from his lips. She touched between his legs and felt his manhood rising.

Nita, knowing she had now lost Terrance for sure, had a big conniving grin on her face. "Well maybe you would find it pleasing to know that I was in charge of providing the entertainment for tonight."

With a *'I don't give a fuck'* look on her face, Sunny said, "And?"

Terrance looked at Nita raising his eyebrows. "What entertainment? What you talkin' bout, Shanita?"

As Nita pulled her shirt over her head and was walking to the closed bedroom door, she stopped as her feet reached a heap of money; some of which was crunched up, some folded, and some lying smooth. As she counted, she looked at both Terrance and Sunny. "Let's see who gets the last fuckin' laugh now."

At that moment, Nita flicked the light switch beside the full-length mirror. And they all watched as their reflections disappeared. Sunny and Terrance stood with their mouths wide open, while Nita stood with her arms folded, smiling, showing all her teeth.

"Sweet revenge, Bitches!" Nita yelled at both Terrance and Sunny.

Sunny couldn't believe what she saw and Terrance was just as baffled, standing there in his underwear. There was complete silence, until Nita started laughing.

Before them, behind what they thought was a mirror was a room full of guys. Some standing, some sitting. The look of shock was all on their faces, as if they were caught on candid camera. They had been busted. Redds tried to hurry and shut the curtains but it was already too late.

From behind the draped mirror someone spoke, "Damn, man this is fucked up. How she gonna blow us up like that. I'ma fuck that bitch up."

Terrance scurried to get his shorts on, realizing fully now what had happened and that all his boys had seen his ass. He looked over at Nita, who gave him the finger and hurried out the room before she was bum rushed by Terrance, Sunny and all the guys in the other room. In such a rush she left behind some of the money. Sunny ran over and picked up the money and threw it at Terrance.

"I can't believe you did this shit to me. How could you humiliate me like this, T? And you claim you got feelings for me, but you allowed me to be treated like a trick in front of your boys!" Sunny was furious.

Terrance never raised his voice. Instead, he spoke with compassion and sincerity. "Sunny, please believe me when I say I had nothing to do with this bullshit. I actually ended up here by mistake, looking for the fuckin' bathroom."

There was a loud bang on the door. Sunny and Terrance looked at each other.

"Damn, more surprises. Who else you invite to the party Terrance?" Sunny asked, with neck swaying and eyes rolling.

"Sunny! T! Open the fuckin' door. What's going on in

there? Open the damn door," Jazz yelled from the other side.

As Jazz banged on the door, Redds was trying to stop her from on the other side. From inside the room Terrance and Sunny could hear Jazz letting Redds have it.

"Get the fuck out my way Redds. I saw that bitch Shanita leaving up out of here and she was bragging on her way out that Sunny was a cunt and got what she deserved, and that my brother was a bitch. Open the door Sunny, its me Jazz."

"Pipe the fuck down Jazz, let me handle this," Jump Man begged.

The door swung open with Terrance standing and Sunny sitting on the bed. Jazz ran in and went straight to Sunny. She gave her a run down on all the activities that took place. At first Jazz was pissed that Sunny had been with another woman, not to mention, the woman was Shanita. But she got over that quickly when she realized her friend was so upset.

Jazz put her arm around Sunny, "Mommi, I promise we will get that bitch back. We'll catch her. I promise you that." Jazz looked up at Terrance, "Told you that bitch was no good. See this game she ran. I promise to fuck her up on sight."

Jump Man jumped in, "Sunny I am so sorry, baby. All Nita told us was she was going to have a show for us, but we never knew it would be with you. She just promised we wouldn't be disappointed." He lied, knowing that if Terrance knew the truth, all hell would break loose. But he knew Nita's word against his wasn't shit and with the shit she just pulled, Terrance would never believe her. "All the guys know how Terrance really feels about you. None of us would have agreed had we known. But once it started it was too late. I mean, we are men and what fool wouldn't want to see you like that," he tried to joke. "But please know, Terrance had nothing to do with this. We had no idea he was coming into the room and he had no idea what was going on in here."

Jump Man threw a pile of money on the bed. "Sunny, please

take this money as our apology. This is the money that was charged at the door. Please take it, this is not a profit that I feel comfortable taking." Then looking at Terrance, "Man T, my bad dude. You know I wouldn't have done this shit had I known it was Sunny. For real Dog."

The two men gave each other pound and a hug. That was a sign of love and that T accepted the apology. Jump Man and Redds left the room. Terrance turned to his sister.

"Jazz, can I talk to Sunny for a minute. You mind waiting for her downstairs?"

"Sunny, is that cool with you?" Jazz asked turning to Sunny.

Sunny smiled at Jazz like she was unfazed, but Jazz knew she was hurt. "I'm cool. Be down in a minute and ready to go."

The door slammed behind Jazz as she walked out leaving Sunny and Terrance alone. There was a lot of tension in the room. After what had just happened, Terrance was hoping that he didn't lose whatever chances he may have had with Sunny.

"Sunny, I am so sorry for what happened. But please know I am telling you the truth when I say I didn't know what was going on. I would never do anything to hurt you. I dig you too much for that," Terrance said with feeling in his voice.

Sunny knew in her heart that Terrance wouldn't hurt her. Her heart softened and she smiled at him.

"Boy, I know you been diggin' me, your sister tells me everything. And I believe you. I know you had nothing to do with this. So, no apologies necessary." Sunny smiled with her head leaned to the side and her hair hanging on her shoulder.

Terrance thought Sunny was absolutely gorgeous and all he could do was smile at her. "Oh, you know Jazz tells me everything too. So I know you been diggin' me too," Terrance said sarcastically.

Terrance stood in front of her sitting on the bed and Sunny rose to her feet. They both looked into the mirror to make sure that this time they weren't being watched. And just to make sure,

Terrance left the room and returned.

"I locked the theater room door from the inside, we should be okay this time," Terrance assured Sunny.

As easily as Sunny had put her clothes back on they were back on the floor again and she was naked on top of Terrance riding his dick.

"Damn girl, you feel soooo good. I want you to be mine."

Sunny looked down at Terrance's handsome face and locked in on his beautiful eyes, "Only if you say please."

"Please baby, please," Terrence whimpered in his best whining voice.

With that Sunny tightened her vaginal walls around his thick dick and leaned back. Her long hair was grazing his knees and Terrance grabbed Sunny's waist to pull her down with each thrust that he gave upward into her. Her pussy was drenching and Terrance could see the white cream on his shaft as she lifted her body. Sunny reached back and began to fondle his balls as she grinded down on him. Terrance began to ball and un-ball his toes, and strained intensely not to cum and ruin the moment. Sunny looked at him and noticed he was struggling not to release and slowed her pace. He was so thankful that she did, he wasn't ready to explode. Terrance wanted to enjoy her lovin a lil while longer.

Suddenly Terrance had the urge to be skin to skin with Sunny and to penetrate her slow and deep.

In a calm and sexy tone Terrance asked her, "Can you lay on your back baby, please? I wanna be close in you."

Sunny didn't question him or hesitate, she did as she was told and laid down. She looked up to admire Terrance. He was a gorgeous man. His body was nice, tight and firm. The ripples on his stomach were a turn on. His caramel skin was smooth and even soft. But what Sunny liked the most was his bald head, and his one dimple on his left cheek that made his smile worth millions.

Just as Sunny was admiring Terrance, he was doing the same.

He took his time appreciating her body from head to toe. He thought Sunny had to be one of the most beautiful women he had ever seen. Her light golden skin was rich and flawless. Her mixed ethnic entities were doing her justice. Her body was toned and in perfect shape. She was thick, but in all the essential places. Sunny's waist was small. In the front it led to a flat pierced belly button, and in the back led to a nice rounded ass. Her breasts were full and firm with just the right amount of jiggle. Her areolas were fresh and pink and looked very appetizing. Her dark long wavy hair lay against the crisp mint green pillowcase and framed her face just right. Her face was angelic, the bone structure perfect, and her hazel greenish eyes were like none ever seen. Her beauty mesmerized Terrance and that increased his desires for her.

Terrance placed himself between her thighs and she felt warm to him. He lay there kissing and sucking on her neck and ears. It was driving Sunny crazy; it was one of her favorite spots and got her wet from the slightest touch. She grabbed the back of his head to let him know he was working her up. She parted her legs further wanting him to enter her, but he didn't. She could feel the head of his penis lying against her slit and tried to maneuver her body so that at least the head would slip in, but she was not successful in doing so. Terrance was driving her crazy.

With short breaths Sunny spoke, "Stop teasing me, put it in. I want you to fuck me."

"Not yet, sweetness. Not yet," Terrance whispered in her ear.

Sunny's juices met the head of Terrance's dick at the damn door. He thought he was going to cum just with his head being in, but he knew he couldn't go out like that. Luckily for him, he had trained himself on how to hold back. Sunny felt so good, her name fit her perfectly cause it felt like the sun was shining down on his dick. His strides were slow and deep and he was hitting every wall imaginable. Sunny's legs were lying wide open and their bodies were squeezed together. They were grinding slow and Terrance was thrusting deep inside her. Sunny could feel her climax rising and didn't want him to stop. She grabbed his ass and dug her nails into it, signaling him that he was hitting it just right.

"Damn boy, ooh, damn. Ahhhh yes. You gonna make me c-c-cum-m-m all over your dick. DAMN."

"Yeah baby go ahead, put it all over me. I wanna feel you cum."

Terrance begin to nibble and lick on Sunny's ear and that was all it took.

"I-I-I'm c-c-u-u-um-ming," Sunny sang out while panting and slowly releasing Terrance's ass.

Terrance had been waiting for her to climax so that he could finally explode.

Sunny looked at him as she was pleased and said, "Put it here," motioning her head downward bringing attention to her breast that she was pushing together.

Terrance raised his eyebrows, "You sure baby?"

Sunny shook her head and Terrance quickly rose straddling himself at the top of Sunny's stomach so that his dick rested right in between her 36 D cups. Sunny continued to hold her breast together as Terrance was now fucking her titties and precum was dripping from the head of his dick. He let his head drop back and he was enjoying this indescribable feeling.

"Fuck girl, them titties feelin good on my dick."

"Cum on them baby, so I can lick it off."

And with that said Terrance nutted all over Sunny's breast and just as promised, she licked it all to the last drop. Terrance collapsed beside Sunny totally out of breath, and unable to say a word. The silence was golden. The only noise was coming from the music that was still jumping on the floor below them. Sunny found her a comfy spot on Terrance's chest and he embraced her.

Hours later Sunny would awaken and untangle herself from the man that just rocked her ass hours before in this unfamiliar bed. Terrance didn't feel Sunny as she got up from the bed and didn't hear her as she quickly dressed and grabbed her things. She found a piece of paper off the night table stand beside the bed and a pen from her purse. She scribbled a short note and left it on Terrance's chest, it read…

"Thanks for the good time, when is the next cook-out?"
Until next time,
Sunny

HONEY DIP

ARETHA TEMPLE

I walked into the store and was suddenly stopped by a big ass facing me. Now you know a niggah cannot resist looking at a big ass so I stood and stared—mesmerized by the beauty of it. The face that belonged to it turned and looked right at me, smirked and walked away.

Bitch is a flirt, I thought.

She was thick and chocolate like I love 'em, with a cute little face and blond hair that hung down to her shoulders. Her lips were thick and glossy. She stood around five feet and was well proportioned.

In my mind, I gave her the nickname, *Ms. Thickness*, cuz there was no escaping it. She'd paid for her stuff while I stood behind her gazing at that ass.

Ms. Thickness' phone rang and she answered the call, while grabbing her stuff and heading out the door. Shorty had my nose open and I didn't even know her. I hurried up and asked for a couple owls for my greens then walked out the store.

When I walked outside, Ms Thickness was sitting behind the driver's seat of a Black H3. *This bitch got paper*, I thought to myself or *that's her niggah's shit*. But I didn't give a fuck; I was certainly impressed with her style.

I walked to my money green Cadillac truck to let her know I had paper too if she was watching and wondering. It was good to let her know that I wasn't a broke ass niggah.

"Hey eye problem!" she yelled out her window.

I turned and looked, but tried to play it cool, even though I wanted to jump in that pussy like a pool on a hot ass summer day.

"What's your name?" she asked.

I licked my lips like LL Cool J and yelled, "Money Green!"

"Money Green? What kind of name is that?" she asked, smiling at me.

"The type of name that fits a niggah like me real tight. I'll let you figure it out," I replied, keeping my composure.

She chuckled, "Yeah, whateva."

I walked up to her Hummer, licking my lips once again. I smiled and hit her with, "What's your name sexy?"

"Just call me Honey Dip," she said.

"Honey Dip huh?"

"Yeah," she said, showing her red tongue ring in her mouth.

"I can get used to sayin' that," I returned, locking eyes with her.

Yeah, they call me *Money Green,* I'm thity-one, single, with no babies running around. But I got many bitches running around—but no rings on their fingers or mine. I got my favorite jump-offs like Yolanda, she's a thick lil' chocolate chick who I have been fuckin with for awhile. She got the bomb head and pussy, and some big ass titties to go along too.

I was born and raised on the south side of Toledo.

That's where the dirtiest niggahs live and kick it. These niggahs do not give a fuck if you were their mama, they will get you. That's why it's called the dirty mo'fucking south! Let me spell that different, durty yeah that's it.

I love myself—sometimes I love myself too fuckin' much. I've had this confident attitude about my looks and dealing with women since my early teens, losing my virginity at thirteen to a fifteen year old girl. I'm six-foot, with thick defined arms that will make 50 Cent look like a fiend. Fuck a six-pack, I got an eight pack. My skin is caramel and my eyes hypnotic and can blind you like the sun.

I rock a tight dark caesar with no hair on my face. I sport two big ass diamonds in my ear, and a platinum Ice-grill in my mouth. And my dick game is long and tight.

"Why were you staring at my ass?" she asked.

"What, it ain't like you got offended," I chuckled then said, "I couldn't help it beautiful, it was calling my name. It was saying, "Monneeeeey!"

Honey dip laughed. That was a good sign.

"I have never seen you around before. You from the east side or something?" I asked.

"Yeah, the east… but not the east side," she replied.

I was confused and didn't know what she was talking about. She must have seen that I was stuck on stupid too.

"I'm from up north, Newark New Jersey"

"All right then Jersey girl, what brings you here to wack ass Toledo?"

"I got fam here. I'm here for my grandparent's anniversary."

"How long you been here? Better yet, how long are you staying?" I asked.

"Let's just say I'm here long enough for me to get to know you better," Honey said looking me in my eyes. She was flirtatious, alluring and so sexy wit' it.

This bitch had me open already, and I didn't even see the pussy yet—which was a first for me.

"Let me get ya number," I said pulling out my cell- phone.

"Nah, baby let me get your number," she said pulling out her blackberry.

Without even giving it a second thought, I was a sucker and gave up mine without getting hers.

"Alright sexy, I'ma call you a little later," Honey spoke as she licked her lips.

"What time you gone call?" my dumb ass asked.

She flashed me that seductive and enticing smile of hers, and then rolled up the window leaving me watching her Hummer leave showing her Jersey plates.

A week and some days had gone by and shorty didn't call a niggah yet. I was even answering private calls. That made me look fuckin' thirsty and I hated thirsty niggahs.

Tuesday came, and I was on my way to take care of a booty call. Since meeting Honey, pussy has been on my mind like crazy, and I needed a quick nut. I had my game face on, and was on my way into Yolanda's house when my phone rang. I looked at the caller ID and it read private.

Yolanda stared at me, ready for some dick. The way she was standing in her bathrobe, knowing she was naked underneath, stirred up the beast in me. I was dying to let it loose, preferably on Honey, but Yolanda would do at the moment.

Yolanda began undressing me, pulling at my belt-buckle and pulling out *daddy-long dong*. She came out her robe and stood naked in front of me. Her tits looked like water balloons and her pussy shaved was like a Marine's head.

She smiled, and then embraced me and started doing what she did best, sucking my dick. Her head game was crazy. I flopped down on her couch and let her get busy on me.

My phone rang again, and I thought, *Hmmm a private phone*

calling at three in the morning. It could have been any of my rats trying to play with me so I let the phone ring. Then it rang again, this time I answered but did not say hello.

"Hello?" I heard Honey say.

"Yeah," I said.

"What's up you busy?" she asked.

"Nah," I lied.

"Well, can you meet me somewhere?"

"Where?" I asked, rubbing Yolanda's wet pussy as she deep-throated me like a porn-star.

"Meet me at the store, where I met you at."

"Alright," I said as Yolanda was about to make me spit up on her.

"Shhiiiiitttt!" I moaned.

"What?" Honey asked.

"I said I'ma be there."

"Alright in fifteen minutes," she said, then hung up.

Damn, I had game. Only a niggah like me can make a booty call with the next bitch, while getting my dick sucked by the next bitch. I laughed it off, and continued to let Yolanda please me.

Yolanda was so naïve. She was so wrapped up in sucking my dick, that she probably didn't even know that I was on the phone wit' some other bitch that I was trying to fuck.

I had time to break Yolanda off right quick wit' some dick, just before hitting her with a line. Yolanda dropped the bomb head pussy on me so tough she made me bust real quick. My shit was still hard though, so she climbed on top and worked her pussy on me while licking her own chocolate chip nipples. She fucked me like crazy, and made me nut like a rocket off to the stars. I shot up a load in her so hard and fast that I thought the condom broke.

When it was over, she got a soapy rag and wiped me off. That's why she was my favorite, she knew what to do all the time without being asked. Damn! I soon had to hit her with the *"I'll be back"* lie. Yolanda knew I was lying but she knew I was coming back, but not that same night.

I climbed in my truck to go meet Honey Dip.

When I got to the store, she wasn't there yet. I sat and waited for what seemed like forever, when she decided to pull up. She parked then got out. She was looking good in her painted on jeans and red and white Timbs that went up her leg—she knew how to freak them shits. She sported a ponytail that made her look like an around the way girl.

When she got in my truck, she smelled like bubble gum and weed. That told me she was a smoker, or was around somebody who was smoking.

"Damn you had me waiting forever," I said, but not really giving a fuck about the wait.

"Quit crying, you got a sweet or sumthin' to roll these trees up with?"

I looked at her as if she was crazy, but still pulled out an owl that was in my pocket. She had some nerve telling me to quit crying after she had me waiting almost two weeks for her to call, and then had me waiting out here almost an hour for her ass.

Honey took the white owl and freaked it, then put the weed in it. She then lit it—puffed- puffed and then passed it to me. I choked like a ma'fucka. Then looked at her thinking why this bitch ain't choking.

"You can't handle this shit yo," she said, laughing."

We got smoked out for a few more minutes, enjoying the night and with me enjoying her company.

"Let's roll… shit, better yet let me drive," she said like I was going to let her drive my shit.

Honey rolled everywhere like she'd been in Toledo all her life. I fell back on my own words and let her drive my truck.

Honey told me she was twenty-three and was going to school for criminal justice and was a C.O. at one of those up north jails. She had no kids and was not trying to have any no time soon. We got so high that we both were looking stupid. Her chocolate skin was glowing and she was so cute with her chinky eyes that were so slanted from the tight ponytail she was rocking.

Honey drove around endlessly and we soon ended up at IHOP to get our grub on. We were ready to order the entire menu, because I had a serious case of the munchies. My dick was rock hard under the table, and I was tempted to rub it thru my jeans. I didn't know if it was the weed or Honey that had me so fuckin' horny—maybe it was the combination of both.

After our stomachs were full we asked for the bill. I decided to drop her off back to her truck, but that did not happen.

"Take me to ya crib, Money Green," she said playfully.

I was like what the hell—but I wasn't gonna deny the invite. I waited almost two-weeks for the pussy.

I pulled up in my garage with a high still lingering and a smile on my face—feeling like grimace and shit. We both got out and walked in from the door in the garage. Like always my bitch was right there waiting. Lady, was my Rottweiler that I had for years. She was the only bitch that I fully trusted.

Honey surprised me though. She wasn't scared. Lady didn't even bark at her. If it were anybody else, she would have been barking up some shit.

"Yo shit is tight Money!" Honey said, going through my shit and looking around.

"Thanks." I grinned.

It was like she knew to take off her boots, but she also took off her socks too showing her pretty manicured toes that were painted red. Lady followed behind shorty like she had been knowing her forever.

Honey and I sat up until four in the morning talking, fooling around, and it was cool. I got to know things about her. She fell asleep in my arms with the television watching us.

The following morning I was getting out the shower and had a bathrobe around me, and was still wet.

"Yo ass is so fuckin sexy!" Honey praised.

I smiled because that I already knew. Shorty stood up and walked up to me. She was so short she had to stand on her tiptoes to hug me. Honey Dip got to kissing my neck then she went for my lips.

"So sweet," she said after the first kiss.

I grabbed her and kissed her as if she belonged to me. Honey opened my robe, stood back and stared at me like I stared at her ass that day in the store. Honey started taking off her clothes, leaving nothing on but her brown satin bra and panties. Her titties were perfect sitting in that bra. Her panties made her pussy look fat.

I was about to find out just how fat that pussy was. Honey pulled me on top of her. Honey was moaning as I sucked on her nipples and rubbed on her clit. I slowly took off her panties and bra; I didn't want her to think I was in a hurry. With my Jones at ease, I kissed her muscled stomach and then I kissed her creamy thighs. I worked my way to that sweet pussy of hers.

I sucked shorties clit so good that she bust like three times. Now it was time for my man to get wet. I laid on top of her, kissing her and letting her taste her own sweet juices.

"Be gentle," she whispered in my ear.

I was gentle alright. I eased the head in little by little; but shorty was tighter than OJ Simpson's murder glove. *Oh my God*, that pussy was so tight and wet, I had to hurry and pull out because the pussy was about to make me spit up in it.

"What?" she asked, as I looked into her eyes.

"Where the fuck you been all my life?" I said jokingly.

Shorty laughed then said, "In Jersey."

At that, I stuck my man back in her, and she stopped laughing and got to moaning.

The sex was so intense. We fucked and fucked until we could not fuck no more. We both fell asleep in the bed, but when I woke up Honey was gone. I didn't worry, I just knew she went to get her some clothes or something, but I was wrong because she never came back.

That was a month ago. No Honey.... No Phone calls—nothing. I was sitting in the car with my niggah listening to some C.D. A song was on with Juelz Santana and some other cat. They were talking about a girl that I could relate to. Guess what the fuckin name of the song was? *HONEY DIP!* Ain't that some shit…

HONEY

Yea, I left him. I didn't leave the city, but I still gave him something he would never forget. My bomb ass pussy. He ain't never had no pussy like mine. That nigga could not handle my little pussy. I ain't gon' lie he had a big dick and it was good, but I didn't lose my cool like he did. *"Aaaaaahhh baby this pussy's good!"* Is all that nigga was screaming in my ear.

I guess you want to know why I made him wait two weeks before I called. Well, first of all it's none of your business. Second, it's none of your business! Nah, I didn't want to be all calling him all early and shit seeming all desperate. Plus I had unfinished business to take care of, and calling his fine ass would of slowed me down so I called when I could.

What that nigga didn't know was I lied about being in Toledo for an anniversary. I was there for other reasons. Money Green is a cool dude. I could see myself being with a niggah like him, but not right now. That niggah had a nice ride, a nice crib and a good head on his shoulder.

That niggah was also sexy than a ma'fucka, and always licking them lips like LL. I caught myself thinking of him, but I had to do what I had to do. A niggah need to feel like he ain't shit sometimes. It's always a niggah who leave the bitch looking stuck on stupid—having her all opened and shit. She can't call him because she ain't got his number. She's only being dealt with when he wants to deal with her. That shit is fucked up and pay back is a bitch!

I knew for a fact Money Green had left bitches clueless on numerous occasions. Calling them only late nights when he had on his drunk or game face ready to fuck something. Then fuck 'em and then leave 'em.

I knew it probably made him say fuck bitches even more –but oh well. MOB (Money Over Bitches) was what niggahs were always yelling. Well we bitches need to scream MON (Money Over Niggahs) but see we can't do that, and I don't know why these niggahs are weak for us. That's why they have like five or six bitches spread around so they won't be caught up loving one.

Will I ever call him again—maybe, but I'ma wait till he forgot about me, and then I'm gonna call and fuck his head up again. But I know this time he will be careful, so I will make sure I'm careful also because he will try to get me back. That ain't happening. It's been a month. I think about him and I know he thinks about me too, but a girl had to do what a girl had to do.

I also found out that we had a friend in common. I was about to do some major business with the niggah too.

I was waiting on this niggah. He said he would be around in ten minutes. Soon, he came pulling up in an all back Navigator sitting on some dubs.

"Damn, Telly you doing it like that?" I said.

Telly smiled showing me his fangs. Telly was a fine niggah, but he was too much for me and plus he was my cousin by marriage. That niggah got two bitches, *Brooklyn* his wife and *Star* who belongs to both him and his wife. Yeah his wife gotta girlfriend. Crazy shit huh?

"What took you so long, yo?" I asked.

"I had to handle some shit right quick girl."

"What the fuck yo ass had to handle that you had me waiting for 30 minutes?"

"I was with my business partner," Telly said, smiling.

I smiled too because I knew what partner he was barking about.

"Stop talking shit and jump yo ass in so we can talk business."

"Alright," I said, getting out my truck and jumping into his pimped out Navi.

"Damn nigga you let Xzbit pimp ya ride?" I joked.

"Nah, little girl, I pimped my own shit," Telly said throwing me a bag of trees.

"Roll an L up right fast," he told me.

Me and Telly puffed and discussed our shit, then he dropped me off at my truck. I pulled out my blackberry and dialed a number. It rang a couple of times. I was about to hang up, then I heard a sexy baritone answer.

"Hey sexy," I said, but got no response for a short moment. "Hello," I repeated.

"Yeah, what's good, luv," he said, trying to act nonchalant on me.

"How are you?" I asked him.

"I'm good."

I tried my luck and asked him, "You missed me?"

"Look Honey, or whoever you are, I don't got time to play games with you," he barked.

"Who's playing games Money? I'm in Toledo and was wondering if I could come see you."

There was a long pause.

"Where you at now?" he finally asked.

"At the BP gas station on Detroit."

"Sit there, I'll be there in a minute."

"Alright, I said then hung up.

I smiled a devilish smile and thought about giving him some

pussy again. Only if he behaved.

I was becoming irritated with his lateness shouting out, "What the fuck? This nigga still ain't here it's been like an hour."

I almost pissed on myself when Money jumped in my truck suddenly.

"You scared me!" I said, holding my chest.

"Oh shut that fuckin' crying. You shoulda had yo doors locked," he said.

"You had me waiting a long time yo."

"Pay backs a bitch, huh?" Money said with a devilish grin.

"Whateva niggah!" I said rolling my eyes

Money was looking and smelling so good. He looked like he had just got a hair cut.

"What's up girl?"

"You," I answered.

"Hmm…is that right. What brings you back here?"

"You baby… I missed you," I said.

"Well, that I don't believe."

"Why?" I whined.

"Because you just left me like I wasn't shit."

"I'm sorry," I whined again

"Yeah whatever!" Money said screwing up his face.

I couldn't believe he was treating me like this. *That's alright I'ma get in that head again.*

"So what's up Honey or whatever yo name is?"

"Money, my name is Renee," I finally confessed.

"Renee Huh? Well Renee what you trying to do?"

"I'm trying to be with you. I missed you."

"Alright, well follow me to my house."

"How's Lady been doing?" I asked like I really gave a fuck.

"My bitch is good...she's knows how to behave herself and knows I don't play when it comes to bitches." At that he slammed my door.

This niggah is on some shit, but I wasn't going to fall for it.

Damn I must've had really fucked his head up. I followed Money to his house, and parked my truck in his garage right beside his ride. We then went through the side door. I stood behind him as he pushed in his alarm code. I acted like I wasn't paying any attention, then he opened the door.

Lady was standing there waiting for him. First she jumped on him then she jumped on me, licking and smelling me. Money fed his bitch then looked at me. I smiled, but he didn't smile back.

"Can I get a hug?" I asked walking up to him.

He stood in front of me looking me in my eyes. I stood on my toes and wrapped my arms around his neck. He hugged me back. Damn, he was smelling good. We looked at each other and then kissed.

My pussy was tingling and I felt his dick growing. He grabbed my ass, and I jumped on him wrapping my legs around his waist. We left Lady sitting there and he carried me upstairs and threw me on his bed. He stood in front of me shedding his clothes silently. I took off my jeans then my shirt and bra. Money took off my panties and went straight to my throbbing pussy. Slurp-slurp is all you heard. A bitch was going crazy.

Money kissed his way up my body, then he entered my pussy.

"Why you leave me like that?" he asked, stroking my pussy slow.

"I had to baby."

"Why?"

"I just had too."

Money started fucking me real hard "Baby slow down!" I yelled.

"I can't, this pussy is good as fuck!" I started fucking him back taking in his thick dick

"Don't move!" he said in my ear.

I moved anyways. Money bit my neck and came all in me.

"I told you don't move!"

"Did you just cum in me?" I asked, not believing this shit.

"Yeah," he said still laying on me.

"Get the fuck off of me!" I said trying to get from under him.

Money looked at me then pulled his limp dick out of me.

"What's wrong?" he asked, with a smirk on his face.

"What's wrong Money? You fuckin came in me. I can't get fuckin pregnant!

"Who says yo ass will get pregnant?"

I blocked him out and went into the bathroom and got in his shower. I let the hot water run over my body as I thought about how my master plan was going to be fucked up all because of me.

As I let the hot water hit my body, I felt Money getting into the shower with me. He grabbed my waist. I turned and looked into his eyes. He and I stood there for a while just looking into each others souls. We both had secrets. I put my head down so he couldn't figure mine out.

"I'm sorry about what happened in there. It's just that it was feeling too good."

"Well, I don't want to get pregnant!"

"Alright, I feel you." At that he kissed me on my wet face, then he sucked on my nipples. I let out a moan. He went further down to my stomach then he went to my sweet spot tasting my juices. I started shaking, it was feeling so good.

Money turned me around, then he ate my pussy from the back. My hair was getting soaked but I didn't give a damn, I was in heaven. I came in his mouth and he caught every drop. Money stood up and his body was looking good wet, and his dick was standing at attention with a curve. I looked at it and grabbed it while licking my lips. I know I shouldn't be going there with this niggah—but damn! I bent over about to suck his dick, but he stopped me. "I don't want that."

I looked up at him while still holding his dick. He grabbed me up and carried me to the bed. He and I were soaking wet. We kissed and rubbed on each other while my pussy felt like fire. I wanted his dick in me, so I pushed him on the bed and straddled him. It took a while for him to enter me. But boy when he did. I started working his ass like I was dancing you know what Juelz Santana said, "If you can dance you can fuck."

I bounced, rolled and grinded all on that good dick. Then I did my shit and squatted on it.

"Shit work that pussy. Yeah Baby!" he yelled.

I felt myself cumming, I was right there, so I laid on Money licking his ear and shit.

"Yo! I'm about to, cum get up," he moaned but I was cumming too so I kept fucking.

"Oooh Shit!" he yelled, as he opened my ass cheeks up slamming my pussy up and down.

"Baby I'm cumming too!" I yelled.

We was both breathing heavy, tired from the nuts we both busted.

"I thought you said you didn't want to get pregnant?"

"I don't," I said out of breath.

"So why you didn't get up when I told you I was cumming?"

"Because I didn't want to stop cause I was cumming too."

"Well you know that's two nuts of mines up in you right?"

"Yeah, well if I'm pregnant, then the clinic, here I come."

"I know that's right, I don't want no babies yet either," he said while rubbing my nipples.

While Money was asleep I was awake, thinking about this shit I was involved in. I was ready to back out, but I needed the math bad. I looked to see what time it was, 4:30 a.m. is what the digital clock said on Money's dresser. I put on his slippers and went downstairs to get something to drink. Lady was outside the door. She looked up at me, looked in the room then followed me down the stairs. I poured me some juice and gave lady some water.

24-36-42 was in my head. I walked into Money's T.V. room that was decked out in a green leather pit. He had pictures of him and other niggahs all around. He even had a picture with the friend we had in common. He had a couple of pictures with some girls too, but they didn't have shit on me. I was having second thoughts about Money, I was really feeling this niggah, and rule number one was never mix business with pleasure.

MONEY

I felt Honey get out of bed, but I just rolled over. 5 a.m. is what my clock read and she didn't come back upstairs yet. I climbed out my bed and couldn't find my house shoes, so that meant she had them on. I went downstairs anyway. Lady must have been with Honey because she was nowhere to be found. When I reached the kitchen I saw a glass on the counter, but no Honey or Lady. I looked in the TV room and there they were. Honey was on the couch sleep, and Lady was on the floor. Honey looked so innocent but I knew she wasn't.

I didn't bother her. I let her sleep and went back upstairs. I saw her purse on the floor by her shoes. I wanted to go through it so bad, but you know what they say when you look for something—you will find it, and soon hate that you went looking for it in the first place. But I wanted to find out what this bitch was about, even though I knew I didn't want to know.

Shit, fuck it! I grabbed and opened the Prada bag. The first thing I saw was her phone. Then a bag of weed along with a lighter and some MAC lipgloss. Then I saw her wallet. I slowly began to look through it. I could not believe what I was seeing. I saw around five fuckin I.D's with different names but with her face.

As I stood there with my mind going, her phone went off. I looked at the caller I.D. I saw the name Biz come up. I just looked at the fuckin phone thinking, *is this the Biz I think it is?*

See Biz was competition to me. Is this bitch working fo this niggah? Nah, this is another Biz, it got to be.

"What the fuck are you doing in my purse?" I heard Honey bark from the doorway.

Think of something! Think of something! I was saying to myself. I was busted.

"This fuckin phone keeps ringing. I'm about to throw this piece of shit out the fuckin' window! It woke me up!" I barked, tryin' to flip it. "Why, you got something in here to hide?"

"Nah, it's just not right for a man to go into a ladies purse!" Honey snatched the purse out of my hands. Took out her phone, looked at it, screwed up her face and said, "Who the fuck is this?"

I looked at her like you know who the fuck it is. Honey needed an Oscar for her acting. The bitch called the number back.

"Did somebody call Honey?" Then she hit them with, "Sorry, you got the wrong number."

This bitch was good, but not that good. She might have got me if I didn't see the name pop on the caller I.D.

Right there that told me this bitch was workin with Biz. See Biz and me only fuck with one another when he needed a couple of them thangs, if you know what I'm talking about. I must of had a strange look on my face because she hit me with the "Baby what's wrong?"

"Who was that?" I asked playing stupid.

"He had the wrong number he was looking for Dink," she lied.

"You really think I'm stupid don't you?"

"No!"

"Well why the fuck you keep playing me dumb?"

"What the fuck are you talking about?" she yelled. Lady ran in and started barking.

"Lady go!" I yelled.

"Look, I don't have to go through this shit. I'm out!" Honey started putting on her clothes.

"Who are you really?" I asked, standing in front of her.

"I told you my name is Renee."

"Yeah, but that's just one of your many names."

She looked at me.

"Yeah, I know about all your identities, they're all in your purse. I even seen who that was who called you." I laughed to myself. "So who is Biz? Your niggah right?"

"No, baby you got it all wrong!"

"Well make it right then!" Honey or whoever she was looked at me with a blank face.

I shook my head at her and told her to get out my house. Honey finished getting dressed and left out. I walked downstairs to open my garage door for her. After turning my alarm back on, I stood in the kitchen looking at nothing in the dark with Lady right beside me. I couldn't believe this shit. I wanted to know what plans she had for me. What did her and Biz have up their sleeves?

I was sitting in my truck watching these niggahs, but they didn't see me. Niggahs are some grimey ma'fucka's! Bitches can't trust bitches and niggahs can't trust niggahs. Your right hand man will envy you and will turn on you in a heartbeat—greedy fuckers. When women have girlfriends who they really trust, they tell them hoes their sex life and how they man fuck, then that trifling bitch goes and fuck that niggah just to see. This world is a trip and you can't trust anybody.

I can't believe Honey's trifling ass. I knew one thing, that bitch was out to get me, but she had another thing coming. What's so fucked up is that I really liked that bitch, but fuck her. I'm off her ass right now.

I was on my way to get the new crispy Jordons that just came out, when I noticed Star. Star was a sexy chocolate chinky eyed bitch, who had body and looks for days. The only problem was she belonged to Biz and his wife.

Star was walking and I followed her phat ass. The jeans she

had on looked like that were painted on. The way the bitch walked I could tell that she had some good pussy. Star stopped at a Lady Footlocker, and I went next door to the jewelry store. I needed to go in anyways to look at this pinky ring.

I was in there for a minute almost forgetting about her sexy ass until I left out running right into her.

"Hey Money!" she said, slowing down.

"What's up Star, how's that ass, I mean how you been doing?"

Star smacked her lips at me. A few years ago Star was a money hungry hoe. You couldn't fuckin' speak to her if you didn't have no dough. I heard that she changed her life—somewhat, but once a hood rat always a hood rat.

"Biz let you out?"

"What, niggah I'm grown," she came back at me.

"I can see that," I said, looking her up and down licking my lips.

"Money you're a trip, I'm out!"

"Wait…why you just gonna leave me like that? I'm just making conversation."

"Because yo ass is a trip," she repeated.

"What you in here buying?" I asked.

"Shit, I want them Nikes, but they ain't on sale yet."

"How much are they?"

"Why?" she asked rolling her head, "you gonna buy them for me?"

"Maybe, how much are they?" I said rubbing my hands together.

"They a buck fifty."

"Damn, for some fuckin sneakers?" I had a lot of nerve when I was about to go pay a grip for the new Jordans but those are Jordans.

"Biz won't get them for you?"

"Nah, he screaming about I already got too many shoes that I don't even wear."

"How bad you want them?" I asked licking my lips.

"It really don't make me or break me if I get them or not," she said trying not to act pressed.

"See, I was about to go get them for you," I said smiling.

"Niggah stop playin with me. If you're buying I want them!"

"Yeah, same ol' Star," I said, laughing.

"That's right niggah, ain't shit changed but my panties!"

I was about to see how far this bitch would go.

"Biz fucking that pussy right?"

Star laughed.

"I'm serious is he? Because if he ain't you know where I'm at."

"Niggah you wouldn't know what to do with this pussy," she countered sarcastically.

"You think?" I said, walking up to grip that phat ass. Some lady walked by with her nose turned up. Star and I both laughed.

"Niggah I know. Plus you don't pay you don't lay!" She hit me with, but that's what I was waiting for anyways.

"Money ain't a thang!" I said, pulling out a rubber band of money out of one pocket and another stack in a money clip from the other pocket. That bitch had slobber running down her greedy lips.

"So what you saying Money?" she asked.

"I'm saying let me hit that!"

"Alright," she responded. "We can talk but first lets go get my sneakers!"

It was 11:30 pm. And I was chilling, getting some good head from Star. Yeah, I got the bitch sneakers, cuz I had it like that, and Star was a money hungry hoe—tricking for some kicks. She sucked my dick and played with her pussy at the same time.

I started sucking on her nice ass titties. The bitch was about to make me cum so I told her to stop. Star pulled a rubber out, opened it, put it in her mouth and went down on my dick one last time while putting it on. She then climbed on top of me.

"You sure you want this pussy?" she had the nerve to ask me.

Did I want it? I had been wanting her pussy for the longest. I opened her ass cheeks and she put her hot wet hole on my dick. "Mmmmmm!" I moaned.

"Damn niggah, I just sat on the dick and you already moaning!" Star laughed at me but see it was me who was going to have the last laugh. "Ride this dick!" I said, slapping her ass.

Star stood up on her feet and grabbed my chest and started bouncing and bouncing. She did that for awhile then the bitch spun around on my dick and was fucking me cowgirl style. I was like *what the fuck?*

This bitch was a ma'fucka for real. Star bent all the way over, so I just rose up with the dick still in her and hit that shit from the back.

"Shit, this pussy good!" I yelled, while she slammed her pussy on my dick. I stopped fucking her and let her do her thang. Star put an arch in her back and did her thang. I pulled my dick out, then put it back in. Her ass was moaning like crazy and I kept doing it. I felt her pussy muscles tighten up, and pussy juice went flying everywhere while she was shaking. I pulled out looking at her still squirting everywhere. This was a first for me in all the bitches I have fucked. I never ran into a bitch that squirted.

Star and I fucked like it was a marathon. I then wondered what she was going to tell Biz or Brooklyn. I didn't give a fuck though. We both were bent from the crazy sex. And I was off to ma'fucking sleep, thinking to myself, *Damn, Biz yo bitch pussy is so good!*

Four months had passed since Star gave me a lot of info about her niggah. I didn't even have to ask the bitch. When a bitch get dicked the fuck down ain't no telling what comes out her mouth. I just stayed quiet and let her run off her mouth like diarrhea. She loved that niggah though, and I couldn't understand why. She also claimed that she didn't want to leave me alone.

But I let her know that we were just fucking—nothing else more.

It's like she be trying to change my mind when she be fuckin me. If I was to be with her it will only be because she had some good snapper and I know the bitch could get some doe. Star's a rat and will always be a rat. I didn't care how much Gucci and Prada she wore, the bitch was still a fuckin money chasing ho.

But I couldn't knock her though because I'm always chasing that paper too. I have to respect her gangsta.

I saw Biz one day, but he didn't see me. He was on Central at the light.

All I could think about was his pussy that be on my dick, and how him and that trick Honey was trying to do me. "FUCK YOU NIGGA!!" I yelled like that nigga could hear me.

HONEY

Money Green didn't know what he was talking about. Money Green thought that I was workin with Biz— that's funny. Niggahs are so stupid, but I'm stupid too. You know why I'm stupid? Because I let that niggah catch me slippin. I thought my ass was slick but I guess not that slick. He thought wrong of me. *Why didn't I explain shit to him?* I asked myself. Shit was already fucked up when he looked in my purse and seen Biz name and number come up.

But I swear it wasn't Biz who was calling me. It was hard to explain, but I thought, in due time. I always kept my line of work personal and undisclosed. I had a lot to think about and my business was getting hectic every passing day. I had a change of heart when it came to Money Green, even though he could become arrogant and cocky, I loved his company. I was really feeling that niggah and I should not have let my feelings mix with business.

My one mistake was letting that niggah fuck me and bust two fat ass nuts in me. Now I'm three months pregnant.

MONEY

There's a saying, *keep your friends close and your enemies closer.* And I needed to take heed to that.

I was sitting in the parking lot of a club called *The Classic,* waiting on this niggah, Biz. *I'm always waiting on somebody*, I thought to myself, chuckling. I soon noticed this red Charger roll up. That ma'fuckin ride was so sick with its candy apple paint job and sitting on 22" chrome, that it made me want to throw up.

"Niggah that shit is nasty!" I shouted.

"Ain't it!" Biz replied, with a Colgate smile.

"What's good, my niggah," I asked.

"Same ol', shit, my niggah…getting this paper and pussy, ya feel me."

"Yeah, I feel you on that."

Me and Biz walked into the club; and I ain't no fag or nothing but I must say that we both were some handsome ma'fucka's and we both was looking fly.

Biz and I both had one thing—well two things in common, we both loved the color green and we both loved Star's pussy.

Biz and I both wore green that night. He sported a green polo shirt and some black jeans with his green Timbs. I sported a green and white Sean John shirt, blue jeans and jacket with my all white leather S. Carters. We both had our bling on and the bitches was staring at us hard. This one bitch that clocked us tough was a dime piece, fo' real, with her open toe shoes. I felt like Damon Dash with the foot fetish.

"You got nice toes," I said.

"Thank you," she replied, smiling and shit.

Ol' girl was thick and too fuckin' cute. And her having nice feet was a plus for me—no hammer time going on.

"What you drinking sexy?"

"Grey goose!" she yelled over the music.

"Stay put I'll be right back," I whispered in her ear.

Her friends started laughing, but were jealous because I didn't step to them. As I was walking, I seen Biz talking to some niggah with a Black Yankees fitted cap on covering his eyes.

I didn't know who the niggah was, but I had to be careful of my surroundings. I went and got me and shorti's drink. I took shorti's drink to her, we talked for a minute, and then I walked over to Biz and his guys.

"Money, this my niggah Jose, he's here for the weekend so show him some love," Biz introduced.

"What's up yo?" Jose greeted.

"What's up," I replied, giving him some dap.

I knew where he was from—the ma'fuckin Big Apple, with the hoody, fitted cap and beige Timbs on.

We all conversed then mingled. Biz and I sat at a table to discuss some shit when Star walked her in. Biz didn't look too happy and she didn't either when she saw that we were together.

"This bitch is hard headed," Biz said, then got up walked over to Star.

Whatever he said to her made her walk off and roll her eyes.

"Let's go man before I smack her ass. I tell her to stay her ass in the house and she comes out anyway." Biz looked over where she was standing then stood up and walked to the door.

"Yo ass rolling with me or you jumping in the truck?"

"Whatever niggah its on you," I responded.

"Well come on we going to the Lion's Den."

I jumped in the Charger then we rolled out. I sparked up a conversation about him and his thing he had with Star.

"Yo ass got it made niggah, you got two bitches," I mentioned.

"Yeah, well these couple months it's like I'm losing Star's ass."

"Why you say that?" I asked.

"For one, the bitch been acting funny. Two, she be staying

out late. Brook be like Star came in around four in the morning."

That's because she be leaving from my crib, I thought to myself.

"She promised me she would stay out the streets, and she was cool for a while, but something done got her back out here. When we fuck it ain't the same. Her pussy be feeling different."

I smiled inwardly because I've been beating that shit up.

"It's just not the same any more man," Biz added.

"Well you know bitches," I said, trying to make him feel a little better.

"So what's up with the New York cat?" I asked.

"Jose, that niggah down here on some business shit. Dude got mad paper, but you will never know because he's laid back and don't floss. My Lil cousin Renee was fucking him for a minute."

"Renee?" My heart skipped a beat.

"Yeah she's my little cousin, little grimy bitch. I think her ass is up to something because when she was here a couple months back. The bitch was asking me mad questions."

I sat back and listened. I didn't say shit.

"One day I walked in and Star was on my phone. When she gave it back to me it was Renee's number on it. What the fuck they got to talk about? They both act like they hate each other."

I was wondering what they had to talk about also.

"But fuck them both," Biz screamed. "We gon' hook up with Jose Sunday at Brook's shop. To make that move you feel me?"

"Yeah," I said as he turned up the music.

It was four a.m. when I was dropped back off at my truck.

"Alright niggah, see you Sunday at two, don't be late, niggah," Biz yelled then drove off.

All kinds of shit was going through my head. It was like when I got high, I began realizing shit. I drove my drunken ass home and lay in my bed without taking my clothes off. Lady was at the foot of my bed. I turned the T.V. on and forgot that I was watching State Property 2, and put it on pause.

I grabbed my phone and dialed the number. "Yo, Listen," I said into the phone.

"I'm listening nigga."

HONEY

My life was so fucked up. Nothing was going right for me. I was pregnant and getting twisted in a crazy ass world. I tried calling Money last week, but he wouldn't answer. I guess he was like fuck, private numbers now. I got a call from Toledo the other night. The caller told me Money and that punk ass Biz been kicking it with each other, ain't that some shit?

I was hoping that everything would go smooth on Sunday. The top dog was already in the T. There's nothing I could do. Biz was a stupid Ma' fucka. How you gon' be out chilling with a nigga you know you don't like, and know he don't like you.

I was about to try Money again. I was missing him. I missed the way he fucked me. He was one of the best I had since I have been fucking, but with Money it wasn't just his sex it was his conversation also. I was feeling bad. I might be carrying this man's seed, and he had the right to know. I redialed Money's number, letting my number show up.

"Yeah," he answered.

"Hi," I said.

"Who is this?" he barked.

"Honey, I mean, Renee.

"Why you calling me?" he asked.

"Because it's something I need to talk to you about," I whined.

"What the fuck you got to talk to me about?"

"Well for one, Money, I'm sorry for the lies and I'm pregnant!"

"Pregnant?" he yelled.

Money didn't say anything after that, it was silence on the phone.

"Look, I can't say I don't want to hear that shit because I know I bust two good nuts off in that pussy, but how you know its mine?"

"Because I'm three months pregnant, and I know it's yours."

"Well what the fuck you want me to do?"

"Nothing, I was just letting you know."

"Alright, you told me now what?" he yelled in the phone.

"I'm keeping it!" I yelled back into the phone.

"Good! Keep it then, but why would you wanna keep a baby by a niggah you can't even keep it real with?"

I couldn't say shit in response, I just let him talk.

"Come on girl you played with me twice for what? I thought we were really feeling each other. I even let you come to my crib that's something I don't do with bitches, but you I thought yo ass was different… but I see you wasn't."

"I'm sorry, Money!"

"Yeah, that's what you keep screaming, but how long is it before you play me again?"

"Come on now don't do this to me. I'm feeling you, baby. I think about you a lot, and now I have your baby growing inside me."

"What are you saying, Renee… that you want to be with me? Is that what you saying? I don't know man, you're full of games."

"I will show you I'm not. I'm going to catch a plane there," I said hoping he would agree.

"Do what you want Renee."

"Alright, I will call you back with the time detail alright?"

"Yeah…whatever," he replied dryly, and hung up the phone.

MONEY

I couldn't believe this bitch called me out the blue talking about she's pregnant. I did nut hard in that pussy double time. But I didn't trust that bitch, and wanted to play her close.

I wanted to shoot over to Yolanda's crib right quick. She was hooking something up for me and I missed her freaky ass. Besides, I needed my dose of that bomb head from her.

An hour later I came out of Yolanda's crib fully satisfied by getting my sex on. I was walking back to my truck when Renee hit me on the hip telling me she was getting on the 7:30 flight—American Airlines.

I told her alright and hung up.

I picked up Honey, ...oops, Renee from the airport and we headed straight for my crib. I had to admit that she looked good—so good, that my anger for her just disappeared. I just wanted to fuck her in my ride—thinking, *pregnant pussy is the best pussy to have.* I wanted to pull up her skirt and just tear that pussy up.

We talked, got shit between us situated, and she had such a strong influence on me, making a niggah feel weak, that I wanted to slap her. But instead, once we got to my crib, clothes came off, her panties got pulled down, and I fucked her like DMX did Taral Hicks in Belly.

We sweated out my sheets so much that we both needed a shower. I let her get hers first, while I lay sprawled out on my back, exhausted, peering up at the ceiling and thinking about that pregnant pussy she hit me off with.

I was feeling comfortable, thinking everything was going to work out with us. I closed my eyes and then heard the phone ring. I sighed, and picked up, being in a somewhat good mood.

"Hello," I answered.

"What's up with you this morning?" he asked.

"Shit, waiting for this day to be over with that's all. What's up with you?" I replied, being a bit irritated that he called, disturbing my peace.

"Same here where is your little bitch at?"

"She in there taking a shower...but yo, I feel kinda bad since the bitch is pregnant. I'm having second thoughts," I mentioned.

"You bitching up on a niggah, now? That's some bullshit!" he snapped. "You get some new pussy and get sprung. I told you to fuck her not fuck with her. Your ass talking 'bout you having second thoughts punk muthafucka holla back!" (((Click)))

Yeah, whatever, I thought.

After that talk, I sighed, got off the bed and asked myself—*what the fuck am I going to do?*

Shit was fucked up! I wish I didn't agree to do this shit. I was stuck on stupid. I didn't want Renee to get pregnant—but when you in some good pussy, shit just happens, right? We got into some heavy talk since she flew in and decided to be together for the baby.

I had to admit to myself, that I was in love with her trifling ass—but sometimes everything ain't what it appears to be—my world was built around illusions.

UNKNOWN STRANGER...

I was Money's fuckin connect. I hooked him up with everything from drugs to guns. And we were cool peoples. But that niggah, Jose' I've been wanting his ass since he robbed and killed my brother on some hoe shit. Her bitch ass was the fuckin bait! Ma'fucka fucked with the wrong one.

It took me awhile to set this shit up. I knew that bitch and that niggah would go around looking for niggahs with doe. So I put a birdie in her ear. I told her that Money had mad paper and was soft on the bitches. Did you think they met each other on accident? Hell nah, they didn't. That shit was set the fuck up—

everything was. Yeah, that little grimy bitch Star put the little bird in the ear for me. That hood rat bitch was always money hungry right. I knew that she fucked Money for some fuckin sneakers!

I sat and watched all these niggahs pull up to the shop. What everyone didn't know was that I was Money's connect. They knew me, but they didn't know that I was the one who'd be supplying them shit. Biz and Jose just knew me from the block back in Brick City when I use to nickel and dime it for my brother. My brother became a major player, and Jose' was just a worker then he put the game down and robbed my brother and straight murked him, and it was time to pay!

The first niggah to show was Money—with his pussy whipped ass. I told him not to fall in love and what did this niggah do? He falls for the bitch just like my brother. She was a dumb bitch too.

While the gang was rolling up, I mashed out to do something right fast, and shit wasn't going to happen till I got back.

As I was on my way to my destination, Biz rolled past me. I chuckled to myself, thinking about all the shit that was about to happen.

I pulled up at the spot. I stopped and thought about the numbers Star gave me. 24-36-42. I punched the numbers into the alarm system, deactivating the shit, made my entry into the house. I thought I was going to be greeted by Lady but she was occupied.

I walked real slowly through the kitchen to the steps. I heard music coming from upstairs. *That bitch must be in Money's room listening to music.* I crept up the stairs and my phone rang. I looked at it. It was Money. His dog Lady scared the fuck out of me coming down the stairs, but she didn't bark she just looked at me with her tongue hanging out.

"What's up bitch!" I said rubbing her. Lady took her fat ass down the stairs. I could hear talking as I walked further up.

I walked into the room finding Renee lying on the bed talking on her phone cheesing from ear to ear. I politely walked in front of her scaring her half to death.

"Damn Renee you act like you see a ghost!" I said, smiling.

"How.. How did you get in here?" she asked, dropping the phone.

"You remember those numbers you gave Star thinking she was gon' help yo ass set Money up... well stupid bitch you got played, just like you played my brother, you and that punk ass niggah of yours. Didn't I tell you I was going to get y'all?"

"I ain't gon' make you suffer like you made my brother suffer. He really thought you loved him, but it was all a game to you."

I had my 9mm in my hand and raised it up as Lady came in the room. She could feel something was wrong so she started barking.

"Lady, go downstairs!" I yelled.

Lady listened and left out.

"So you gon' do kill me?"

"Kill you is right. I was going to make you suffer, but fuck that I don't have time to play games," I told her.

I raised my gun up to her face.

"Wait! Wait!!!" she begged.

"What bitch?"

"Let me help you get Jose. He was the one who made me do all this shit!"

"So you let a niggah fuck yo head up and make you do shit like this?"

Renee didn't say shit so I cocked my gun.

"Please... please don't kill me, I'll help," she begged again.

"Nah fuck that, I don't need yo help!"

POP... POP...

I shot that bitch twice in the head just like her niggah did my brother.

I left that bitch dead in the bed with two to the head. I ran down the stairs where Lady greeted me. We looked at each other then I went through the kitchen and out the door. Lady followed and we both jumped in the car and left.

Fifteen minutes later I was sitting in my ride and watching these niggahs talk amongst themselves. They were all visible from the street through the big ass windows Biz's bitch had in her shop.

"It's time Lady for me to give some payback." Lady barked like she knew what I was talking about. I pulled out my phone and called Money.

"I'm outside."

"What did you do with Renee?" he asked in a low tone, like he didn't want to know the answer.

"What the fuck…that bitch is 187 across your bed…stank bitch."

"Yo, you got Lady with you?"

"Yeah, she right here."

"Alright let's do this!" Money said, then hung up.

I hung up and got out the car and walked slowly to the door. I opened the door and soon had all eyes on me. Everyone was shocked but Money. Jose's bitch ass acted like he didn't want to look at me, but I made him.

"Yo what's up J? I haven't seen you in a long time what's good with you?"

"You know me the same ol' shit, yo!" he answered.

"Yeah, I knew you was doing the same ol' shit, you and yo bitch!"

Biz looked over at Money.

"What she doing here?" he asked.

"Shit, niggah she's the connect," Money said, lighting a swisher then puffed it.

"This the mo'fucking connect?! So all this time I have been

getting my shit from her?"

"That's right niggah. I'm the man!" I said still looking at Jose' who looked like he was about to shit his pants.

"I remember my brother was once the man till this niggah killed him. Got jealous and shit!"

"Wait... who was your brother?" Biz asked.

"Oh you don't remember Biz? Well you bought yo wife this shop with some of his money," I informed.

Biz twisted up his face a little, then he realized who my brother was.

"I... I didn't have nothing to do with that shit!"

"Oh yes you did, you was one of the niggahs who tortured my brother.

"I know everything, like how you ran yo ass here to Ohio to try to dodge the police and shit. But Jose' here he ain't never scared he didn't run. He stayed and kept doing the same o same shit, don't you know too much of something is bad?"

"What the fuck you gon' do?" Biz asked underestimating me.

"You'll see!"

"What bitch?" Biz said, but was shocked when he heard Click.

"You heard her!" Star said, putting the gun up to Biz's head.

"What the fuck you got to do with this shit?" he asked her.

"You remember that half brother I told you about? Well," Shay said, still holding the gun to his head.

"Yeah, niggah you were set up for the okie!" I said laughing like a mad man.

I looked over at Money who passed the swisher to Biz.

"Niggah it look like you need a lift," he said, also laughing as smoke came out his nose and mouth. Biz took the swisher and pulled on it for dear life.

"All I want to know is why this niggah ain't saying shit?" I said still looking at Jose'.

"What the fuck you want me to say... if you gon' kill me then kill me bit.....”

That niggah didn’t get it all the way out because I popped his ass.

Then I turned my heels to Biz’s punk ass. I watched as Star shook while holding the gun.

“You gon’ kill me now bitch?” I let him slide on that bitch shit.

“Nah niggah, yo bitch is,” I said.

Star looked at me scared to death.

“You remember our deal right?” I asked her scared ass.

“Yeah, But....”

“But nothing, if you don’t do it, then there’s no money for you.”

“I knew yo ass was still a money hungry ass ho!” Biz yelled.

“Tell him how you was fucking and sucking Money for a little of nothing, Star.”

Star looked at me like what the fuck was I doing? Biz looked at Money with his face twisted up.

“Oh yeah, yo girl got some good pussy. The first time I hit that it was for some buck fifty dollar sneakers.” Money smiled

“All this shit wasn’t planned y’all! Why y’all going there? Telling him this shit?” Star cried out.

“Because you a stank bitch who helped them ma’fucka’s set my brother up. You was the only one who knew a lot of the money shit, and the hiding places, you and that bitch, Renee. That bitch is dead; now it’s yo turn ho if you don’t kill this nigga!”

“Alright... alright I’ll do it! If I kill him you going to let me go with the money... right?”

“Ain’t that what I told you?”

“Yeah!”

“Alright then!” Star stood in front of Biz and closed her eyes. POP! POP! The bitch hit him in the neck. I don’t know where the other shot went.

Biz was in the chair holding his neck. Money got out of his seat and walked over to the door, leaving me and Star face to face. Her ass was crying like a baby. She really loved that niggah, but look what money will do to you; it will make you kill the person you love.

I didn't need that bitch anymore, so I popped her ass point black in the face.

"Yolanda!" Money yelled.

"Why kill her?"

"Because the bitch crossed her own niggah for some doe so she would have crossed me too... plus she told them where Milton's Money was."

"Alright let's get out of here, Yo, you got the money?"

"Hell yeah I got the money," Money said.

I smiled as we walked out the shop. What's going to happen when they find Renee's body? Well, we will be long gone... and that house wasn't in Moneys name it was in one of my dope fiends name that they will never catch up too because he's dead, and no one knew Money lived there... As for Biz and them well Brooklyn will find her bitch and her husband dead... and she will find Jose also. I don't give a fuck! I did what I wanted and I got the money...

We got in the car and Lady got to barking and shit when she saw her master. Money turned on the radio and guess what was playing... that song Honey Dip, ain't that some shit...

DEEP

MEET THE AUTHORS

ERICK S. GRAY

The author of the urban sexomedy BOOTYCALL *69 has been known for his well thought out plots and ability to keep readers interested with every turn of the page.

This entrepreneur is also the owner/founder of Triple G publishing and is making moves in other markets as well.

Being born and raised in the south side of Jamaica, Queens, this gifted author has brought himself out on a high note with his first endeavor. He continues bringing you good stories as he shows in his collaboration with Mark Anthony, and Anthony Whyte, STREETS OF NEW YORK VOLUME 1 , Ghetto Heaven, Money, Power, Respect. Nasty Girls and It's Like Candy.
Erick S. Gray is showing that young African-American males don't all fall into the same categories of drug dealer/thief/statistic. His future is filled with promises of more intriguing and diverse stories for the masses to digest.

Books By Erick S. Gray

It's Like Candy - In Stores Now
Ghetto Heaven - In Stores Now

Also By Erick S Gray

Money Power Respect
Booty Call *69
Nasty Girls

Myspace: www.myspace.com/ericksgray

ANNA J.

Anna J is a writer from Philly who also walks the runway in her spare time as a full-figured model. Co-author of Stories To Excite You: Menage Quad, Anna put her writing skills to the test in this hot collaboration that was released during the fall of 2004. Her debut novel, an Essence magazine best selling novel, My Woman His Wife is high on the charts and a good read for those that enjoy a steamy love affair with a little bit of drama to boot. The continuation of the drama can be found in The Aftermath, Anna J's second novel under Q-Boro books where Monica is still off the chain, and drama is still a main factor.

If your Anna J cravings still aren't satisfied you can also find other hot stories of hers in Fetish: A Compilation of Erotic Stories, Morning Noon and Night: Can't Get Enough and Fantasy: Erotic Short Stories in bookstores nationwide. Anna J. was born and raised in Philly, where she still resides and is finishing up Get Money Chicks, her newest work of fiction that will be released in September of 2007.

Books By Anna J

The Aftermath - In Stores Now
Get Money Chicks - September 2007

Website: www.askannaj.com
Myspace: www.myspace.com/phillyauthor

Also By Anna J.

Stories To Excite You
Morning Noon & Night (Anthology)
Fetish (Anthology)
Fantasy (Anthology)

K'WAN

K'wan is without a doubt one of his generation's most talented and gritty writers. Born the only child of a poet and a painter, creativity was imprinted in him from day one. He is the national best selling author of Gangsta, Road Dawgz, Street Dreams, Hoodlum,Eve, Hoodrat, and most recently BLOW for G-Unit Books. He is currently hard at work penning the sequel to his #1 Essence Magazine Best Selling title "Hoodrat" entitled "Still Hood". K'wan resides on the east coast with his family.

Books By K'wan

BLOW (G-Unit Books) - July 2007
Still Hood - October 2007

Also By K'wan

Gangsta
Road Dawgz
Street Dreams
Hoodlum
Eve
Hoodrat

Website: www.kwanfoye.com
Myspace: www.myspace.com/kwanfoye

BRITTANI WILLIAMS

Brittani Williams was born and raised in Philadelphia, PA where she currently resides. She began writing when a seventh grade English assignment sparked her imagination. After many years she was given the opportunity to become a published author. Along with her debut novel Daddy's Little Girl released in February 2007 she has participated in two anthology projects and her second novel scantily titled Sugar Walls will be released in winter 2007. She is currently hard at work on a third novel and planning to participate in as many anthologies as she possibly can.

Books By Brittani Williams

Daddy's Little Girl - In stores now
Sugar Walls - November 2007

Website: www.brittani-williams.com and
Myspace: www.myspace.com/msbgw

Also By Brittani

Fantasy (Anthology)

JUICY WRIGHT

Juicy Wright, as she is affectionately called, hails from the Washington, DC Metropolitan area. Her talent as an erotic writer was first noticed by Life Changing Books in 2007. She immediately began working on an anthology with some of the most well known authors in the African American industry.

Juicey's desire is for her readers to walk away from her books, "soaking wet."

BEWARE… she is currently working on her hot upcoming release, in stores 2008…be prepared to keep a towel handy!

ARETHA TEMPLE

Aretha Temple was born in Queens, New York. As a child knew she had a talent for writing when she was in the 7th grade and started writing poetry. As Aretha got older she discovered that her passion for writing expanded beyond just poetry. She began writing short erotic and urban stories and sharing these stories with her various online groups. Aretha was then recruited by best selling author Noire to write a column for her online magazine Noiremagazine.com called "Re-Re's Got the Scoop". Aretha's first novel will be released this year entitled "A Hustler's Ambition". She is currently working on her second novel as well as her second anthology. Aretha currently resides in Toledo, OH with her two sons, Dominique and Da'Jaun.

ORDER FORM

MAIL TO:
PO Box 423
Brandywine, MD 20613
301-362-6508

FAX TO:
301-579-9913

Date	
Phone	
E-mail	

Ship to:	
Address:	
City & State:	Zip:
Attention:	

Make all checks and Money Orders payable to: **Life Changing Books**

Qty.	ISBN	Title	Release Date	Price
	0-9741394-0-8	A Life to Remember by Azarel	08/2003	$ 15.00
	0-9741394-1-6	Double Life by Tyrone Wallace	11/2004	$ 15.00
	0-9741394-5-9	Nothin' Personal by Tyrone Wallace	07/2006	$ 15.00
	0-9741394-2-4	Bruised by Azarel	07/2005	$ 15.00
	0-9741394-7-5	Bruised 2: The Ultimate Revenge by Azarel	10/2006	$ 15.00
	0-9741394-3-2	Secrets of a Housewife by J. Tremble	02/2006	$ 15.00
	0-9724003-5-4	I Shoulda Seen it Comin' by Danette Majette	01/2006	$ 15.00
	0-9741394-4-0	The Take Over by Tonya Ridley	04/2006	$ 15.00
	0-9741394-6-7	The Millionaire Mistress by Tiphani	11/2006	$ 15.00
	1-934230-99-5	More Secrets More Lies J. Tremble	02/2007	$ 15.00
	1-934230-98-7	Young Assassin by Mike G	03/2007	$ 15.00
	1-934230-95-2	A Private Affair by Mike Warren	05/2007	$ 15.00
	1-934230-94-4	All That Glitters by Ericka M. Williams	07/2007	$ 15.00
	0-9774575-2-4	The Streets Love No One by R.L.	05/2007	$ 15.00
	0-9774575-0-8	A Lovely Murder Down South by Paul Johnson	06/2006	$ 15.00
	0-9791068-2-8	Changing My Shoes by T.T. Bridgeman	05/2007	$ 15.00
	1-934230-93-6	Deep by Danette Majette	07/2007	$ 15.00
	1-934230-96-0	Flexin' & Sexin by K'wan, Anna J. & Others	06/2007	$ 15.00
	1-934230-92-8	Talk of the Town by Tonya Ridley	07/2007	$15.00
	0-9741394-9-1	Teenage Bluez	01/2006	$10.99
	0-9741394-8-3	Teenage Bluez II	12/2006	$10.99
		Total for Books:		$
		Shipping Charges (add $4.00 for 1-4 books*)		$
		Total Enclosed (add lines)		$

For credit card orders and orders for over 25 books please contact us @ orders@lifechangingbooks.net (cheaper rates for COD orders)

**Shipping and Handling on 5-20 books is $5.95. For 11 or more books, contact us for shipping rates. 240.691.4343*